FROM THE ASHES . . .

Then, through his hazy left eye's vision, he could see the source of the smoke. My God! They'd burned down his cabin. A few charred logs in the wall were all that was left of it. How long had he been out? The notion only added to his pain and misery.

Sun was up, so he'd been out a while. Then he saw Cob at the hay stacked in the shed, still saddled and bridled. If he could get to him . . . Then he noticed the blackened ground—those no-accounts had tried to burn his shed, too. Even crawling on his hands and knees was a pain-filled chore.

He paused for Cob to settle down at the sight of him on the ground. The horse snatched another bit of hay, switched his tail and then turned back to look at him.

It must have required twenty minutes for him to finally get the horse settled and to get ahold of the trailing reins. Exhausted, seated on his butt, he spit the copper taste of blood out of his mouth, realizing that the rip in his upper lip was serious. But how to get to his feet and in the saddle was a bigger obstacle at the moment than any wounds. They must have caved in his ribs. If he didn't hug himself, the pain was excruciating.

He looked at the sun time—mid-morning. He began to crawl to the wall of the tack room. That took all his strength. Cob came along, snorting in the charred hay. Herschel's back forced to the wall and his feet braced, he began by gritting his teeth to raise himself, using one foot to boost himself and the other to hold what he had. This way his arms were at his sides and he could stand the most of it. At last he was on his unsteady feet. If he ever found out who did this, they'd regret leaving him alive . . .

THE
Horse Creek
Incident

DUSTY RICHARDS

JOVE BOOKS, NEW YORK

THE BERKLEY PUBLISHING GROUP
Published by the Penguin Group
Penguin Group (USA) Inc.
375 Hudson Street, New York, New York 10014, USA
Penguin Group (Canada), 90 Eglinton Avenue East, Suite 700, Toronto, Ontario M4P 2Y3, Canada
(a division of Pearson Penguin Canada Inc.)
Penguin Books Ltd., 80 Strand, London WC2R 0RL, England
Penguin Group Ireland, 25 St. Stephen's Green, Dublin 2, Ireland (a division of Penguin Books Ltd.)
Penguin Group (Australia), 250 Camberwell Road, Camberwell, Victoria 3124, Australia
(a division of Pearson Australia Group Pty. Ltd.)
Penguin Books India Pvt. Ltd., 11 Community Centre, Panchsheel Park, New Delhi—110 017, India
Penguin Group (NZ), Cnr. Airborne and Rosedale Roads, Albany, Auckland 1310, New Zealand
(a division of Pearson New Zealand Ltd.)
Penguin Books (South Africa) (Pty.) Ltd., 24 Sturdee Avenue, Rosebank, Johannesburg 2196,
South Africa

Penguin Books Ltd., Registered Offices: 80 Strand, London WC2R 0RL, England

This is a work of fiction. Names, characters, places, and incidents either are the product of the author's
imagination or are used fictitiously, and any resemblance to actual persons, living or dead, business
establishments, events, or locales is entirely coincidental. The publisher does not have any control over
and does not assume any responsibility for author or third-party websites or their content.

THE HORSE CREEK INCIDENT

A Jove Book / published by arrangement with the author

PRINTING HISTORY
Jove mass-market edition / November 2006

Copyright © 2006 by Dusty Richards.
Cover illustration by Ben Perini.
Cover design by Steven Ferlauto.
Text design by Kristin del Rosario.

ISBN: 0-515-14217-4

JOVE®
Jove Books are published by The Berkley Publishing Group,
a division of Penguin Group (USA) Inc.,
375 Hudson Street, New York, New York 10014.
JOVE is a registered trademark of Penguin Group (USA) Inc.
The "J" design is a trademark belonging to Penguin Group (USA) Inc.

PRINTED IN THE UNITED STATES OF AMERICA

10 9 8 7 6 5 4 3 2 1

This book is dedicated to a great cowboy, the late Mike Gorsalka of Sheridan, Wyoming. He was a rancher, a great father, husband and neighbor. When the boy from down the road, hardly out of his teens, drew a moose permit, he came right over and asked for Mike's help. They went up in the Bighorn Mountains, the youth shot his huge trophy, and Mike helped him get it down to the pickup. The task required all day.

"Lots of work?" I asked, imagining the enormous size of the bull.

Mike nodded as if it wasn't any big deal. "He was a big one."

But that was his way. His preschool granddaughter could burst in with some wild tale about the horses in the pasture and he always had time for her. Like most cowboys out of the north country, he loved and recognized good bucking horses. "Now, that one could really buck."

Everyone who knew him misses him. I'll cherish the short time I spent trout fishing and visiting with him. But I figure he'll have the coffee on and the camp already stocked with split wood when I get to that big roundup in the sky.

Special thanks to his wife, Ann Gorsalka, an extraordinary lady, a great writer, and a generous friend, or the development of this series would not have been possible.

To the wonderful staff and facilities in the Sheridan, Wyoming, and the Billings, Montana, Public Libraries, for all their work and assistance, I give my deepest gratitude.

For more information about my current and upcoming books and activities, check my website: *dustyrichards.com*.

Gracias, mis amigos,

DUSTY RICHARDS

ONE

Their voices singing, "Now he'll carry me o'er the water," were fraught by the bitter north wind. A mound of fresh dirt salted with dry snow powder sat with the new pine-board box beside the hole. The preacher led the singing. Herschel Baker stood in the back of the small gathering, mouthing the words. His eyes narrowed against the cold's sharpness and the notion Jack Diehl died for no good reason he could fathom. Hannah, his widow, and their four kids stood wet-eyed, huddled in the front of the small crowd.

Someone needed to pay for Jack's death. But no one would. Shot in the back by parties unknown. Someone knew who did it. The law wouldn't look hard for the ones guilty. All that would be said about Jack's death was that another two-bit rancher was dead. One of them "rustlers" up on Horse Creek. John Diehl never took a copper penny didn't belong to him. Herschel'd just better cover his own backside—for all he knew he might be next on their death list.

"Herschel Baker—"

He stared down into the face of Marsha Allen. She was wrapped in a brown blanket that half-covered her head and her red nose and cheeks appeared frostbit. Her tight mouth looked colorless before she spoke above the wind. "Come by the house and have supper with us."

Before he could say no, she gripped his arm with both hands and gave him a shake. "Not taking that for an answer. Come eat with me and the girls, tonight."

"All right."

She swept the lock of graying hair back from her face and smiled her Sunday best at him. Marsha was only twenty-eight. He'd known her for years. When her husband Mel was killed in the wagon wreck two years earlier, he wondered how a young woman would survive with three small girls up there. But folks did kind things and helped her.

He walked her to the wagon where the two spindly horses stood with their tails to the north gale, and he assisted her up on the seat. Then he lifted the girls, one at a time, into the box and received a polite thank you and smile from each of them.

Feeling uncomfortably obvious standing there, he gave a head toss to the roan horse he called Cob. "I'll be trailing you."

"Don't get lost," Marsha said with a grin and clucked to her team.

"Oh, I won't."

"See you at our house, Mr. Baker," the girls shouted, busy wrapping themselves in blankets for the ride home in the back.

"Sure," he said, wondering why he had agreed to her invite.

He tied down the scarf bound over his wool cap and under his chin. Then after checking the saddle girth, he swung a leg over the roan's back. Never spoke to none of the others. There'd be plenty of time for that later, he imagined. He pulled his kerchief up over his nose for protection and booted Cob after the wagon winding its way south toward her place.

Her stout-looking cabin was nestled under the brow of the hill. A high shed barn, corrals, several haystacks, sat in the Horse Creek bottoms. Mel'd left her a nice enough place, Herschel decided, dismounting heavily and stomping his cold feet. A weak winter sun hung low in the west when he helped her down from the seat.

"You girls run on and put some wood on the fire."

"Yes, ma'am." They rushed off, trying to ball up their trailing blankets, acting as if grateful for the chance to escape the cold.

"I can put the horses up," Herschel offered.

"I put them up myself all the time."

He turned his face away from the north wind. "Go on to the house."

"Oh, all right. Feed bags're in the tack room, give 'em some oats. Better give the roan some, too." She clutched the blanket, looking up at him, pursing her lips.

"I can do it," he insisted. "Go ahead."

"I don't doubt you can do it. I just feel guilty not doing it myself."

"Marsha, I'm not being punished unharnessing them."

"Well, good." She leaned over and hugged his arm as if out of an impulse. "I'm glad you came today. I'll go fix us some coffee and hot food, since you're doing all the work."

"I'll be along."

"Don't be too long." She rewrapped the blanket over her shoulders and ran off toward the house.

He climbed onto the seat, undid the reins and backed

the wagon into the alleyway, so it wouldn't be buried in the next snow if she needed it. Then he busied himself unhitching the horses and removing the harness. To carry each set required him to scoot sideways between the wagon and the stalls to reach the tack room that smelled sweet with oats and harness oil. He filled three homemade feed bags with oats and hung them on the team horses' and Cob's heads. For his last trip, he removed his saddle and put it in the room.

Be too late to ride to his place after they ate. Reckon with the girls and all there it wouldn't look too bad him staying over—if she invited him to. Standing inside the shelter of the barn and smelling the sweet hay, he leaned against the wall. The notion of whoever shot Jack Diehl still churned in his mind. Why? He closed his eyes to the cold weather and the bitterness of losing a close friend. There would be no escape from either.

When the horses had finished eating, he gathered the feed bags. With the ponies in the lot and enough hay forked in the mangers for them to eat, he headed for the log cabin bathed in the bloody red of sundown. How long since he'd eaten with her and the girls? Months. In the fall he came by looking for a team of horses that ran off from a freighter. He stopped over with them, coming down and again going back with the team. Caught that pair of percherons down on the Crow Land. Earned him a hundred dollars reward. Lots of money for a week's worth of work.

The heavy front door opened before he could touch the handle. Kate, the oldest, smiled big as the gatekeeper.

"We was getting worried you might freeze out there."

He took off his gloves, undid the scarf and removed his cap. "Naw, Kate, I had to feed those horses."

"I know," she said and wrinkled her nose. "I was only making talk." Her hand out, she took his scarf, cap and then his heavy, wool-lined canvas coat. It weighted her down, but she smiled big and dismissed his concern. Standing on a stool, she put them on the wall pegs.

He looked around, rubbing his hands. The big braided rug in the center of the room, under the lamp. Flames dancing in the rock fireplace, and the other two girls busy setting the table. A warm, snug place, he decided—Marsha arrived with steaming coffee in a mug.

"Had some left over and I heated it."

He looked into her blue eyes and nodded. "That'll be fine. Anything would do to be out of that weather."

"Yes, it would. Kate, bring Mr. Baker a chair."

At first, he wondered who else was there. *Mr. Baker.* He'd forgotten his own name. He shook his head to dismiss the notion of a seat; he'd planned to simply squat there on his boot heels in front of the fireplace and warm clear through.

"Use the chair and relax," she said privately. "Supper won't be long."

"Ah, thanks, Kate," he said and took the cup with one hand, then with the other carried the chair to the side of the hearth. He'd squatted there and not felt conspicuous, but in the straight-back chair, he'd stick out. He moved around so he could observe them better.

The coffee was hot. He focused his attention on it until the youngest, Sarah, came over with her rag doll.

"Have you ever met my Betsy?" She held up the wash-worn baby.

"No. Does she go to school?"

"No, she's too whittle."

"Sarah—" Marsha spoke to stop her, but he held up his hand.

"Does she talk yet?"

"Oh, yes, all the time to me."

"Well, I bet you're a good momma."

"I twy to be."

He winked at her and she ran off bubbling about Mr. Baker and her Betsy. Somehow him accepting the doll had given her the confidence to tell the world. Her older sisters, however, weren't that elated with the news.

"I hate to bother you," Marsha said, standing beside his chair. "But before spring I'll need two new shorthorn bulls. Men don't like to deal with a woman and I hate to think I've been robbed."

He glanced up at her. "I'll be on the lookout. Good ones won't be cheap."

She stared in the fire. "I can afford good ones."

He nodded. Looking down at the pegged floor, he wondered how she managed running her ranch. Three Crows cowboyed for her part-time, but each fall, she managed to sell some top cattle. Keeping good bulls was part of her success.

"Supper's about ready if you'd like to wash up now."

"Oh, yeah. I was sitting here getting warm and forgot about my manners."

She nodded sharply. "I know you've got lots on your mind."

"I'd say a wagon load." Then standing, he forced a smile for her and the girls. "Guess after we eat, I could find that harmonica."

"Yes!" came from the girls.

Their mother's frown toned them down and he went to wash. "Don't bother, Mr. Baker."

A disappointed, obedient "Yes" followed.

Supper was served on the long table. Kate asked the Lord's blessing and they all said amen. The fresh bread, brown crust with a cast of white flour, looked so tempting the saliva about washed his mouth away. And real butter. Marsha put a large slice of sugar-cured ham on his plate before he could choose a smaller one. Then she passed the platter to the girls.

The meal felt like a feast for him. No fancy Billings restaurant could have ever come close to matching her delicious food. After his own get-by meals of beans, oatmeal, or cheese and stale crackers—he felt like someone important.

"Will the law do anything about it?" she asked.

"I don't know. I was planning to ride up and talk to Sheriff Talbot about the matter."

She paused eating. "Reckon that's smart?"

"Won't hurt to ask." He frowned. No law against asking if the law would investigate a murder.

"Well . . ." She turned her lower lip inward as if in doubt about what to say to him. "You know that Talbot works for them big outfits. Nosing around might make you a marked man, too."

He looked hard at the potatoes and gravy left on his plate. "Still, he's the law."

"We ain't got any law. Them big ranchers have got the law."

He bobbed his head in agreement and swallowed a big lump in his throat. "Don't always have to be that way."

"It's the way it is."

"Maybe—you're right." Maybe as long as folks accepted it like sheep it would be like that—and they'd do nothing about things that're dead wrong.

"I-I just don't want to see you get hurt either." Her hand shot out and she squeezed his wrist for a long second.

"Aw, I'm a big old boy. But I promise to be careful."

His reply made her smile, and she acted pleased he'd at least listened to her warning.

The dishes cleared and washed, the girls set the kitchen chairs in a circle facing the fire. Marsha had stoked the fireplace with more wood. She sat on her small sewing rocker and waited. He grinned at them and made a big deal out of searching in his vest pockets.

"You reckon I went off and left that rascal at home?"

The girls all looked concerned—then he pulled the little silver harmonica out of his pocket. "Ah, here it is. But first, Kate, go over in that coat and in the right-hand pocket is a bag."

"Candy!"

He turned his head to the side as if thinking about it. "Might be chawing tobacco."

"Aw!" came the disappointed cry.

"One piece is all," their mother warned as the others clustered around the oldest to see their prize. Then Marsha looked to the ceiling for celestial help.

With a hunk of hard candy in their cheeks, they retook their seats and he began with "Red River Valley." Then he livened things up and did "Turkey in the Straw." The girls were up and dancing around the room. A waltz tune next and they swayed like ballroom dancers. After each number, he would beat the spittle out on his canvas pants leg and play another for his enthralled audience.

"You've earned your supper, Old Dan Tucker," Marsha finally said.

"You girls can go change for bed over in that corner. Mr. Baker won't look, and then hustle up in the loft to bed."

She brought him another cup of coffee and he thanked her. His face, tender from the windburn, felt ablaze in the reflected heat of the fireplace. He noticed she'd put something shiny on her red nose and cheeks.

Her girls scrambled up in the loft like squirrels and were under strict orders to go to sleep. The two of them sat and listened to the fire snap and crackle. He rubbed his palms on his britches. Like usual, he felt trapped alone with her. Why he had such a feeling he could never say—but a few feet from Marsha Allen and alone, the caged sense set in on him.

With a dress to repair in her lap, she threaded a needle

by the fire's light. "I thought you'd come back to see us sooner."

"I intended to."

"The girls really look forward to your music."

"Guess I get so busy making a living—time just flies by."

"You aren't going to do anything foolish over this, are you?"

"Like what?"

She never looked up from her sewing when he glanced over at her.

"You can't do nothing about them big outfits. They've got the law on their side and the money." The stitch tied off, she bit the thread in too close to the dress, then set the garment in her lap and looked hard at him.

He stood and stretched his arms over his head. "I'm not going to see the small ranchers up and down Horse Creek get potshot like some kind of ducks on a pond."

"Oh, Herschel, I was so afraid you'd say that. Why do men have to act so much like some . . . some kind of knights?"

"'Cause wrong's wrong. Being filthy rich or owning half of Montana don't make you a king in this country."

She jumped up, threw her arms around him, burying her face in his vest. Holding her tight to his body, he felt her sobs and was overcome with his own helplessness to stop them. He stared over her head into the surging flames and the small explosions in the hearth. That inferno must be what Hell was like—and he'd see that Jack Diehl's killers went there.

TWO

B UCK Palmer used his hairy ham of a fist to snatch Cooter Daws's shirt in a ball and jerk the skinny cowboy out of the chair. With the blanched-faced Texan inches from his own face and the strong smell of whiskey on Daws's breath in his nostrils, Palmer spoke. "You dumb ass. Shooting that damn rancher is only going to make them fight that much harder."

"We—we had no choice. Honest, Buck. The sumbitch was going to shoot us."

"How come was he shot in the damn back then?"

"Hell—B-Buck, we couldn't do anything else."

"I sent you down there to look around for ways to root them damn two-bit ranchers out—not kill them. Not yet anyway." Palmer let him go and shook his head, deep in thought. Those two would be the ruin of him if he wasn't more careful about what he put them up to do.

In flight from Buck Palmer's fiery anger, Cooter Daws turned over a chair and scrambled around like some kind of clumsy ox, to get at a distance from his boss. Denver Smith, the taller one of the two hired hands, knocked into the other table backing for the outside exit.

"You want us out, then pay us and we'll light a shuck for Texas," Smith said.

"I want some damn results. I ain't paying you fifty a month to lay around here and rut with that damn Sadie all day, either."

"What in the hell can you do when the damn country's froze up tighter than a damn bull's ass at fly time?" Smith asked, making certain there was nothing between him and the back door.

"Now I've got to calm folks down. May cost me big money to shut down a damn investigation. Money don't grow on trees. But how the hell would you know?" Palmer used his fingers to comb through his wavy blond hair. That pair were too stupid to do anything unless he drew them pictures. If anything was done down there on Horse Creek about them two-bit ranchers, he'd have to do it or be there to show them how.

"You two keep low. You sure that no one saw you?" He narrowed his gaze at them.

"No one saw us."

"Both of you go out to my place and stay there till I send word. Feed the damn cattle. And for Christ's sake stay out of sight and any more trouble."

"We could go—"

"Hell, no, don't you go down there on Horse Creek. You ever heard of Montana vigilantes? Well, this ain't Kansas, and this ain't Texas. You get a bunch like them swelled up at you and they'll come after you with a rope. And they won't stop till they hang every jack one of us between here and Canada. That goes for anyone they might even think had a hand in his death."

"We need to torch a few of 'em. Then the rest'll pull

stakes. They ain't that tough." Daws made a braggart face like that would be easy.

"Not till this Diehl killing blows over. I don't want it tied to us. Get out there and go feed my stock. I don't want to see yeh till I send word or drive out myself."

"We can't come in Saturday night?" Smith frowned at him in disbelief.

"I said stay out there! Are yeh deaf? Less you're seen, the less they can point a finger at yeh."

"All right. But first get us a couple of bottles of hooch to take along, and we'll leave," Smith said, sharing a nod with Daws.

Palmer agreed. He'd get the money for it out of their pay. "Stay in here."

They nodded and started dressing to go out the back way. In the hallway, Palmer closed the door to the room he used for his meetings and some high-stake card games. At the end of the hall, he could hear the tinny piano and the squeals of the women out in the saloon. The plunking of the roulette wheel and the noise of a good crowd tinkling glasses. He slid around the end of the bar, nodded to Earl in approval of all the trade in the smoke-filled room and took two bottles of cheap whiskey from a wooden case.

"I've got a little business to tend to," he said. Earl, behind the big mustache, nodded.

In the rear room again, he issued them the liquor and reiterated his orders. "Stay out of sight."

"Yeah, we heard you," Smith said, sticking the bottles down in his long coat's side pockets.

"I better go to covering up your tracks," Palmer said and shook his head ruefully after them.

"If'n ever figured it'd get this gawdamn cold up here, you'd not hired me for less than two hundred a month," Daws said and went out the door after his partner, letting in some dry snow and more cold before he closed it.

Maybe hiring them had been his biggest mistake. Big Texas gunfighters. He shook his head at the notion and went out to the barroom. Before he was done with those two, he might need to send them floating facedown in the Yellowstone River.

Back in the Antelope Saloon's main room, Palmer helped work the bar. Talked to the customers. Frowned at one of the girls who got too loud, and he loaned Wolford Doone a ten-dollar bill.

"I'm going up and spend the whole night with that Lucille." Doone held up the bill and smiled at it. "Pay you back on Friday."

"I know you will. See yeh, Doone."

"Sure is busy tonight," Earl said, coming by behind him.

Buck nodded in approval, then made a sign for him to hold up. He looked across the smoky room to watch his man and Lucille talk, get excited and then go skipping off together.

"Earl?" he said out of the corner of his mouth

"Yeah, Buck?"

"See if that damn Lucy's holding out on us. Wolford Doone just paid her ten bucks to spend the night."

"I'll see what she turns in."

He knocked the ash off his cigar. "If she's holding out, bust her ass good."

"I'll handle it."

"Yeah. " If he had one man hired that did things right— it was Earl.

Palmer looked up and saw the sheriff of Yellowstone County come in the door. The big man took off his thick wool overcoat at the entrance, gave the place his usual stern appraisal. Used the web of his hand to flatten his mustache, then he spoke like a politician to several customers in passing.

Sheriff Sam Talbot waded up to the bar, laid the expensive coat on it and nodded to Palmer, who held out a fresh cigar to him.

Palmer waved away his reach for his money. "On the house."

"Thanks," Talbot said, then used a jackknife to cut off the end of the cigar.

"Whiskey or beer?"

"Beer'll be fine. Got to go by and speak to the veterans up at the hall in a few minutes."

Palmer ordered him a beer over his shoulder, then he struck a match for the lawman to light up. Earl quit everything and delivered the big mug.

With a nod from his boss that would be all, he left them.

"I've got a problem, Buck," Talbot said after his first taste of the foamy brew. He wiped his mustache on a folded white handkerchief, then replaced it in his pocket.

"Oh?" Palmer said.

"Some rancher named Diehl was shot down on Horse Creek."

"I heard something about it."

With the glass in his hand, Talbot looked around to be sure they couldn't be overheard before he said, "Hear anything else?"

Palmer shook his head.

"Keep your ears open for me. You hear anything, you let me know. I don't need a range war."

"You think that's what it is?"

Talbot stopped drinking and shook his head as if to dismiss the matter. "I think this Diehl got in the way of a bullet. Period."

With a bar rag, Palmer made a swipe at the water ring from the sheriff's glass. "I'll do my gawdamndest to keep it that way for you."

"Good." Then Talbot took a puff off his cigar and blew the smoke over Palmer's head. "You let me know if you hear a peep about it."

"I promise you'll be the first to know, Sam."

"Damn right. I knew I could count on you." He closed his right eye and made a pleased nod.

You bet, Sam Talbot, you can trust me as far as you can throw me. One thing for certain—Talbot had no idea who did the shooting. Seeing he didn't find out anything would be number two. Then he wished the lawman good luck talking to those war veterans.

A few minutes later, the sheriff left the Antelope in his fancy wool coat and Boss of the Plains silk-edged hat, smoking a free Buck Palmer twenty-five-cent cigar. With the bar rag in his hand, Palmer watched him exit. Damned old bag of wind.

"For you," Earl said and passed him a small envelope.

Buck never flinched. He jammed it down in his pocket like he'd put his hand in there for something. A blank envelope meant one thing. Only person in Montana send him a note like that—his boss. Rupart MacDavis wanted to see him. Shit fire and save matches, all he needed was MacDavis upset over this shooting.

"Handle things here. Looks quiet enough," he said to Earl. "I've got to get up early and take care of some business."

"No problem."

Moments later, dressed in his sheepskin-lined coat, wool cap and scarf, he eased out the back door of the saloon, letting his eyes adjust to the night's darkness. The snow and stars made the shadowy journey to Tal Street on the crunchy frozen mess underfoot an easy one. He stayed on the various cleaned-off porches going to the livery and eased inside the office to awaken the boy sleeping face-down on the desk.

"Ah, Mr. Palmer." The bleary-eyed youth shot to his feet.

"Have my horse hitched and ready to go at five a.m."

"I will, sir."

"He ain't ready, I'll kick your ass up between your shoulder blades. Hear me?"

"I-I'll sure have him ready."

"You better." Palmer left the neat foot-oil-smelling office and went on to his room in the Fargo Hotel.

He'd tried boardinghouses. His hotel room was better. If he wanted female company, he could bring her up there. No damn rules for him at the Fargo. They changed his sheets once a week. Kept his clothes washed and pressed. Not the coldest place in town either. In the basement sat a large coal-fired furnace that most nights kept the pitchers of water on the bureaus from freezing.

After lighting the coal-oil lamp on the dresser, he removed his heavy coat and put it on a hook. Must be below zero outside, he decided, sifting on the bed to untie his lace-up boots. Too cold to piss out the open window; he'd use the pot under the bed. Opening the sash would let out all the meager heat in the room, and it would never warm up again. All the hotels in Montana had those telltale stains under every window—this night he'd refrain.

At last, still fully dressed, he pulled the covers over his head and went to sleep. The knock on the door awoke him. Wake-up call.

"It's four-thirty, sir."

"Yeah, yeah." He sent them away like a growling grizzly bear. How long had he slept? Ten minutes? No, it was ten when he came in. No matter, he had to meet Mac-Davis, midday at the line shack, or else have him ticked off. Folks didn't intentionally make MacDavis mad.

Yawning and shaking his hurting head, lacing up his boots, he dreaded the cold drive up there. Maybe when the sun came up—hell, no matter, it was winter and that meant Montana was on the edge of the north pole. That place might even be a suburb of Billings.

He came downstairs, never said a word to the boy at the desk who offered a good morning, and rattled the frosted glass in the front door going out. At the Real Food Cafe, Maude brought him a stained mug full of steaming coffee. He nodded and she wrote down without asking: three scrambled eggs, four flapjacks and ham.

"I've got your order," she said and drew a grunt from him.

The steam off the coffee softened the edges of his beard stubble. He dared sip some and knew all day he'd regret the heat damage to his tongue. Elbows on the counter, he hadn't noticed any of the others in the room. Not that he feared anyone that could be in there, but it always paid to know who was around him. So between sips that grew less painful by the minute, he inventoried the customers. Mostly people in the local coal- or wood-hauling business, stablehands and a few store clerks. All familiar faces. He settled down, letting his mind open like a melting ice block on the top of a hot range.

What would he tell MacDavis about the dead rancher? He had hired stupid men. It wouldn't be easy to root that bunch off Horse Creek. Hardheaded bunch of bumpkins anyway. Of course all that deeded land they held would fit MacDavis and the rest of the big outfits for a good water supply. Then that range east and west of the creek would be covered with their cattle. All for a song. Plus cut out the petty rustling that made MacDavis so mad. Hell, everyone in Montana, including him, ate the other guy's beef. That wasn't stealing, that was getting by.

"Here, you want some mustard?" she asked with a mischievous grin on her face.

He shook his head. "That real chokecherry syrup you got there?"

"Real as it gets." She left the pint jar half-full of the red juice beside his plate.

He watched the pats of butter melt and run off the crown of the brown flapjack pile as he stuffed eggs between each layer. Then he soaked the stack in the blood red syrup. When he set the jar down, he grinned at the sight. Be a real feast. Be his last one, too, until late that evening when he got back to town.

After he left the cafe, he went to the livery and found his horse hitched and ready. He took a buffalo robe and a heavy horse blanket out of the box behind the light buckboard's spring seat. Robe spread over his lap, horse-sweat-smelling blanket wrapped around his shoulders, he nodded for the boy to open the barn doors. He drove the thick-coated half-Morgan, Chester, out through the double doors into the dark night.

Chester pulled the rig with the pride of a great gaited horse. A pleasure to drive, grain-fed, he could cover a lot of miles in a day and never tire. In the lights from the various businesses, Palmer drove the empty street in haste and soon was headed uphill. If he didn't freeze to death, he should be at MacDavis's by mid-morning. Still the cold froze his whisker stubble under the scarf. Must be thirty below he decided.

By the time the dull sun began to fill the wide horizon in the southeast, Palmer figured he was well over halfway to the shack. At this time, he knew the coldest temperature on the mercury had been achieved; anything else would be a gradual upturn.

Mid-morning, with the weak sun still hanging in the distant south, he drove over the last rise, seeing the snow swept valley, the box elders sticking out of drifts and the sagging roof beam of the old shack. Beside the corral sat the carriage and the fancy black team stuck their heads over the rails to nicker at Chester.

Grateful to be there, Palmer also dreaded the next hour or so of interrogation. MacDavis was a hard man to work for and satisfy.

MacDavis's black driver, George Washington, came out and took Chester's bridle. "I's put him up, Mr. Palmer."

"Fine. When he cools some, put this blanket over him." He swung the one off his shoulders when he stood. His legs held him when he stepped down, and he felt lucky after sitting that long on the spring seat tensed up by the cold. Stomping his boots on the hard frozen ground for more circulation, he headed for the front door. The swirling wind brought him a smell of wood smoke and he hoped the room was already warm.

Inside, the large bulk of the rancher's body under a Scots-plaid blanket was sprawled in a leather-wood chair under a coal-oil lamp reading a book. He looked up mildly, and the flames in the fireplace reflected off his round gold-rimmed reading glasses.

"Have a good trip?" MacDavis asked.

"Uneventful," Palmer said, stripping off his mittens then the gloves underneath them. The room's warm air stung his face, especially the skin around his eyes.

MacDavis unhooked the glasses from behind his ears and put them in a small case. "Warm some."

"Thanks, I shall," Palmer said, holding his hands out to the heat source and hoping his numb-feeling feet in the boots weren't permanently frostbit.

"They tell me Jack Diehl is dead."

"He, ah, had a mishap."

"Mishap, hell, they said he was shot in the back."

Palmer whirled to face him and defend the killing— then he saw the sly smile on the man's shiny full face.

"Unlike the wagon wreck victim of two years ago. This one owes the Billings Bank and Trust lots of money. Convenient for us, isn't it?"

"Yeah."

"I want you to go down there and buy that place at the sheriff's sale. You need a place to headquarters your men down there."

Palmer nodded. That would put his operations right in the middle of things. Might be good, might be bad—but he'd do it.

"If one of the big outfits tried to buy it, they might rebel on the notion. You aren't associated with us per se."

"You think anyone will bid on it?"

"They may try. You simply buy it. The money will be in your account."

"Easy enough." He began to unbutton his coat. "I put a thousand dollars in the special account for the last month's profits at the Antelope."

"Profits are holding up well despite the cold." Mac-Davis nodded in approval. His double chins made one fat jowl.

"They keep talking about a railroad coming."

MacDavis nodded as if the matter was no problem. "It will in time. Raising big capital in the east is hard right now."

Palmer put his coat over a straight-back chair. Mac-Davis never asked him to sit down at these meetings. Once he took the liberty, and the man's obvious scowl of disapproval made him pop right up to his feet.

"Is there anything else?"

"What does the sheriff say?"

"Talbot's looking for the killers. Not hard. Asked for my help if I heard anything."

"You think Sam's getting a little old for the job? Maybe a little too smug?"

Standing feet apart, Palmer rubbed his callused hand over his whisker-stubbled mouth. What did MacDavis want to hear? Talbot was beginning to get smug about his job? Too big for his boots?

"We may need a new man for the badge," MacDavis said.

"Who're you thinking about?"

MacDavis shook his head, the thick graying locks on his shiny forehead staying in place. "I don't know. I thought you'd know someone good for the job."

"I'll be working on it."

"You'll also have to tell Talbot when the time comes to graciously step aside."

"I can do that."

"No doubt you can. I wonder—" MacDavis compressed his lips and looked hard at him. "Who will be the real opposition to come out of Horse Creek next over this shooting?"

"I don't know. Guy named Walter Ferguson. He talks a lot."

The big man shook his head and shifted the robe over his shoulders. "I figure he'll talk. A talker won't get much done. But that isn't a bunch of mice we're dealing with down there. I'd bet a hundred there is some festering going on down there right now."

"Give me a little time, I can learn who it is."

MacDavis squeezed his double chin. "Do that. I want it cut off at the knees before it ever starts." His flat hand sliced the air like a sword.

"I understand."

"Next time have a wagon wreck. Shootings can bring out the vigilantes."

Palmer nodded that he understood. "Montana is notorious for them."

"Yes, and raise your prices so my share of the Antelopes take is fifteen hundred this month. I have a sizable investment down there in that place."

"I'll do all I can."

"Come in, Washington!" he shouted at the man knocking on the door. "Nothing going on in here you can't hear."

"Yes, sah. Ain't getting no warmer outs there."

"Won't till spring either." MacDavis turned back to Palmer. "You be damn sure no one gets that bunch down there organized."

"I'll handle it."

"I knew you would. We should not have to meet again until it gets warm outs there," he said, mimicking his servant's words.

"You's need you hoss?" Washington asked, standing up from his chair at the side of the shadowy room, lighted by the fireplace's blaze.

"Yes, go hitch it for him, Washington. Buck wants to go back and snuggle with some whore. It'll beat our company a lot."

"Surely would," the older black man said softly and went out the door buttoning his coat.

The door shut, MacDavis cleared his throat. "You live a fine life for an escaped felon, Palmer. But Alabama still has your name on a list of wanted men."

"I know, sir."

"Just don't forget it either."

"I won't and I sure appreciate—"

"Cut the butter talk. No more damn shootings. You can't handle it, then I'll get me a man who can."

Palmer bobbed his head.

"I want all those gawdamned rustlers off that creek in twelve months." His green eyes glowed in the fire's light. Hard lines formed around his pursed lips. The situation sent a cold chill up Palmer's spine despite the room's warmth.

"Twelve months," MacDavis repeated.

"I got yeh." MacDavis had never cut a deadline before. This time he had. He better go to making plans how to uproot that bunch. His deal in Billings and the Antelope was too sweet for him to lose them.

THREE

THE weather after the Diehl funeral proved cold. Herschel had left Marsha's place early the next morning, after promising her he'd be careful. On the ride up to Billings, he stopped at the Fergusons', the Gentrys' and MacDuffys'. They all shook their heads and told him he was on a fool's errand asking for the sheriff's help, but he rode on anyway.

Four hours later, Herschel sat fidgeting with his cap between his knees and waiting in the sheriff's outer office. The chief deputy before him sat behind a desk and busied himself with paperwork. A slender man with hollow cheeks and a pencil mustache, he wore a cheap brown suit, white shirt, red sweater and a black tie that showed some wear. Matthew Copelan.

Herschel looked up when a man he didn't know came out of the door marked "Sam Talbot, Sheriff" on the frosted glass pane. Copelan nodded to the stranger in the suit who without a word left quickly. Then the deputy ventured over to the open door.

"Man out here to see you, Sheriff. Herschel Baker from Horse Creek. Says he only wants to see you."

"Why, you send Herschel right in."

"I will, sir."

He stepped out. "You may go ahead, but be brief. Sheriff Talbot talks to the Ladies Aid at three."

Herschel nodded and went in the office. The room was bigger than his shack, with its own blazing fireplace. Talbot rose and offered his hand. They shook.

"Good to see you, Baker. Have a seat." He indicated one of the three captain's chairs in front of his fine polished walnut desk. Seated again, he nodded. "What can I do for you?"

"I'm here to ask about you investigating the shooting of Jack Diehl." He looked at the plaid cap in his hands, then raised his gaze to the lawman for his reply.

Talbot leaned back with a creak of the springs in his chair's swivel mechanism and tented his fingertips. "You have any notions about who did it?"

Herschel shook his head. "I'm not the law here. That's your job."

Talbot cleared his throat. "Kinda hard to do anything when folks down there won't cooperate with the law."

"You didn't even send a deputy down to investigate."

"You telling me how to run my business?" Talbot's pig eyes narrowed and his shiny face turned red on the cheeks.

Herschel moved to the front of his chair. "No. But Jack Diehl was shot in the back by some no-accounts, and it's your job to find them."

"Some? How many? You know who they are?" Talbot's face began to glow redder.

"If I knew that, they'd already been fed to the magpies."

Herschel was standing on his feet. "Maybe the governor'll do something about it."

"Why in the hell don't you go ask him?" Talbot shoved off from his desk and jumped up, looking even more heated.

"I just may do that."

"You better mind your own gawdamn business if you know what's good for yourself." Talbot had his index finger out shaking it like a gun barrel at him.

Herschel stopped and looked him in the eye. "Are you threatening me?"

"Take it however you want." Talbot used his finger to jab at the desktop. "I run this sheriff's office the way I see fit. You and that bunch of rustlers down there on Horse Creek can go to hell for all I care."

"Only till the next election," Herschel said in anger, wishing at the last minute he'd kept his threat to himself. Now Talbot and the rest would be warned of his plans to field a candidate.

He jerked on his cap, stormed out through the office and past the flush-faced chief deputy. In the hallway, he had started down the stairs, when the notion struck him—he needed a petition from the clerk's office. His breath rushing through his nose, he strode past the open door of the sheriff's office and could hear Talbot shouting at his chief deputy. Good, he had them upset, if nothing else.

A matronly lady in the clerk's office met him at the counter. "May I help you?"

"I need a petition to fill out for the office of sheriff." He remembered his manners and swept off the cap.

"Republican or Democrat?"

He shook his head. "Neither. You have any others?"

"Independent?" Her facial expression took on a look of disbelief and concern.

"They don't have a county convention, do they?"

"No, sir. But I must warn you no one has ever been elected in this territory that wasn't with one or the other major political party affiliations."

He nodded. The political parties on both sides were run by the big ranching interests. No way he'd ever be able to get one of his men on the ballot at their county conventions. Independent would have to work.

"Whose name goes on it?" she asked

"I'm not sure. Can I fill it out later?"

She mildly shook her head. "I'm sorry. A petition must have the candidate's name on it when it leaves here. See, if you changed the name, the people who signed it could be doped into thinking they were signing for someone else."

Herschel drew a deep breath up his nose. So far, he'd not talked to enough folks about this business of getting some new law in the county. What should he do?

"Herschel Baker." He indicated for her to write his name in.

"Office you will seek?" She looked up from writing his name.

"Sheriff."

With a quick check around, she half smiled. "Good for you. I hope you win." Then she blew on the ink and handed him the paper.

"Fifty voter signatures or Xs that are witnessed and a forty-dollar filing fee must accompany it to file for the election."

"Forty dollars?" He'd never expected such an expense.

"That's what they set the fee at. Not mine."

"Thanks. Opal Johnson, is it?" he asked, recalling her name.

"Yes, Mr. Baker. And—" She looked around again to be certain they were alone. "Good luck."

Carefully folded, he placed the petition in the inside pocket of his coat and started to leave.

"That must be turned in by April fifteenth or you won't be on the ballot."

He stopped and turned back. "What then?"

"Well, then you could become a write-in candidate. But no one has ever won a—"

"I know. No one ever won an office running as a write-in." He smiled at her and started down the hall.

His temper had overcome him again. This time it might turn out to be his own undoing. He'd come there to convince the sheriff to investigate Jack's death. Here he was with a petition for Talbot's job in his pocket and leaving without getting any action taken on a murder investigation.

Outside the courthouse, he studied the dropping sun. Another day was gone. Not a lot more of them left, either, until April fifteenth. How many folks would have the guts to sign his petition? For them it might be like signing their own death wish. No way to guarantee anyone's safety under the present regime. He headed for the diner for a quick meal. Late as it was, he'd have to stay in the wagon yard for the night.

His supper of roast beef, potatoes and canned corn wasn't bad, but hardly the quality of Marsha's the night before. The memory of holding her in his arms stabbed his heart. Worse yet, she'd be angry over him taking on this political campaign. Last thing she said—*Don't get involved*. So much for that.

In a soiled white apron, Buster Corey came out of the kitchen rolling a cigarette in his yellow stained fingers. The former cowboy had married the cafe owner, Maude, and ended his cowboying days.

"Sit down," Herschel said to him.

Buster sat sideways on the seat across from him and bent over to finish his smoke-making.

"Sorry to hear about Jack," Buster mumbled.

"So were we all."

"You know a pair by the name of Smith and his pard Cooter?"

"No." A cold chill ran up Herschel's neck—Buster was telling him something important and he'd better listen.

Buster looked over at him, the cigarette in the corner of his white lips, and nodded as if to say, *You know enough.* Then he struck a match on the side of his pant leg and arced the blazing flame to the crimped end of the misshapen tube. Making sucking sounds, he soon exhaled small snips of smoke and shook out the match.

"Watch 'em," Buster said, then he put his hand on the tabletop for support and rose stiff-like. "Sorry I can't talk more with you. Got lots of dishes to do."

"Good to see you, Buster."

The older cowboy nodded he heard him and shuffled off in his carpet slippers for the back room.

Herschel wondered how long he must have thought about those two guys Buster named—Smith was one. The other Cooter? His food was cold when he remembered to try to finish it.

After his meal, he considered going in one of the saloons for a glass of red-eye, but decided to save the treat and headed down the snow-piled street for the wagon yard. Maybe some sleep would make him feel rested enough for this job he'd taken on. At the moment, he felt depleted, with a million questions on his mind. And he'd need to raise forty dollars cash by April fifteenth, too.

He went by the stable office and spoke to Lem Paschal. "Guess I owe you two bits more. I'm sleeping here tonight."

The bearded man smiled and nodded. "Credit or cash?"

"Better pay you. I'd hate to have to muck out this barn next spring to work off my bill."

"Aw, them horses' backs ain't close to the rafters yet." Paschal grinned big.

"That's when you clean out?"

"Unless I get industrious before. A little litter makes heat for them ponies."

Herschel agreed. He paid the man, took his bedroll and went into the bunk room that stunk of sour socks, chewing tobacco and cheap booze. The potbelly stove in the center glowed cherry red in spots on the sides, and the sawmill snores of a dozen men filled the air.

Damn sure wouldn't be like the night before, him sleeping under her buffalo robe in front of the open fireplace. Marsha, Marsha. How he wondered and fretted about what he should do about her. Then, in the top bunk, staring at the loft over his head and his covers pulled up to his chin—he tried to comprehend how the whole deal about his running for sheriff would turn out. One thing he knew, someone was going to pay for shooting Jack Diehl. His eyes closed.

FOUR

Herschel stopped at Larkin's store. The too bright sun offered no warmth. Wind out of the north carried shards of fine ice. He hitched Cob on the south side of the building and stomped up on the porch. His feet felt stiff in his boots. The warmth of the place struck his face first as he pushed inside the room that smelled of cinnamon. A quick check and he saw several familiar faces seated around the stove. The owner, Marvin Larkin, nodded to him. Larkin was a round-faced man, bald-headed, who always wore a congenial smile.

"Good to see you, Herschel," Larkin announced.

"Good to be in out of the cold. I could smell the missus' sweet rolls baking clear up the road." Herschel swept off the scarf and unbuttoned his heavy coat.

"Better get a couple. That bunch hugging my heater have ate three pans-full already." Larkin indicated the pan on the counter.

"Aw, Larkin, we only ate two pans of 'em," Walt Ferguson protested. The others laughed. "How've you been?"

His mouth full of pastry, Herschel nodded at the Texan in his thirties, full mustached and blue eyes tightening in the corners when he looked up at Herschel.

"The sheriff is selling her out," Rielly said.

"Who?" Herschel frowned and hesitated talking another bit.

"Jack Diehl's place."

"I was up there yesterday—I mean—" He swallowed hard. "I was in Talbot's office. He never said a word."

"That banker told her yesterday, she couldn't pay the money that Jack owed, he would have the sheriff sell it in ten days."

"Who was that?" Herschel searched their faces.

"A man named Hertz."

"How much does he owe?"

"Twenty-five hundred."

"Why, his cattle would bring that in the spring—but now they won't bring nothing. You reckon they know that?"

"We figure they want us all out."

"Who?"

"Them big ranchers that run things up here. You do any good talking to Talbot?"

"None."

Walt Ferguson smiled. "I figured as much."

Herschel nodded and poured himself a cup of coffee from the pot on top of the stove. With a shake of his head, he then blew on the steam. "Lost my temper was all."

"Over what?"

"I asked him to investigate Jack's death."

"What did he say?" the big swede, Hansen, asked.

"Oh, how we wouldn't cooperate."

"So what's he going to do?" Ferguson asked.

"Not one damn thing."

Seated on a nail keg, Herschel set his coffee cup on the checkerboard, took off his wool cap and scratched an itch in his scalp. "Boys, I know it might be signing your death warrant, but I have a petition in my pocket to put my name on the ballot next November to be sheriff of this Yellowstone County."

"I'll damn sure sign it," Walt said. "Give it here."

"Boys, your name on this document might be like a death list when they get it up there in Billings."

"I'll sign it." Hansen stood up and stuck out his hand.

"After Walt," Herschel said. The Texan took it to the counter and used Larkin's pen. He handed it over to Hansen.

"Republican or Democrat?" Rielly asked.

"What the hell difference does that make?" Ferguson asked over his shoulder.

"Independent," Herschel said to intervene. "I could never get on the ballot at either one of their conventions."

"So you're running for sheriff?" Max Tagget nodded his head like the idea had him worried. "They may kill yeh."

"Like they killed Jack Diehl?" Herschel asked.

"Ain't no joke." Max looked over the others with a serious glare. "Man's a damn fool in this country not to mind his own business and not stick his head into others'."

"Why you dumb honyacker—" Ferguson started for him.

"Whoa!" Herschel jumped up and stopped him. "We ain't having a war over signing that petition. I said, 'Don't sign it.' I don't want to be the cause of any bad feelings in this county. If I can find fifty voters, I'll be on the ballot. That's it."

"Maybe you'll be next," Ferguson said to Rielly. "We let them lord over us and kill us, we may all be sprouting daisies before the election."

Hansen handed Herschel back the petition, and he put the paper back inside his coat. "What can we do for Hannah Diehl?"

"She says she's going back to her folks in Dakota with the kids," Walt said.

"Why, her stuff won't bring nothing." Tall Nels Hansen shook his head in disgust.

"Jack's worked hard," Walt said, sitting back down in the old chair again. "His cattle next spring would easy clear his debt. They're taking cattle, homestead and all, this way."

"Could we buy the bank off for more time for her?" Herschel asked.

"Who's got any money?" Rielly asked.

"We could raise some," Herschel said.

"Hannah ain't Marsha Allen," Ferguson said with a wary shake of his head. "I ain't speaking bad for her, but Hannah ain't a tough outdoors woman. We might stave them wolves off till the grass greens, but she could never run ranch hands and do all that."

"She'll get what the bank don't take then?" Herschel asked.

"I figure they'll take a loss, too, on the sale," Nels said "So she won't get nothing."

"What'll it bring?" Rielly asked.

"Pennies on the dollar," Herschel said in disgust.

"Then why don't we all go over there and bid pennies on it," Walt said. "And tell the rest not to bid a thing."

"Bank may have ringers there to up the bid," Herschel said.

"We can stop them, too," Walt said and shared a nod around the circle.

"Long as we do things legal, they can't do nothing," Herschel said. He rose and assured everyone, "I'll be there to help you all. We better get some things done."

"Good luck on your campaign," Nels said, and the others joined in. Herschel thanked them.

He ordered a bag of hard candy and licorice at the counter. Three signatures was all he had out of them. He had expected a hundred percent participation from the Horse Creek men. Instead he'd have to look elsewhere for his support. Even Larkin acted anxious over the matter, handing him the sack of sweets across the counter. Maybe he'd taken on the impossible. No, he owed Jack Diehl more than that.

He rode on down to Marsha's. If he'd gotten around quicker, he could have reached her place before midafternoon. She came out of the house, wrapping up against the north wind, and greeted him with a hug.

"I'm glad you're back. Let's put Cob up in the barn— What's wrong?"

"I don't want you to get the wrong idea."

She swept her hair back and looked him in the eye. "What idea?"

"I just came to talk."

"Good. Put Cob up and we can talk inside where it's warm."

"Marsha—"

"Go on. I'll make some coffee." She shoved him toward the barn with both hands on his back.

"All right. I'll be there."

"Good." She laughed into the wind and he left her, shaking his head in amused defeat. Nothing he could do with her. Walt was right, Marsha was an outdoors woman.

He stomped his feet on the porch, and on cue she opened the door. "Girls are over at the Fergusons' playing with Molly today. They'll be upset they missed your harmonica."

"Well, I brought them some candy, so I'll leave it."

"You're spoiling them."

"They can use some of that, too." He let her help him out of the greatcoat and she took the scarf and cap. When she turned back from hanging them on hooks, he put up the coat. His move trapped her between him and the wall. Awkward as the situation felt at first, she slipped inside his arms and hugged him tight.

"I wish this winter would fly by," she said, her cheek resting on his vest.

"I'll be glad to see the spring breakup, too."

"Cattle are dying and we've got months to go." She disengaged, hurried to her boiling water and added ground coffee to the pot.

"I knew you'd be mad, but I did it anyway—well, when I lost my temper."

"What's that?" she asked, putting the lid down.

"I took out a petition to be on the ballot as sheriff."

She closed her eyes as if pained and then shook her head in defeat.

"I knew it would pi—I mean make you mad."

"Herschel Baker, I sure ain't—well, mad. I'm worried—not about anything but them back-shooting you." She herded him to a chair in front of the fireplace and brought another to sit on.

"When Talbot said he wasn't going to do nothing—I lost it. And decided justice would only come if folks got upset and ran him out of office."

She nodded and chewed on her lip.

"Couple of hours ago, I stopped at Larkin's and I learned this ain't going to be as easy as I figured."

"How's that?"

He went to his coat, came back and handed her the petition. "I only got three out of six up here to sign it."

"Walt Ferguson. N. Hansen, Loren MacDuffy" she read. "How many more you need?"

"Forty-seven."

"By when?"

"April fifteenth."

"You want my help?"

"Ah, Marsha, you've got girls to raise, a ranch to run."

She leaned forward, put her hands on his knees and looked him hard in the eye. "You want to be sheriff of Yellowstone County, I'll help you get elected."

"It may be a fool's race. I'm opposing both the Democrats and Republicans."

"I can't think of a tougher battle, but I know you'll win in the end."

He wished he had her confidence. His lack of acceptance at Larkin's store earlier had disappointed him bad enough he'd almost torn up the paper riding down there. Maybe he could win—for Jack Diehl anyway.

Before he knew it, she was sitting on his lap, holding his face and kissing him. "To the next sheriff of Yellowstone County."

Damn, he felt afraid to even touch her. Lordy, this was going to be hard. The run for sheriff, the fear he saw in some of those men's faces around the stove—that was what had Larkin upset. And what should he do about Marsha? His arms encircled her. At least he had one more supporter. That made four. He hoped she or the girls didn't get hurt over his hardheadedness to pursue this election. Then he kissed her hard and tasted the honey in her mouth.

FIVE

Buck Palmer drove Chester out to his small spread. He paused on the rise and counted the snowcapped haystacks. If this winter lasted through March, he'd be out of feed. Lots of folks would be worse off, that didn't have any feed at all. No way anything could paw down to grass under all the frozen snow and ice coating the land. Even the usual windswept valleys were clogged with the damn white stuff. Besides, the summer's drought had shriveled all the feed up anyway. Nothing for them to dig up.

Folks were heading for a real bust if a chinook didn't blow in early and relieve them. Another place to operate from might be all right—this Diehl outfit down on Horse Creek would be his only on paper.

He clucked to Chester and slapped him with the reins, and snow flew from the thin rims of the buggy's wheels.

The saddle horses and draft animals had hay in the rack; he hoped those two'd fed the bawling cattle something.

Disgusted and already mad, he hitched Chester and headed for the bunkhouse.

"You two ever do anything up here?" he demanded, bursting in the door.

"Damn right. We pitch off a heaping load of hay every other day to them crying cows of yours," Smith said, looking up from his bacon cooking in a skillet.

"What day was that?"

"Yesterday. Them sons bitches got the hollow belly." Smith turned back to tending his bacon. "You want to eat?"

"Sure. It's my damn food ain't it?"

"I just asked if you was hungry."

"How long's the hay going to last?"

"Six weeks at a load a day," Daws said, standing up and stretching.

"We better cut them to one every other day."

"Your hay, your cows," Smith said. "Don't guess you can buy any?"

"Those horse people can pay more than I can for it." Palmer shook his head and looked hard at the two. "There's a sale coming up in two weeks. Your buddy Jack Diehl's place. I want you two there, but don't raise no ruckus. Avoid me. If I need you, you'll know about it."

"Damn, that was fast," Daws said and frowned.

"He owed the bank a lot of money. They ain't taking no chances on losing it or having it disappear."

"What are we going to do there?" Daws asked.

"Just show up two weeks from Wednesday. The auctioneer's coming from Dakota. They didn't want anyone from around here connected with them damn rustlers doing the sale."

Daws nodded, went to the feed store calendar on the wall and circled the date with a pencil. "We'll be there. Any more trouble?"

"Ya, some guy from down there by the name of Baker took out a petition to run for sheriff."

Daws looked at Smith, who shrugged. "Never heard of him."

"If he gets too big for his pants, you boys can trim him down. But not yet—I get word of anyone's signing that paper, we might sign them on, too." Palmer took a seat at the wood table. "We're gonna be busy, boys. Keep your noses clean and stay out of sight. Might even be a bonus in it for you two. Say a couple hundred."

"Now you're talking," Daws said, sitting down on the other side, ready to eat.

"What's this guy Baker's full name?" Smith asked, putting a pan of biscuits on the table from the oven, then going back for his skillet-fried potatoes and bacon.

"Herschel Baker. Some cowboy about thirty. Got a place north of Larkin's store," Palmer said. "If all he gets are a few of them rustlers to sign it, fine, we let him have his fun. But if it gets serious, we will get that way, too." Palmer broke open a steaming biscuit and lathered it with cow butter from a bowl.

"We'll check him out," Smith said, "when we're down there."

"Just don't draw any attention."

"Hell—" Smith refilled everyone's coffee cup. Then standing back, he smiled. "We're just cowboys feeding hay."

"Make gawdamn sure you stay that way." Palmer nodded over the flavor of the biscuit he had bit into. "Hell, ole Daws ain't never getting married with a cook like you around."

They all laughed. Palmer wasn't all that amused, but he needed loyalty out of the two Texans. They were stupid, but also callous enough to kill whoever he said and maybe do it even before if he didn't keep them on a rein. No time to start training new ones—MacDavis wanted those rustlers cleared off Horse Creek in twelve months. Diehl was the first to go. Baker might be next.

Palmer chewed on his fried bacon and listened to the wind in the eves of the shack. Damn winter anyway—wouldn't ever even let up. He double hated the northern plains—give him the warm south, gulf breezes and white cotton boles. This snowballs and icicles two feet long were for the stupid.

"We'd like to slip into Billings and share some old gal's bed," Daws said.

"Yeah and get hooched up and go to talking." He scowled at the Texan in disapproval.

"Naw, just go in and get right out."

"I've got a shack on the south side of the Yellowstone. Monday afternoon before that sale, you two ride up there and build a fire in the stove. My man Earl will bring some floozy over there and leave her."

"For all night?"

"All night, but if you beat her up or mark her, you won't ever get another chance."

"Hellfire," Smith said, on the edge of his chair. "We'll treat her like a damn princess."

"You know the place?"

"Yeah," Daws said. "We met you there once."

"I'll handle it, and she don't need to know nothing either. You two keep your mouths shut."

"We will. Could you send a bottle or two out with her?" Daws asked. Both Texans hung on his answer.

"Yeah and things go good at Diehl's sale, I'll do it again."

"Her and the whiskey?" Smith asked, waiting for his reply.

"I said that."

"Fine." He went to gathering dishes. Daws dressed to

hitch the team to the hay sled. Those two fed in the warmest part of the day—ten degrees below zero on the door facing.

Palmer left his place for Billings. The gray bank he studied in the northwest was a harbinger of more damn snow. He made Chester trot fast. No need in being caught out in a blizzard. He drove past the bawling herd on the bedding ground. They were alive so far. Didn't look too thin. Wolves would be a problem soon as the cattle grew weaker—he'd need to send a note to them Monday. They'd better start killing some lobos.

SIX

Monday the storm let up and snow only blew parallel to the ground. Herschel rode up to see Barley Benton, a horse trader in his late forties who lived with a squaw north of Billings. Herschel's plan was to talk with the longtime friend and sometime advisor and get back home by Tuesday afternoon to feed his own stock.

Barley was married to a Crow woman, Big Heart, who he called Heart. She answered the door when Herschel knocked. Her small figure shocked him for the moment. Heavens, he decided, she wasn't much taller than Marsha's ten-year-old, Kate.

Heart smiled and ushered him in.

"Man, it's a cold damn day for you to come clear up here. Must be serious." His big pipe bowl in his hand, Barley used the stem to direct his wife to take Herschel's things as he undressed. Walking over, the slender-built man stuck out his hand, and they shook.

"Serious enough," Herschel said. "You've heard they shot Jack Diehl in the back."

"Small piece in the paper last week."

"Billings Bank and Trust is having a sheriff's sale a week from Wednesday."

"Hmm," Barley grunted and motioned toward a chair in the fireplace's circle. "They sure didn't take long."

"Said it was to protect their interests, since the man was gone."

Barley's glare focused on the flames in the fireplace. He nodded and then sucked on his pipe. "Things can get done that ordinarily take months, if you have some power."

"Actually I rode up here for some advice and help."

"Well, Hersch, I don't know how much I can help, but fire away."

"I went to the sheriff and asked him to investigate Jack's murder."

Relighting his pipe, Barley nodded for him to continue.

"To make things short, he turned me down. Said folks down there wouldn't help him, and the rest amounted for me to go to hell."

"We all know Talbot works for the big outfits."

"So—I got mad and took out a petition to run for sheriff as an Independent."

"Sounds serious."

"It is. I'll need fifty signatures of qualified voters to file—and I thought I could count on the folks up at Horse Creek."

"No luck?" Barley frowned his frosty brows at him.

"Three out of five. Six counting Larkin, who passed, too."

Heart brought them steaming coffee in tin cups and Herschel thanked her. He turned back for the older man's impression.

"Them big boys got hired guns and toughs on their payrolls. Family men like that lot down there have to think about their families. They've got wives and kids that you don't have. Jack's death was one more thing to make them jumpy. No, I can see them not signing."

"What do I do?"

"Start having meetings at the various schoolhouses around the county. Give me a week and I'll have you two up here. One at Vernon and the other at the Sharky School. We can do one on Monday night and the other on Tuesday."

Herschel dropped his gaze to the worn flooring. "I'm not no speaker."

"That ain't the issue. You tell them what's in your heart and they'll listen." He used the stem of his pipe to point at the small beaded shield hanging around his neck. Some totem from his scouting days for the army, Herschel decided, as Barley continued, "It will come out of you and convince people."

Herschel took a deep inhale then blew on his coffee. The crackle of the fire grew louder, and uncertainty swallowed his forwardness. "Jack Diehl was a good man."

"Aw, killing is always useless. But obviously he got in someone's way. Who's buying his stuff and place?"

Taken aback by the question, Herschel blinked. "Lordy, I never thought about that being the reason. Kill Jack so they could buy his place?"

Barley shrugged, bent over with his elbows on his knees and sucked on his pipe. "You said how fast they rushed it. Was he behind bad or had he missed his payment?"

"No." Herschel's stomach churned over the notion. "The excuse was to protect their assets—like she couldn't do that or someone would steal a handcart."

The aroma of pipe smoke mixed with the burning pine

filled his nose as he sat back arms folded and considered the sale. It meant he needed to be there and observe it all. Clues to Jack's death and the killers might be found in the ones who raised their hands to bid.

"Week from Monday too soon?" Herschel asked, thinking about Barley's offer to draw folks to a community meeting.

"Naw, folks are looking for an excuse for a break and a potluck dinner. Been a tough winter. I ain't going to want to count the losses of stock come springtime."

"And that'll be months from now. Which reminds me I have to get home and feed mine."

"Got enough hay?" Barley asked.

"I think so, but I'll use all of it this year."

"Them big outfits ones are going hurt."

Herschel nodded. "Those years of open winters spoiled them. I bet that many didn't put up even enough horse hay."

"Last summer's drought hurt, too. Ain't no feed down there under all this ice and snow."

"There sure ain't. I'll be ready for spring," Herschel said, standing and stretching.

"Better eat a bowl of her elk stew. Keep your insides from rubbing together going back." Barley indicated for his wife to get him some.

"I won't turn that down."

Barley's long hand clapped Herschel on the shoulder. "Good sign you ain't lost all your senses since jumping into politics."

Heart knelt in front of the fireplace, drew out the iron pot hanging on an arm, removed the lid with a pot holder. She stirred the stew, then used a buffalo-horn dipper to fill a tortoise shell of the steaming brew.

Barley went after a spoon for him and laughed. "Using

our Sunday go-to-meeting china there." Indicating the bowl, both men laughed.

Saliva filled his mouth at the first sip off the spoon. Elk stew held a hearty flavor all its own that Herschel couldn't spell out, but he savored every spoonful. Sometime he'd make a trek to the high country in the fall and shoot a couple elk for winter meat before they were all gone. Folks talked how only a few years before they'd shot them along the Yellowstone River around Billings. But he'd only seen a few in his three years on Horse Creek.

"I've got some advice," Barley said and relighted his pipe.

"That and your help is why I came up here."

"Oh, Hersch, I'll do all I can, but you need to watch your backside. These guys won't play square. It ain't no game for them—it's real and down dirty."

"I'll do that—and thanks, the stew was wonderful."

"Hell, go to bragging on her cooking and she'll run off and find her a real man."

"No, Barley, she's got him."

"Well, that's arguable. Week from Monday here."

"I'll try not to embarrass you."

"You need to plan on spending the nights here."

"Yes, sir. See you. Bye, Heart. Thanks for the wonderful stew." He headed for the door and his coat.

He spent that night at the livery bunk room, and in the predawn, breathing vapors, he headed south on Cob, gnawing on beef jerky for his breakfast. Plenty enough things to do at home. Feed hay and all. He needed to get back and see Marsha and the girls, too. For certain, he didn't want to lose that contact—he'd begun to notice how he could even be with her alone and not be nervous. Must be a sign, but getting on the ballot came first and April wasn't that far away. Why was getting fifty signatures so hard?

Then he recalled—he hadn't even gotten Barley's on the paper. One thing for certain, he had to press for more signings or he'd never get in the election.

By noon, he'd finished forking off the last of the hay to his cattle and horses. He drove the team of Belgiums on the large sled back to the barn. Young and fresh, he planned to sell the pair of draft mares and break him another team in the spring. Marsha must get a real workout every day feeding her stock. Tough woman—not man-tough like Calamity Jane, who hung out around Billings—Marsha was the gritty get-it-done kind. Man could find a lot worse ones than her.

The big mares unharnessed and in the pen, he headed for the house. Snow crunching under his boot soles, he opened the door and barged in. Be cold inside. No fire in a couple of days. He found the water bucket frozen solid—dang, he'd forgotten to empty it. On his knees, gloves off, he began to build a fire in the potbellied stove. The acrid smell of ashes in his nose and his belly growling, he'd be glad when he had some food in it and was in bed. Cold weather sure wore him out.

When he struck a match on the side of the stove to ignite his kindling, he heard someone shout outside. Who was that? He put the flame to the splinters and rose to go see. Late for company.

"Herschel?" a rider on horseback called out. "Mark Rielly, sir."

"Yes, I know you. Get off the horse and come inside," he said to the teenager.

"No, I can't. Dad was in a horse wreck this afternoon and broke his leg. Maw asked if you'd come set it?"

"I ain't a doc—"

"Doc's in Billings. He can't travel that far, besides you've set broken legs before and they're up walking."

"Get off that horse, come inside. I need to grab some grub and I'll go with you."

"Good. Maw said, you would if'n I asked you real nice."

Herschel closed the door behind the boy and shook his head at the boy's words. Turned, he could see the fire was started and he needed to close the stove's door. "Been gone to see a friend and just finished haying."

"Paw says you're running for sheriff." The youth stood close to the still-cold stove as if hoping for some heat.

"If I get the signatures I need." No time to cook food. He found some raisins to put in his pocket for his supper and gave some to the boy.

"Oh, I bet you will." Mark popped some in his mouth and nodded in approval.

"Wish I was that sure. Stove'll be all right," he said, closing the door on it and turning the damper down. "We better get over there and see about your dad. You can tell me what happened on the way."

Sweet raisins in his mouth to chew on, he caught Cob up and resaddled him. He could hope for one thing. He hoped he could help Rielly when he got there. The afternoon wind had settled some, and a ghostly white world swept the rolling country as they headed southwest. Still cold as the Arctic for Herschel's part. He felt elated when they topped the rise and the low sun shone on the glass-bottle windows at the Rielly homestead.

"That you, Herschel?" Ruby Rielly shouted, wrapping a cape over her shoulders as she came out. "Mark, you put up his horse and grain him. My lands, am I glad you were home."

"I just got home and finished feeding when Mark rode over."

"Hated sending for you, but I had no one else I could

think about could do this. Rielly's leg's busted and you were the only one knows how to set one."

"A doc might be better." He swept off his cap and nodded to the pale-faced rancher in the chair as he unbuttoned his coat. "How're you doing?"

"She hurts. For something not supposed to have feeling, she hurts powerful." He rubbed the outstretched leg stretched on a long board to the next chair.

"It'll hurt for a while, too. Can you tell where it's broken?"

Rielly shook his head, looking faint. "I guess below the knee."

Herschel bent over when Rielly lifted his pants leg, and when he saw that the underwear was distended, he nodded. "It's pretty swollen. Guess we'll need you on a bed and undressed."

"Let's get it over with," Rielly said.

"Better wait for Mark," Herschel said. His head pounded with all the things he should be sure to do in the next short while. A man's life and livelihood depended on him—a man without any medical training. How many broken bones had he set? Several for cowboys hurt in wrecks with cattle and horses. Fixed Billy Johns's busted arm when he fell down the cathouse steps in Ogallala. And a dozen or more broken ribs he'd set and bound up, legs and arms, even set a collarbone, but never knew if it would've knit—the patient, a rowdy Texas cowboy, was shot to death three days later in a card-game scrap.

"He had any painkiller?" he asked her.

"Yes."

"Give him some more. This won't be fun."

She agreed and rushed off for the bottle. A big spoonful of the laudanum and Rielly made a face. Then nodded that he understood.

When Mark came in, he got under one shoulder and Herschel the other while Ruby cleared the way to the bed.

"Take off his pants and cut off his underwear bottoms," Herschel said, while they held him.

"Damn, she really throbs—" Rielly said, trying to be tough, but the beads of perspiration popped out on his unsuntanned forehead as big as match heads.

In minutes, she had his pants off and she used a scissors to snip his underwear off above the knee. Shame to waste them, but he'd hurt worse on his back with them fighting them off of him.

At last, they eased him down and let him lay back on the spread. His eyes looked rheumy from the drug when Herschel sent Mark after some thick sticks and Ruby to start making strips out of cloth.

"It's going to be a few minutes before I can set it," Herschel said, sitting on the edge of the bed.

"Fine—fine—damn fool thing, me trying to chase that colt. Horse I was riding went down and fell on my leg. I heard it pop when we went down."

"Where's the colt?"

"Got away—"

"I'll get him up for you in the morning."

"I was going to halter-break him."

"Mark can do that while you heal."

"How long?"

"Better stay off it two weeks and don't ride for a month."

"He's just a boy." Rielly shook his head. "He can't do everything needs done around this place."

"Maybe you fell on your hard head, Tam Rielly. That's the first time you ever said that in your whole bloody life." She ripped apart another two-inch-wide strip from a white sack.

"Damnit woman, he's got to live in a mighty tough world. I want it so he survives."

"Well, if he does, it won't be because you didn't try to kill him."

Mark came in with an armload. Herschel went to select some to use for splints. Then he used a hatchet to shorten a few and split one board. They looked like they would work. That chore completed, he went back to the bed.

"I want you to lie flat. I need Mark to hold his shoulders down. Ruby, you hold his leg at the top. Try not to kick."

"I'll try. . . ."

For a brief second, Herschel closed his eyes and prayed. Then he took Rielly's foot and carefully turned it as the man moaned. He felt underneath the swollen calf and hoped against hope that the broken bone was coming into place. When Rielly screamed and flinched, Herschel knew the bones were together. Both feet looked equally straight. Maybe he wouldn't limp too bad when it healed.

"Mark, we need the splints." He nodded to Ruby when she shot him a questioning look. "The strips. Yes. I'll hold the leg in place. You two have to splint it. Don't move, Tam."

Under his directions, the leg was soon bound up. At long last, he sat back and wiped the sweat off his face on his sleeve. He felt clammy all over and wondered if they had done it right.

She shoved a cup at him. He looked up at her, realizing it was whiskey, and nodded.

"I'll fix you some food," she said. "Mark told me yeh had raisins for lunch."

He laughed and shook his head. "I hadn't had time to cook anything yet when he got there. It was all I could find."

She acknowledged his response and covered her sleeping husband with two blankets while Herschel stood up, sipping the whiskey.

"I'll cook you some real food in a minute. My Lord, the moon must be in a bad phase. Been more bad things happened in the past few weeks." She swept off to fix the meal.

Sun must have set; he closed his eyes to the lamplight and considered everything. Save for Marsha and the girls, his life hadn't been running too well either. He hoped Rielly's leg healed straight. Nothing more he could do for him, but pray.

SEVEN

Nels Hansen agreed for his boy Toby to tend to Herschel's cattle while he campaigned up in the northern part of the country. So Herschel fed early on Sunday morning, then rode down to meet Marsha and the girls at the Box Elder Schoolhouse for church. He joined them in the back row between hymns. Services had already started, and the four females all nodded in approval at his arrival.

"They ain't took up the collection yet," three-year-old Sarah said loud enough some folks and kids nearby snickered.

"Hush," Marsha whispered.

Sarah gave her mother an exasperated look up. "He needed to know that."

"Not so loud everyone else heard you. Now sing."

After the services, and before Herschel passed out into the brilliantly sunlit but still cold outdoors, Reverend Macken shook his hand. "Good luck on your campaign, Herschel. God bless you."

"Thanks, Lewis. I'll need all the help I can get."

The man nodded as if he understood and then spoke to the party behind them.

"We better get home and cook some dinner," Marsha said as they headed for the wagon.

He agreed, exchanging pleasantries with others as they all separated in the schoolyard.

"Maybe some of them would sign that petition," she said under her breath.

He looked ahead at her wagon and team with Cob hitched to the tailgate. "I ain't so desperate yet to go to funerals and church services to ask for their support."

"Just an idea," she said.

"I may need lots of them."

"Surely you'll get several at those meetings your friend Barley has set up."

With a "Here you go," he helped her onto the seat, then began loading the girls. "Sure can hope so. But this petition signing isn't like dropping your name that you'd do this or that. Your signature is a matter of public record that you're supporting the opposition."

"I know," she said, untying the reins. "But it looks to me, with all the ill feelings, someone would have the guts to do it. I sure would if I was a man."

He laughed at her huffy words and winked at the amused girls busy bundling themselves up in the back of the wagon. "You would, too. Want me to drive?"

For a long moment, she looked at her gloved hands holding the reins. "Oh, yes," she said as if taken aback by his offer. "That would be very nice of you."

"You girls aren't afraid of my driving, are you?" he asked, climbing up beside her on the spring seat.

"No! You drive," came the chorus.

Marsha pursed her lips and nodded. "I'm just used to doing it."

"You'll soon be so self-sufficient you won't even want me around." He clucked to the team, swung them around another rig and headed for the east road. The snowy ruts hard-packed and frozen, the shod horses had no trouble starting up the long grade.

She slapped his knee with her gloved hand. "That's not so. I know how hard it was for you to feed and get down here in time for church. Beside having to ride to Billings this evening."

"I wasn't complaining about that. Why, I'd've had a dinner of oatmeal by myself if I'd not come down here."

"Oatmeal for dinner?" one of the girls demanded.

Marsha turned and gave them a frown.

"That sounds good to you?" he asked, feeling mischievous as the horses topped the rise and headed down the backbone atop the polar cap.

"Not for dinner," Kate said.

"Mr. Baker does not raise a garden or can, like we do."

"Why don't they call me Herschel?" he asked her.

"Because that wouldn't be proper."

"It would be to me. I'm not some old stuffy judge or old man."

"No, but you'll be the next sheriff of Yellowstone County."

He gazed across the silver-clad landscape and shook his head. "I wish I was that certain."

She bumped him with her shoulder. "Better get ready, Sheriff Baker."

He clucked to keep the horses in a jog. This whole idea of running for office had taken on a somber note for him. If he'd only pushed someone else into taking the job. Maybe they would have impressed everyone, and his campaign would have gone like a wildfire. For the moment, Herschel's feeling was that the campaign was little more than a smoldering fire in a wet pile of old hides.

While she cooked the noon meal, he forked a load of hay onto the sled for her to feed later. Kate was helping him and he was amazed at the young girl's ability to fork the sweet alfalfa.

"That's enough," she finally said, when the pile on the sled reached shoulder high on him.

"You're sure?" he said to tease her.

"Oh, yes. Mr. Baker. The hay has to last till spring." She took the forks and headed for the shed to put them up.

"I guess that's right," he said, trailing along.

"You can sure pitch hay. It takes mother and me twice that long."

"Maybe because I'm a man."

She looked up at him, squinting against the too-bright sun. "I've thought about that, too."

"You have?"

"Yes. If I ever marry someone, I'm going to be sure he can pitch hay that fast, too."

Herschel chuckled and hugged her shoulder. "Good idea, Kate."

Pitchforks in the barn, they headed for the house. The big collie, Rand, bounced around in the snow, anxious to play.

"Go on," she said. "Hersch and I aren't wanting to play—oh, I wasn't supposed to call you that." She put her mitten to her mouth.

"Hey, I won't report it."

"Good. Mom would be upset."

Rand stopped and began to bark. Herschel could see two riders coming up the creek road. He paused and tried to make them out.

"You know who they are?"

She looked at them hard, then shook her head.

The pair rode in close and reined in their fume-breathing ponies. One was short and thicker-set, the other a beanpole. Both were dressed like stuffed dolls. The short one spoke. "We're missing two big work mares."

No hello, no nothing—just a hard look at Kate that Herschel considered indecent.

"I guess we ain't met before," Herschel said.

"Name's Daws, he's Smith."

"Baker's mine."

Daws, the shorter one, nodded. "Seen them mares?"

"No." He looked at Kate.

She shook her head. "They haven't been with our stock."

"Probably stolen," Daws said. "Well, we've got to get on."

"Nice to meet you," Herschel said, thinking about what Buster Corey told him about the pair. *Watch out for them.*

"Sure," Daws said and they turned and rode on.

"Who were they?" Marsha asked, holding open the door as they went inside.

"Two men looking for work horses."

Herschel stopped in the open doorway for a moment to be sure they'd rode on. Then he removed his cap and went inside.

"Something wrong?"

"Those two weren't looking for any lost horses. They were sizing things up. Keep your shotgun loaded," he said to her under his breath.

"I didn't see them good enough—"

"I did, Mom," Kate said. "I'd know them anywhere. Kind a creepy. That Smith guy never said a word."

"What did they really want?"

"I knew that I'd be a wizard. Hay's on the sled," he said to change the subject. He took the harmonica out of his pocket and began to saw on it with his mouth. "Old Dan Tucker" soon filled the warm room. The girls quickly started to frolic and dance around the floor, until Marsha called them all to come eat.

Kate and then Herschel washed their hands. "I always like your music," Kate said. "It sure livens things up."

Marsha closed her eyes and shook her head. "It's delightful."

"Aw, we all get too serious at times. Music switches the mood," he said and took his place at the table. Despite the uplift in tempo, he still wondered what those two rannies were up to.

"It sure does." Marsha put her hand on his forearm. "Kate, ask the grace please."

"Our dear heavenly father . . ."

That evening, Herschel had a late supper at the cafe in Billings, but Buster had already gone home for the day, they told him. Later, he stopped off at the Antelope Saloon and drank one red-eye, made small talk at the bar with a couple cowboys he knew, then set out under the stars for the livery. The frosted crust crunching under his soles, a block from the Antelope, he stopped in the deep shadows of a business porch. He thought he was being followed. Whatever had triggered the notion—he could not explain. More a gut feeling than anything else.

Controlling his breathing and listening hard, he decided whoever was behind him had stopped as well. An ear turned, he listened to the muted sounds of the saloons, tinny player pianos, and raucous laughter of some doves. Nothing.

After a few minutes, he hurried on to Paschal's stables and joined the log-sawing crowd already in their bunks. On his back under the cover, he stared in the flickering candlelight at the ropes that held the bed above him, and wondered why he felt so jumpy. He'd better learn more about Daws and Smith, too. Then past forever fretting about them, he finally fell asleep.

EIGHT

THERE were lots of rigs in the schoolyard at Vernon. Smoke poured out the chimney. From the seat of his buckboard, which he shared with Heart, Barley nodded in approval at them when they drove up. Grateful for the numbers, Herschel agreed. Impressed at the sight of them all, he felt better about the meeting, and it was still early. Cob hitched to the wagon, he followed the two of them inside.

Some of the men he knew from meeting them earlier at auctions, horse trades and sales. Others shook his hand and smiled. He felt welcome in the school building bustling with children and busy-talking grown-ups. The situation even eased up some on his gut-wrenching worries about what he was going to say to them.

"Barley says you want to be sheriff," a man with white billy-goat whiskers said.

"Yes, I would, sir."

"That's a damn shame."

"Oh, no, we need a new sheriff that—" The man's head shake made him stop his explanation.

"I mean is I only vote for Democrats."

"I can understand that."

"Well, long as you ain't mad."

"No, that's why we live in America. So we can all vote like we want to."

"Democrat."

Herschel thanked him and moved off to speak to another man he knew: Bill Carr. Under a high-crown Texas hat, a broad smile crossed Carr's face.

"How've you been, Hersch?"

"Fine so far. Too cold not to be."

"Ain't that the truth. Barley says you're taking them all on."

"Yes, I figure if we'll ever get any law in this county, someone needs to run for office."

"Somehow I never imagined seeing you someday in a fancy-dan wool overcoat and a hundred-dollar hat speaking to folks."

"We need less speaking and more work."

Carr laughed, then dropped his voice. "I'll send you some money by Barley. You'll need it for ads and things—expenses."

"Thanks," he said and nodded in approval. The gesture reinforced things in his mind; people were upset by the current law in Billings and where its loyalty lay.

The tables of food were set out at six, and serving began. Two women hustled the embarrassed Herschel to the head of the line, and to keep from hurting feelings, he tried to sample every dish. That soon proved impossible. Before he reached the end of the line, he was down to saying thanks and how he'd try it later to the anxious women behind the table, who each stood ready to dish out her favorite recipe.

He took a seat at the first table he came to. In an instant, a dark-eyed brunette put a piece of huckleberry pie in his face.

"I know you wanted this," she said in a deep drawl. "My name's Katherine Hines. I live on Crab Creek and you can come by any time and have more . . . pie."

Herschel felt his face heat up. "Well, thank you, ma'am. I'll remember that."

"And make sure her husband ain't home," Barley said under his breath, tucking a white towel in his shirt collar for a bib.

"Oh."

"Ain't no secret, Katherine 'entertains.'"

"I appreciate that."

"Better get comfortable with those sort of things; she won't be the last."

"I shall, Barley."

At last, a preacher named Conley introduced him as the next sheriff of Yellowstone County.

"Thank you," Herschel began after the applause. "There's two kinds of law up here in Montana. One's only for the big ranchers and they have their man in office. But I think we need equal protection.

"My best friend, Jack Diehl, was shot in the back a few weeks ago, and no one down there in Billings has turned a hand to investigate his murder. Tonight, I need you that are willing to face up to the other forces. By signing this paper and allowing me to run as an Independent, you will be exposing yourself, because it will be on public record when I file my petition.

"That's enough politics. Let's dance."

They applauded him and then began moving the tables back. In his best buckskins, Barley came to stand near him. Many came by and shook his hand, thanking him for running, but none asked for the petition. At last a man with an obvious bad hip came by and asked to sign it.

"Wils Reynolds is my name. I ain't afraid of them bullies. Let me sign it."

"Sure." His heart racing, he whipped out the paper and pencil. "Here."

The older man's steel eyes looked hard at him. "I hope you whup ass and fill the jail with half that bunch or more."

Herschel chuckled at the man's words and shook his hand before he left. Barley signed the petition after Reynolds, and a burly man, Phineas Green, another horse trader, walked over to autograph it.

"I hope they read my name on this," Green said. "I'm so tired of that rude bunch overrunning our ranges with their damn cattle and thinking they own it all. Good luck, Herschel."

"I figured more would sign it when they came up," Barley said after Green left and no one moved toward them.

"Those big outfits got these folks all scared."

Barley bobbed his head. "Yeah and a lot worse than I even imagined."

"It's one thing to talk bad about 'em and hate 'em, but signing your name to a public document is a different story."

"I'm learning," Barley said, and with disgust he shook his head.

The next evening in Vernon, four more men came forward and signed the petition at their dance and potluck. They took up a collection for Herschel's campaign by passing the hat through the crowd and earned him twelve dollars and thirty-two cents. He thanked everyone and started to leave early to make Billings for a few hours' sleep. He didn't want to miss the Diehl foreclosure sale the next day.

"Sorry we didn't get more signatures," Barley lamented, beating his gloved hands together in the starlight.

"Hey. We tried. Maybe tomorrow, I can get some more at the sale."

"Listen, I can twist some more arms. Come back in a week and I'll have them."

Herschel agreed and booted Cob into the night after thanking his friend for all the hard work he'd done arranging the meetings.

"No problem. They love them. Watch your backside!" Barley shouted after him.

"I will," Herschel promised, dreading the night ride to town and wondering if he would ever get fifty brave souls on the line.

NINE

MARSHA Allen loaded the girls in the wagon shortly after daybreak, as well as several food items she was bringing for the community meal at the sale. Her heart filled with dread over what this day would bring. She clucked to Essie and Clyde, then began to drive the pair up the Horse Creek Road. She wanted to be there early and help set up.

"Will the Diehl girls still be there?" Nina, her middle one, asked.

"I don't know. They may have already left. There will be other children to play with."

"It ain't fair."

"What's that?" Marsha asked over her shoulder, the sharp wind cutting her eyes above the face scarf.

"Selling them out," Kate said, from the back.

"It's the law."

"It won't be when Herschel—I mean, Mr. Baker is the sheriff."

"We can't count on that yet."

"Oh, he'll win. Everyone likes him."

Marsha looked at the azure sky. *I hope so.*

When they arrived, the homestead was buzzing. Each girl took something to the tables set up on boards atop barrels. Sarah carried two fresh loaves of unsliced bread wrapped in a basket and trekked after the other two. Marsha carried the still-hot dutch oven.

Nelda Hansen directed her to the fire with the oven. "We can keep it warm here till the fire burns down. Then shovel hot coals on it later."

Marsha agreed and talked to the others as they spoke to her.

"Where's Herschel?" one woman asked, looking around for him.

"Campaigned up at Vernon Schoolhouse last night."

"Oh, he won't be here."

"No, he's coming. The sale may be started by then, but he's coming."

"How is the petition-signing coming?"

"Oh, he needs more, but many are coming forward now." She wished what she'd said had been the truth. Deep in the pit of her stomach she was concerned—not only about his safety, but about the lack of support they'd shown him. What was wrong with these people? Then she turned to the sound of loud voices arguing.

Sam Talbot in his expensive wool topcoat and fancy high crown hat was making tracks for the house.

"What's happening?" Marsha asked one of the other women.

"I think some of the men are making a stand against the sheriff and him selling her personal things."

"Oh, dear God—" She bit on a knuckle and wished Herschel was there. Where were her girls? There might be shooting. Oh, dear God. . . . She located Nina and ran through the moving throng. Sarah? Where was she?

"Kate. Kate Allen!"

At last she saw her eldest face's weaving through the people and coming toward her. "Where's Sarah?"

"In the house playing with a doll."

"We ain't standing for you selling her personal things," Nels Hansen said from the porch, blocking Talbot's hired flunkies ready to remove them. Joe Gentry and Max Tagget stood on each side.

"You're interfering with the law here," Talbot said, out of breath

"Wait!" Marsha said.

All heads turned as she came though the throng. "My baby is in there and I'm going to get her out before the shooting starts here."

"There will be no shooting," Talbot said.

"Never mind what you say." Marsha shrugged off a deputy on her arm and stalked for the porch. The titter of the crowd's laughter at her telling him off was loud enough. Past Hansen, she scooped up her wide-eyed child, turned and headed back for the circling mob.

"You ain't selling her things." Hansen stood defiant. The slant-eyed ranchers flanking him nodded the same.

"Then I'm arresting you three for obstructing justice."

"Talbot, you do, you'll regret it," Hansen said.

"You three can't buck the law, Hansen. I have a court order to sell everything. Arrest those three!"

The four deputies armed with shotguns moved toward the porch.

Marsha saw Hansen size the situation up and then raise his hands. Obviously, with all the people there, he didn't want any trouble or anyone hurt. The other two did the same. Ignoring all Sarah's questions and her other two girls with her, Marsha watched them disarm the three men and march them to a buckboard. An eerie silence had settled over the crowd. No one liked what was happening, yet they didn't know how to stop it short of bloodshed. Hansen shook his head for the others not to do anything when they handcuffed him and the other two men in the bed of the wagon.

"Talbot, you better enjoy today. You won't have many more behind that badge," Hansen said, taking a seat in the bed.

"I'm doing what the court instructed for me to do," Talbot protested. "You men are violating the law opposing those orders. You will be tried before the judge in Billings, sentenced and fined."

"Turn them loose, you old blowhard!" a woman shouted.

"Yeah!" went up the cry. But with the sheriff backed by his four shotgun guards, the crowd backed down.

Marsha watched the deputies all mount up, but for the one who drove Talbot's buckboard.

"We'll bail you out!" one of the men shouted.

"How much?" someone else shouted at the sheriff.

"That's for the judge to say. I imagine on the magnitude of the charge, two hundred fifty apiece."

His stinging words silenced the crowd. Marsha knew seven hundred fifty dollars was a king's ransom to these people. Maybe he was bluffing. She hoped so. Anxious about everything, she looked to the north for any sign of Herschel. She kept her girls close and headed for the food table. Maybe after that show of force, some more of them would sign Herschel's petition.

Buck Palmer stood on the sidelines, to himself. He winced at the entire performance of the sheriff. What in the hell could be worth ten cents in that house? Sending all his deputies back to Billings—what if the others caused another riot? These Horse Creek folks were waiting for any spark to set them off. Where in the hell was Baker anyway? He hadn't seen him all morning. Talbot was out of control. Only thing this show of force could do was propel Baker's candidacy like a rocket. Of course, Baker couldn't win; but it would damn sure make his job to see that he didn't get elected ten times harder.

The auctioneer from South Dakota was a slender young man in his early thirties. Palmer figured that smart idea was Talbot's, too. The local ones might have favored these folks and not the bank's interest. The auctioneer opened up with a short speech on how all terms were cash. Then he and the town trash that Talbot hired to help started the sale with harness.

"Someone give me twenty dollars, hey anywhere twenty—"

"One penny," a man from the crowd bid.

"Why, I'd give a dollar," another man said.

Palmer knew that the moment the man had given the bid, someone behind him had given him a swift blow to the kidneys. His face blanched and whirled, then he melted.

"One dollar, one dollar, give a dollar and half anywhere?"

"Sold a dollar." The auctioneer was looking for Talbot. Palmer watched them exchange confused shrugs and he about laughed out loud. Horse Creek folks planned to control the sale, and anyone who bid anything up was going to soon be pressured out of the bidding.

The next item was a Studebaker farm wagon. Ellis Hardware in Billings's name was on the side boards as the sale agent.

"One penny," came the bid.

The auctioneer dropped his gaze to the snowy packed ground. "Anyone knows that wagon is worth a hundred dollars."

"I'm bidding one cent," Loren MacDuffy said. "You got any higher bidders?"

"Yes," Talbot said. "I'll bid ten dollars."

"You better have deep pockets, Talbot," Loren said and stepped back.

"I do. You want to go to jail with your criminal friends?"

Loren laughed aloud. "Who's going to take me? You?"

Talbot waved his finger at the man; then, red faced, he spoke to the auctioneer. "Go on, Colonel. I'll take this wagon."

Palmer watched them sell item after item to the sheriff. He knew the bank would cover the man's purchases, but still it only made the crowd fester more. Talbot was only cooking his own goose. Palmer shuddered under his wool-lined leather coat to think what Rupart MacDavis would say about this day.

In the crowd he'd seen his two men, Daws and Smith. No doubt they were wondering about the deal and what to do. Best they did nothing; the whole thing was going wrong for the sheriff—for himself, he best let Talbot bid in the place and then he could buy it from the bank. Not interested in the items that were selling, he went back and bought a cup of coffee and pie from the women. He knew the Allen widow, and he was up on the gossip about her and Baker. She was busy at the fire stirring something in a large kettle with a wooden paddle.

"How are things selling?" the ample-bodied woman serving him the pie asked.

"Talbot's buying it all."

"Guess he'll have a big bill when this is over."

"Yes, ma'am," Palmer said and took his pie and steaming coffee to the side. Shame he never could do anything about having an affair with that Allen woman. Good-looking, too. Baker must have caught her eye. Maybe with him owning the Diehl place after this sale, he could work his way in with her and put Baker out.

He watched her straighten and speak to the girls who were hand-warming at the big cooking fire. Too far away to hear her words, he knew she was only acting motherly. Nice damn figure on her; even under the heavy clothes, he could imagine it.

"What're we going to do?" Daws asked, under his breath at his side.

Palmer took the cup down, never looked at the man, then said in a sharp whisper, "Not one damn thing and don't get in the way. Talbot's messed it up good this time."

Daws blew on his coffee, nodded, and was gone. When Palmer turned back, he saw what the Allen girls were shouting about. Herschel Baker had arrived, was off his horse and hugging them. Hug them hard, Baker, you might not be doing that for much longer.

TEN

❧

"WHAT'S going on?" Herschel asked Marsha, looking around with a scowl. His gut feelings told him things were not right at the sale. He could hear the auctioneer rattling away and getting no bids.

"Plenty. They took Loren and two others to jail for blocking the sale of her personal things. Under armed shotgun guards, mind you." Marsha made a put-out face at him.

"What else?" He could hardly fathom such a thing—Montana had turned into a police state.

"They've penny-saled things and Talbot's been the only buyer."

Herschel nodded in deep thought. Was their resistance working or not? No way to tell, but he couldn't believe they'd hauled three men off with guards.

"How many signatures did you get?" Her face was fresh-looking and beaming.

"I have thirteen now."

"Give me that petition." Her blue eyes glared. "I'll go get it signed."

"I don't want to hide behind your apron."

She pounded him on the coat sleeve and looked up imploringly at him. "You aren't. I want to show that snotty Talbot what people think of him."

"Well, in that case—" He reached inside his coat and handed her the paper and the pencil. "See what you can do."

"You girls stay here," she said to them, and they agreed. "Get some food, Herschel. Marge, fix him a plate. He probably hasn't ate in half a day."

"Why, sure," the woman said and grinned big. "Going to be a damn sight different when you're sheriff."

He nodded and then he winked at the girls. "Might be even tougher."

"No, Hersch, it'll be lots better," Kate said and the other two agreed.

To eat the plate of steaming beans and ham Marge served him, he sat on some benches the woman had set up out of the wind. Accompanied by the girls who sat around him, he glanced up when the shadow fell on him.

"How's the campaign going?" Buck Palmer asked. The tall, blond-headed, blue-eyed saloon keeper from Billings looked out of place in the wool-skin-lined leather coat and high crown hat.

"Good enough," Herschel said between bites. "Been to Sharky and Vernon. I'm gaining support. Folks ain't use to an an Independent running, I guess."

"Guess you're getting lots of help up here?"

"Oh—some." Herschel was uncertain about what side of this situation the big man was really on. Maybe a fence straddler was all, but he would bear watching anyway. Nevertheless the food was filling a big empty gap in his intestines.

"Well, good luck. Guess you'll be up at Billings next looking for votes."

"I may drop by your place," Herschel said, waiting for his reply.

"Oh, sure, come anytime."

"Good. I wasn't sure where you were in this deal."

"Me?" Buck threw a thumb at his chest. "I just have to be careful. I can't afford to piss off too many folks."

When the big man left, Herschel considered their talk. Maybe he'd been too hard on the man—he needed to sure be careful on who were his friends and who weren't in this deal.

"What's 'piss-off' mean?" Nina asked.

Embarrassed, he thought for a moment. "That's a bad word. He didn't intend for you girls to hear him say that."

Kate nodded that she understood. The middle one shrugged it away and went back to talking to Sarah.

Out of breath, Marsha arrived back and showed him the paper. "I've got fifteen more."

"That easy?" He rose and handed her his plate in exchange for the petition. "That's twenty-eight."

"The three in jail will sign it."

"Loren already has, but that makes thirty with the other two."

"Folks're upset. Her personal things wouldn't've brought that much at a real sale."

He looked down into her blue eyes and agreed. For two cents he'd have kissed her, but with all the folks around and everything, strong brakes on his impulses held him back.

"They're going to sell the place next," Marsha said and sent him off toward the crowd. "I know you want to see it sell."

He put the petition inside his coat, hugged her shoulder and headed for the group.

". . . one hundred sixty acres. You folks know and have seen it. Surveyed and a valid deed. What's my starting bid?"

"Five hundred dollars," Talbot said, and he then looked over the crowd.

Herschel had never noticed before the expensive wool coat the lawman wore. Better dressed than most businessmen in Billings. The crowd stood and waited and listened. Save for a Shanghai rooster crowing in the barn, no one made another bid.

"Sold!" the auctioneer said.

The crowd, still grumbling among themselves, began to move toward the tables and food setup.

"Nice place," Buck Palmer said to Herschel when he turned toward the lunch setup. "Wonder what the bank'll want for it?"

"I have no idea," Herschel said, watching the sheriff talk to the auctioneer. "Maybe Talbot will move down here."

"Not likely." Palmer chuckled at the notion.

"He couldn't even come down here to investigate a murder. Surprised me he came today."

"You don't know? A sheriff gets ten percent of all fore-closure auctions."

"That explains that then. Better go shake some hands," Herschel said. "You might buy it cheap. There ain't many around got much money."

"He have many cattle?"

"You buying them, too?"

"Cheap as I can get them."

"His sale of steers next year would have gotten him out of debt." Herschel shook his head at the thought of what was happening to all Jack had worked for.

"All they've got to do is live till spring, huh?"

"Jack had lots of hay." Herschel indicated the white-capped stacks down the valley.

"Getting someone to fork it out is all."

"There's enough chuck line riders coming through to get that done." Herschel reached inside. "Would you sign this petition?"

Palmer paused for a minute. "You know that might hurt my business."

"You don't have to."

"What the hell, give me that pencil. We need some kind of law up here." He scrawled his name out on the line and grinned big. "Good luck to you."

"Thanks," Herschel said and shook his hand. The petition back in his coat pocket, he nodded and went off to talk to someone else. He was soon shaking Marley Fender's hand, still taken aback by Buck Palmer signing his petition. One thing, he sure must have the saloon owner down all wrong.

"Wishing yeh some good luck," Fender said. "Talbot showed his ass today. I got ten dollars here. You go get them boys out of jail, will you?"

"Herschel," a rancher named Greene from over at Butterfield said. "Here's five to get them out."

"I signed that petition of yours," and older man said, coming in to talk. "I've got two dollars to help get them out."

Before they were done, Herschel guessed he had over seventy dollars for the men's release. Palmer was gone and Talbot's men were loading all they could into wagons. It would require several trips to get it out of there.

"What're you going to do?" Marsha asked.

"Guess ride back up to Billings and speak to a lawyer about getting them out of jail."

"Why, it'll be dark soon."

"Dark don't matter; those men shouldn't have to sit in jail. They didn't do anything that bad."

"No."

"I'll go see what I can do for them."

"Thank God for you," Nelda Hansen said and clapped him on the sleeve.

"Guess Talbot showed us all, huh?" Herschel couldn't believe what the man had done. Still he had a long ride on his hands. And perhaps not enough money in his pockets to bail them out.

"You be careful," Marsha said when he hugged her shoulders.

"I will. You girls stay warm and take care of your mother. I'll see if they've sold out all the candy up there."

"They have," Nina said. "Guess we'll be pissed off."

"Nina!" her mother said, shocked.

"Easy. Buck Palmer said that today." Herschel shook his head at her with a disgusted look.

"I'll wash his mouth out with soap, too."

Herschel had a hard time to control his chuckling. "Yes, ma'am."

"You can't talk like that, young lady," Marsha said and took her toward the wagon by the arm.

"Marsha, wait," Herschel called out and caught them. "Nina didn't mean no harm. She won't say it again. Things went poor enough here today, save for you getting those names for me. Why, Buck Palmer even signed it, so I can't be too mad at him either."

"He did what?"

"Signed it."

"Well, I'll be . . . Nina, you ever use that word again—"

"I won't, Mommy."

"You better recall, because Herschel saved you from a bad whupping."

"Yes, Mommy."

Herschel felt relieved and gave Marsha a peck on the face. "I better ride up there and see what I can do for them." Armed guards—the man had lost his mind was all Herschel could think, but it worked in his favor he knew, parting from Marsha and the girls.

Buck Palmer dropped by his own place riding home. He would have to see Hertz at the bank in the morning. But he better sic his dogs on Baker—this day would not set well in MacDavis's eyes. Besides he sure needed that petition back, or destroyed, with his name on it. To sign it suited the occasion at the moment and insured he was not listed as opposed to small ranchers.

He rode up the lane and dismounted in front of the low-roofed cabin.

"That you, Boss?" Daws demanded from the lighted doorway.

Palmer listened to the cattle bawling in the distance. Then he looked up at the man. "You two ever feed them?"

"We did like you said and cut back. In case you didn't know there's been lots of cattle drifting in, so we ain't only feeding yours, but others, too."

"We'll see about that. I've got a job for you two."

"Come in, we've got some coffee."

He took off his hat and scarf and nodded to Smith, who eyed him tough-like from across the table.

"Sumbitch Talbot has got them damn ranchers all riled up." Smith shook his head then combed his too-long hair back with his fingers. "Does he want war?"

"You mean Talbot?"

"Yeah, your dumb sheriff."

"He won't be sheriff much longer. But this Herschel Baker ain't taking his place. You know him?"

"Ya, he's that Diehl's buddy," Daws said, pouring the coffee.

"All right, I'm setting the rules this time. I don't want him dead, but I do want you to get that petition off him and burned. I want you to discourage him from going after another one."

"We can handle it."

"I don't want him shot or anything." He looked hard at the pair of Texans. "But I want him discouraged."

Daws grinned at his partner when he set the coffeepot back on the stove. "We can do that. And we'll get the petition and burn it."

"He carries it inside his coat."

"You know where he's at?" Smith asked.

"Yeah, went to Billings to get his buddies out of jail."

Daws nodded he'd heard him. "We may ride over to his place tonight, and when he gets back home, we'll convince him."

"Wear masks."

"Yeah, we can do that."

Palmer blew on his coffee. "Make this good and there's a couple of hundred in it. One for that petition being destroyed and the other for how convincing you two are."

Daws scrubbed at his mouth with his hand. "And another round for us with that Lucie at your river shack?"

"That, too."

Smith nodded in approval at his partner.

"But it better go right this time." Palmer looked hard at both of them for an answer.

"He won't run for nothing when we finish with him." Daws tossed his head at Smith, who agreed.

"He ain't stupid. Be damn sure he don't know who you two are."

"We'll be careful about that."

"What Talbot did today will sure help him. Whatever you two do better undo that as far as Baker's concerned."

"You want something to eat?" Daws asked.

"No. I've got to get back. That land deal needs attention in the morning."

Daws blinked at him. "Tomorrow's Thursday, ain't it?"

"Yeah." Palmer damn sure didn't care what day it was, just so this pair took care of Baker and he closed the land deal. Things MacDavis expected—like he expected all those small ranchers at the sale to be off Horse Creek inside of a year. Wary of it all, he closed his eyes, then stood up and looked at both of them. "Don't mess this one up."

ELEVEN

A FTER a five-hour ride and darkness, Herschel found Emerson Sparks, the lawyer, in his living room reading a newspaper. The man's wife showed him inside.

"Why, Herschel Baker, what brings you to Billings this time of night?"

He shook hands with the man. "There was some trouble today at the sheriff sale."

"Trouble? Have a chair and tell me all about it."

Herschel explained about the arrests, and Sparks shook his head at the end. "I would say Talbot has overextended himself. No way a judge will fine them that much."

"Well, he threatened them anyway."

"I can get them out tonight on ten dollars bond."

"I'd sure appreciate that. In fact I can pay that kind of bond."

"Let me get my hat and coat. We'll go to the jail and get them out. You been up there yet?"

"No, the sheriff and I had some words the other day

over another matter, so I'm not too welcome. I also took out a petition to run for sheriff."

"I heard somewhere about that. How's it going?"

"I guess I'll get that petition filled out after today."

"I should hope so. Nita, I'll be back in a short while," he said to his wife, and they left, walking the three blocks to the courthouse in the starlight, Herschel leading Cob. At the rack before the public building he hitched him and they went inside.

"What do you two need?" the night jailer asked.

"We're here to bond out the three men arrested today," Sparks said.

"That Swede and them two Texans?"

"Mr. Hansen, Mr. Gentry, and Mr. Tagget."

The jailer looked through some papers and at last held one up to read it. "Says here two hundred fifty each plus expenses and mileage for four deputies on each one."

Herschel's heart sunk.

"If I have to get Judge Stone down here, there will be some heads roll. Talbot can't set bail that high," Sparks said.

"I'm just doing what I'm told."

"We're paying you ten dollars a man, and next Monday I will have them in Judge Stone's courtroom—" Sparks turned to look at Herschel.

"They'll be there."

"This ain't what—" the jailer protested.

"Make a damn receipt for each of them and now," Sparks insisted, using his index finger to stab at the table-top.

"The sheriff ain't going to like it."

"Be lots more in this world that he don't like."

The man began writing out the receipts and handed the copies to Emerson. Herschel paid him thirty dollars. Then, scratching his thin hair and grumbling to himself, the deputy went back in the jail with a ring of keys.

In minutes, a grateful Hansen, Gentry, and Tagget all stood at the desk as the jailer issued them their things.

"Sure good to see you, Hersch," the tall Swede said. "We were about to give up ever getting out of here tonight."

"Monday, you three have to be in court with Emerson," Herschel explained.

"We'll be here." And they shook the lawyer's hand.

"You can rent a rig from Paschal to get home tonight. Sorry I never brought your ponies along."

"We'll be fine," Hansen assured him.

"Good. I'll ride back then." Herschel got ready to leave.

"See you and thanks," Max said. A quiet man, his involvement in the standoff shocked Herschel when he thought about it.

"Wait," Joe said, and when they were in the hall and away from the jailer, they stopped. "Give me that petition. Me and Max want to sign it, too."

"You're damn right we do."

After they did so, Herschel put the paper and pencil back inside his coat and thanked them. Emerson told them what time to be in court and they parted. Herschel thanked the lawyer, who refused any pay.

"They can pay me later," Emerson said. "Sounds to me like your campaign just got a big boost today."

"Looks like it did. Thanks anyway." Herschel checked the girth, mounted up and headed south under the stars.

Cattle to feed in the morning, lots of miles to cover. He about chuckled aloud headed for the grumpy ferryman that would take him over the Yellowstone River for ten cents. Nina's off-color remark came to his thoughts—well, Talbot would be pissed off, too, when he learned that them three were bailed out.

Long past midnight, he dropped off the ridge and could make out the haystacks and the corral, plus his cabin in the ivory setting. Sure no smoke coming out of that stovepipe. He dropped heavy out of the saddle at the barn—a crude shed made from rough-cut lumber and hand-hewed posts. Out of nowhere, a sledgehammer hit him in the kidneys and he cried out. Too late two people were beating him with clubs and he fell under the onslaught, unable to fight back. Even his thick winter clothing wasn't dampening their efforts. Facedown in the hay base, he was beat, stomped, and kicked. His assailants never said a word either—who were they? The world went black.

How long had he been out? He awoke to the smell of smoke and his finger felt his lip. The upper part of his lip was split wide open and he couldn't see out of his right eye. When he tried to get up, the pain struck in his side like lightning. Glistening on the snow was a silver button. He managed to pick it up and pocket it in his coat, but paid dear for the effort in more racking pain.

Then, through his hazy left eye's vision, he could see the source of the smoke. My God! They'd burned down his cabin. A few charred logs in the wall was all that was left of it. How long had he been out? The notion only added to his pain and misery. Who were those two? Yes, there had been two of them he felt certain.

Sun was up, so he'd been out a while. Then he saw Cob at the hay stacked in the shed, still saddled and bridled. If he could get to him . . . Then he noticed the blackened ground—those no-accounts had tried to burn his shed, too, but for some reason all that caught was the loose hay and it went out—thank God. Even crawling on his hands and knees was a pain-filled chore.

Cob snorted at his approach.

"Easy," he said in a voice that sounded so coarse he wasn't sure it was his own.

He paused for Cob to settle down at the sight of him on the ground. The horse snatched another bit of hay, switched his tail and then turned back to look at him.

It must have required twenty minutes for him to finally get the horse settled and to get ahold of the trailing reins. Exhausted, seated on his butt, he spit the copper taste of blood out of his mouth, realizing that the rip in his upper lip was serious. But how to get to his feet and in the saddle was a bigger obstacle at the moment than any wounds. They must have caved in his ribs. He'd had broken ones before, but this time it was much worse. If he didn't hug himself, the pain was excruciating.

He looked at the sun time—mid-morning. He began to crawl to the wall of the tack room. That took all his strength. Cob came along snorting in the charred hay. Herschel's back forced to the wall and his feet braced, he began by gritting his teeth to raise himself, using one foot to boost himself and the other to hold what he had. This way his arms were at his sides and he could stand the most of it. At last he was on his unsteady feet. If he ever found out who did this, they'd regret leaving him alive.

No way to get his foot in the stirrup. He leaned on the horse and pushed him to the corral. If he could climb the fence—maybe he could get in the saddle. Dizzy headed, he tied the reins to the rail and started up. The world went swirling around and he lost his balance and fell down.

He awoke to Cob's snort in his face. *It's all right, pard.* Getting his bearings again, he managed to push his way to his feet and then mounted the corral fence using an elbow to steady himself. On the rail, he needed Cob to get closer. The horse stood away and whined to the others in the trap. No doubt he was tired of this business, too. There had to be a way.

He'd never felt so helpless in his entire life. At last he bent over and managed to untie the reins. Then by jerking and pulling and grousing at the gelding, at last he coaxed him in place. He stuck his right boot toe in the stirrup and half dove across the saddle. For a long moment he felt like he would fall off on the far side, but somehow managed to stay aboard. He fixed the reins, speaking softly to settle Cob. Bent over in the saddle, at last, he rode out in a long walk under the crossbar over the main gate.

To stay in the saddle in case he fainted, he roped himself in using the lariat. Several times in the two-hour ride, he jerked himself upright from a dizzy spell grateful for the restraint of the lariat. When he crossed the last rise and could see smoke coming from Marsha's chimney, he sighed in relief.

"Mother! Mother! Come quick, a grizzly bear has gotten ahold of Herschel!" Kate screamed wide-eyed from the open front door.

It hurt him to try to smile, sitting bent over hugging himself and knowing at last he was there.

"We wondered why you missed coming— Oh, my God, Herschel, who did this to you?"

He shook his head and fumbled with the rope. Her fast fingers took it loose and she helped ease him down. "Who did this?"

"I ain't sure. But they meant for me to know they did it." He stood beside the horse. "I can't put my arm . . . over your shoulder—broke some ribs."

"I'll kill them." She swept the lock of hair back and gave him a defiant look.

Unsteady, he started for the front door and the wide-eyed girls. Marsha supported him on the right side. Even out of his blurred vision he could see the horror in their eyes. Must look bad.

Inside, a shiver of cold made him shake as she carefully removed his heavy coat.

"Who did this to you?" Sarah asked, standing before him holding her rag doll.

"Don't bother him," her mother said. "Kate, go put up his horse. Nina, go boil some water."

"We going to have to give him a bath?" she asked, looking disturbed.

"If we have to—yes," her mother said. "Now, do as I say." She shook her head inspecting him. "Sit down or lay down?"

"Maybe I better lay down on the floor."

"No. You can lay on my bed."

"But my pants are so dirty."

"You can shed them and your boots."

"But the girls—"

"They saw their paw in his underwear; won't shock them that bad. Besides they have to grow up, too."

In no mood or shape to argue, he did as he was told. Teeth gritted, he sat up as she managed to remove his boots then his pants. At last lying on his back in her bed, he closed his eyes and drifted off from the world of sharpness. He awoke and looked her in the eye.

"Your lip needs to be sewed. That's going to hurt and I'm not sure if I do it it won't leave a scar."

"Right now a scar don't worry me."

"It may later. You need to see a doctor."

"I can barely see you."

"Don't be funny. This is serious."

"I'm sorry—I didn't mean to be a burden. . . ."

"Oh, you silly—you needed to come here. We can help you. I just don't want you mad at me."

"Don't cry—"

She threw herself on him and tried to hug him. "Oh,

Herschel, this damn sheriff deal did this to you. I should have convinced you—"

"No."

She raised up her eyelashes filled with tears. "What?"

"It ain't your fault or anyone's, but my own. I should have been watching my back." He swallowed a hard knot in his throat. "I let down my guard against them and they used it. Just a tough lesson. Don't cry over me, girl. They ain't killed me, and that scar might just be reminder enough no one ever does this to me ever again."

She bobbed her head in agreement and tried to compose herself sitting on the edge of the bed. "I have some laudanum. You'll need it for me to stitch that lip."

He agreed and nodded at her. "Get on with it."

"Probably hurt me worse sewing it than it does you." A small, forced smile on her face, she struck the errant wave back and went after her things.

"What else they do to you?" Kate asked, returned from putting Cob up.

"Burned my house down and tried to burn my barn—it went out."

"Girls, he don't need to answer your questions."

"They're—" He cleared his throat. "They're fine."

"Why would they do that?" Nina asked.

"Just mean, I guess."

"Must be, from what they did to you."

"Aw, you can build new cabins and your maw can sew me up—"

"Take this," she said, administering a tablespoon of laudanum. "Girls, let him rest."

At last alone, he laid back and let the medicine float him away. He stared at the shingled underside of the roof, the fireplace cracked louder, and soon he fled into a faraway land. He could feel her gingerly touch his swollen lip, even felt the pinprick of a needle. Then the cinching together as she pulled tight on the thread. He could see the hard set in her eyes as she worked, and the long thread she pulled through each time. Then he went asleep.

He woke up under the covers and discovered his ribs were bound up tight in some cloth strips. His tongue felt the swollen side of his lip—the gap was closed. To his side, she sat in her sewing rocker and worked on a dress in her lap.

"Was the petition in your coat pocket?"

"Yes."

She set the dress aside. "How much money did you have?"

"The bond money. Why?"

"They got all the money, and the petition is missing."

He gazed at the shingles. One more thing he owed them for.

"And I found this silver button. Yours?"

"No. it was the first thing I saw when I woke up lying there on the ground."

"Came from them, you reckon?"

"It might have."

"I'm going to Billings and get some more medicine in the morning."

"I'll be fine—you don't—"

"No, you'll need more. It will be days before you can even do much of anything. Kate rode over and told Walt what happened." Her fingers smoothed the whisker stubble on the side of his face. "He's getting Hansens to feed your stock and he'll be here to sit with you after he feeds."

"I don't need—"

"The county clerk have those petitions?"

"Oh, Marsha, don't bother with that."

"You won't be happy until you have one again. I can do that while I'm in town."

"You have stock to feed—firewood to get up."

"Tommy Black Hat is bringing me a wagonload of wood he owes me. Kate and I already fed while you slept, so they'll be fine while I'm gone. If I make good time, I'll be back in late afternoon."

"I hate to be—"

"A bother—well, you ain't. Now, what can we feed you? Soup? With that swollen lip you look awfully tough." Then she chuckled and he tried to smile.

For his supper, she spoon-fed him beef vegetable soup. Keeping it in with the numb swollen lip proved hard. So she could learn how, even Kate fed him some. The first nourishment in a long time set well enough on his stomach, and after the next spoon of medicine he fell asleep.

He awoke and his hand touched strange material in the bed.

"You all right?" she asked in a sleepy whisper.

"Yeah, fine," he said, realizing the warmth he felt was hers.

Those thugs stole his money and the petition—somehow that paper must have been their real goal. Who hired them? He didn't know his enemies well enough. Oh, he'd seen MacDavis and his black driver in Billings, knew John Lake on sight, and a few more of the big outfits' ramrods he knew—but not well enough to know who'd sent those men to his place.

In her sleep, she threw an arm over him and snuggled close. The pressure on his chest hurt, but he smiled, the nicest thing that had happened to him in twenty-four hours.

TWELVE

MARSHA dressed for the trip and checked on him one last time. Seeing his swollen face and purple-black eyes made her stomach churn. Those devils did that to him deserved some real mean treatment.

"Nothing else you need?" She pushed him back down. "You rest. Walt's coming over. I'll be back here by dark."

"Let the petition go."

"Let them win? No."

"Be careful."

"I will," she said and gave her girls their instructions. "These are very trying times. You can miss school one day for emergencies. Watch after him. Keep the fireplace going and keep his soup hot. Kate, you can feed him." She hoisted her purse ready to leave. The .30-caliber pistol weighed heavy, but she could shoot it if necessary. "Anything else?"

They shook their heads, and she went over and kissed him on the forehead. "You behave."

"I will."

Outside the sun had warmed some. She stepped onto the wagon and made herself a place. Grateful that she and Kate had harnessed the horses earlier, with the robe over her lap she headed for Billings.

The team kept at a trot up the valley, and over the Horse Creek Bridge she paused at Larkin's store—told the men around the stove about his beating. They looked aghast at one another, but kept their words quiet in her presence.

"Oh, I have some things at the stage depot," Larkin said as she prepared to go on.

"I'll get them," she said and prepared to leave.

"They burned his cabin, robbed him and took the petition, too?" Max asked her.

"Yes, I'm getting a new one of those today."

"I'll sure sign it." The small man made a sharp nod about his intentions.

"We all will," Rielly said.

"Thanks," she said, pleased at the circle of encouraging men by the stove. The tight muscles in her back eased some when she went outside, listening along the way to Larkin's instructions on picking up his freight.

First thing when she arrived in Billings, she went by Doc's. He shook his head over Herschel's beating. "No idea who did it?"

"No, sir, none whatsoever."

"Sounds like you've done all I could do for him. I'll get you some laudanum, and he gets worse, I'll drive down there and check on him. He's that beat up, he's better not moved."

"I worry about the scar?"

"Wouldn't be no worse than if I'd done it."

"I guess not."

"What did they want anyway?"

"They got it."

Doc frowned at her.

"Herschel took out a petition to run for sheriff. He had thirty of the fifty names on it and close to fifty dollars."

He took off his glasses and polished them with a clean kerchief. "I didn't know that he'd done that, but I suspect those men had a high old time down in the saloons on his money."

"You may be right." She nodded, took the two bottles and went to the buggy after paying him. Wrapped in cloth to keep them from freezing, she stored the bottles in the wagon box behind the seat. Her next stop was the stage depot. The handlebar-mustached clerk found the packages and secured them for her in the back.

At the diner, she had a bowl of chili with crackers at the counter. Maude Corley stopped and spoke to her, busy looking at the orders on her pad.

"How's things up on Horse Creek? I heard that Talbot arrested some of the ranchers at that sale last week."

Marsha looked around, then spoke under her breath. "They burned out Herschel Baker and beat him half to death."

Her eyes widened and brows raised. "He dead?"

"No, but close to it."

"Over that petition he took out—" Maude nodded as if she already knew the answer.

"They wanted it bad and took it."

"Lands, girl, you all be careful—" Then she dropped her voice. "I hear a word about it and I'll let you know."

"Thanks." Marsha smiled at her. There were some folks in this world that would help her, though she wondered if knowledge about who had done the beating might only end up with him getting hurt worse or even killed. She left the cafe and drove to the courthouse.

Inside the clerk's office, a young man offered to help her.

"I need a petition for the office of sheriff," she said.

"Oh, women can't run for office in Montana."

"Not for me." She gave him a peeved look.

"Well—you better come back when Opal gets back—I mean, she will have to clarify the matter."

"When will she be back?"

"Oh. . . ." He looked at the schoolhouse clock on the wall. "At two p.m."

"Fine, I'll be back." That would make her late getting back home, but getting that petition filled out might encourage Herschel enough to speed his recovery. She left the office and went down the hall. On a whim she went around a corner. Her heart was palpitating under her rib cage. Then she heard the scurry of feet on the floor and peeked around in time to see the same boy go into the sheriff's office. No doubt reporting on her effort to get the paper. Damn.

Her back pressed to the wall and out of sight, she waited until she heard him run back to the clerk's office. What should she do? No, in another hour and a half she would have the petition and be driving home. That was her goal and she intended to do it.

So she went looking at merchandise in the nearby stores and returned to the courthouse to find a gray-headed woman behind the clerk's desk.

"I'm Opal Johnson. How may I help you?"

Marsha explained, and the woman looked very disturbed. "He must be your intended?"

"Sort of." Marsha felt the color rise on her face.

"Well, that boy Paul is sometimes a little too stiff about things. Under the circumstances, I'll make you a new one and I hope he recovers and can campaign."

"Oh, he will."

"Good."

Marsha left the clerk's office feeling much better. When

she closed the frosted glass door and started down the hall-way, a thin-faced man with a pencil mustache strode up the floor headed for her.

"What's your business in here?" he demanded.

"None of yours," she said and ran her right hand into her purse.

"I'm the chief deputy, and an unattended woman has no business in this courthouse."

"Unattended?" She drew the Colt and drove it in his gut. "My husband would have killed you for calling me that. I still may. Now stand aside or get ready to die."

"You . . . you can't—"

"You ready to die?"

"No. . . ."

"Good. Get over there, and you make one move toward me and you will die."

"I'm the law!"

Using the barrel as a pointer, she waved him aside.

"Lady, you're messing where you don't belong."

"I know where I belong; you're the one's got problems. Don't try nothing." She turned on her heels to leave, halfway expecting to hear him charge after her. But all he did was shout after her back.

In the buckboard, she clucked to the team, cast a last look at the two-story courthouse and sent her team for the ferry. Only on the south bank of the Yellowstone did she relax any. Then she repeatedly looked back over her shoulder, expecting to see the law after her—the heavy purse in her lap, the pistol close if she needed it.

Long after sundown, she left the packages on Larkin's dark porch and drove on south under the stars. Her whole body ached and her eyelids felt leaden. Coming down the creek road under the star-flecked night sky, she saw that some of the snow had been worn out and the dark surface showed tracks marking the way.

She swung the team around the bend and started up the steep slope to the bridge, and the horses stopped. Clyde and Essie never balked.

"Get up," she said, standing and not seeing anything. "What's wrong with you two?" She clucked, and slapped them again with the lines. But no amount of encouragement would make them go on. With her teeth she pulled off her right glove. As she looked around, her hand slipped inside the purse and her fingers closed on the pearl handle of the Colt. Was this a trap?

Nothing moved. The only sounds were her weary horses snorting in the darkness. She made a three-hundred-sixty-degree check of the snowy dark landscape, then she released the pistol grips, satisfied they were alone.

Impatiently angry with the pair, she dismounted from the seat and went around them. It was only when she held Clyde's bridle ready to lead him across that she could see the missing planks.

Her breath caught in her throat. The horses would have wrecked had they not stopped. "Oh." She pressed her face to his nose and shook her head. "Thank God, you two could see that."

On the seat, she backed them up and then drove down beside the high bridge, getting off again to check the ice. It appeared solid enough. So the ice was sufficiently thick to hold up the horses was her main concern, and she began to lead them across the frozen surface. Glancing high up at the gap in the missing boards, a cold shudder went through her body under her heavy clothing. Step by step she crossed, grateful for the rough surface making it easier on the horses' footing. At last across, she climbed onto the seat and drove them up the steep bank onto the road again.

Had that been deliberate? Those boards missing. No local would have left them off without flagging the bridge somehow to keep folks from falling through it. Was that what had happened when her husband was killed? She tried to shut that out of her mind. Her horses jogging, harness jingling, the iron rims crunching the frozen ruts—she knew she better not tell Herschel that Copelan had called her an "unattended woman."

THIRTEEN

THE empty envelope reached Buck Palmer. When his bartender, Earl, handed it to him, he pocketed it and went on without a word. MacDavis must be upset about something. Word about the fracas and Talbot's force had no doubt reached him.

"I have to run up north in the morning," Buck said. "And check on a deal."

Earl told him he could handle things. Light night again anyway. Be hard to make MacDavis's profit this month—bad storms kept pushing through. Hurting his business. He hoped the next blizzard stayed gone until he had his meetings done with "the boss." Then the matter of that Allen bitch coming in and getting another damn petition. Copelan had reported to him he'd tried to stop her, but she drew a gun on him. How that courthouse bunch—Talbot and his dumb chief deputy Copelan—let her get away doing that, he would never know.

Shame his own plan to wreck her and her rig had failed.

Maybe if he'd stayed around down there after prying up them planks—oh, well, Baker was still out of commission and no word they knew who did it. For once those two Texans did something right. He could always burn another petition. That wasn't hard.

After he left the Antelope, he went by and told the livery boy to have Chester hitched up at five a.m. or he'd cut his privates off. Then he went by the cafe and ate a big steak and some potatoes with biscuits and butter. No grits in Montana. Some folks never knew what was good to eat.

The wake-up knock on his hotel room door the next morning forced him to grumble aloud he was getting up. Not looking forward to meeting this soon with MacDavis, he wondered what the old man wanted this time. Something was burning him up or he'd not come down from the ranch again this soon. Palmer finished his breakfast in a few minutes, seeing no one but the usual bunch in the cafe.

Under the horse blanket and robe, seated on the spring seat, Buck sent the light buggy off in a good jog. The big, fresh horse could move fast. This was how he'd easily beat her to the Horse Creek Bridge and was long gone on to his new place—the Diehl Ranch—before she got there. Been handy having the new ranch down there in the midst of them rustlers. His man Starr couldn't get much to drink down there, and maybe he'd feed the cattle enough to get them through. Lots of drifting, starving cattle all over the country. Spring couldn't come too soon for his sake as he squinted against the too-bright sparkle off the winter-locked, rolling landscape.

Smoke coming out the chimney told Buck "the boss" was warming up inside. He left Chester for MacDavis's man Washington to blanket after he cooled. He knocked on the door and MacDavis shouted for him to come inside.

"You know this winter may bankrupt some big ranchers if it don't break soon?" MacDavis said, looking him over.

"I know it's a sumbitch."

"Who's damn dumb idea was it to confront those rustlers and arrest some of them?" Anger radiated from MacDavis's green eyes.

Palmer shook his head. "Damn sure not mine. Talbot's. He got pretty upset down there. I couldn't get to him and stop him in time. Doubt he'd even listened to me anyway."

"Well, you've got the Diehl place, huh?"

"Like you said for me to do. I've a man up there feeding them cattle, too."

MacDavis sat in the leather-cushioned chair with the Scotch-plaid blanket over his legs. He looked up when Washington came in the room. "Get in here, before you freeze your black ass off."

"Yes, suh." The black man checked the open fireplace, then took a seat on a wooden crate in the rear of the cabin.

"I think that Talbot needs to retire." MacDavis turned back to Palmer, tented his fingers before his nose and then pointed them at him. "Who would be our man?"

"Copelan ain't smart enough, that's for sure. That Allen bitch bluffed him out."

MacDavis frowned. "What was that about?"

"Well, we had him out of the race and his petition burned. She came up and demanded a new petition. Instead of Copelan taking it away from her in the hallway, he claimed she drew a gun and told him she'd kill him."

"And his boss arresting those rustlers at the auction fits right in this Baker's lap. We definitely need Talbot to retire. And we will put in our next man."

"Who do you have in mind, Boss?"

"Walter Sears."

Palmer nodded his head in approval, shrugged his shoulders and shifted his weight to his other boot. "I can get him elected." Sears was no gunfighter—he was a businessman, but not directly connected to the big outfits. He also should be a man Palmer could direct. Talbot had gotten too damn big for his own britches.

MacDavis closed his eyelids and shook his head in dread. "Baker's going to polarize those small ranchers everywhere."

"Naw, I'll have enough voters to fill every ballot box between here and the Milk River."

"No mistakes."

"No mistakes about it."

"I think personally you'll have the fight of your life ever beating him."

"Naw, not since he had his accident."

"And his cabin burned?"

"Tried to make an impression on him."

"Much better than the last one—your boys shot *him* in the back."

"Much better," Palmer agreed.

"I'll speak to the others. Sears will be our man. The Democrats can put up a token candidate, so he won't draw too many votes away from Sears."

Palmer looked hard at the man. "Will they do that?"

"They will by damn or suffer the consequences. If they don't want a damned rustler for sheriff."

"I'll handle the Sears deal?"

"Yes and get him whatever he needs. Hire some campaign workers, too."

Palmer looked around. He knew the answer to the next question and dreaded it. "I'm to get rid of Talbot?"

"Exactly. He won't go, then he can go feet first for all I care about that buffoon."

"I'll handle it." Like he did the rest. Damn, Talbot might have to go feet first. He could also be like a rattlesnake, whirl and strike them. No way, Palmer grinned to himself.

FOURTEEN

B OARDS out of the bridge . . ."
     Sore through and through, Herschel sat up on the side of the bed, trying to piece Marsha's story together. His mind clogged with cobwebs and still half-asleep, he tried to get past the racking pain in his body to better understand her words.

". . . three or four planks had been pried up and left a gaping hole there."

"What happened?"

"Essie and Clyde balked for no reason I could see. Even standing up I could not see the missing planks in the dark. I was furious when I got up to them, and then I saw the missing boards."

"No idea—who could have done such a thing?" Even in his quandary, he knew the same ones that beat him must be involved. The thought knifed his heart; they were low enough to even endanger a woman's life.

"I have no idea. I backed the team up and led them across the frozen creek."

He held out his arms and quickly put them down when the lightning-hot strike ran through his chest. She dropped on her knees and buried her face in his shirt. "We've unlocked the devil, haven't we?"

"No, it isn't the devil doing this, Marsha, it's some evil men with no respect for human lives." He held her as tight as he could afford. Sore as he was, there was no way he could ever campaign for weeks—and that petition she brought back from town needed new signatures. How would he ever? No end to his problems and now he even had her in harm's way. What would they do next?

"Maybe Walter can go look at the bridge and tell us something. He'll be back here by mid-morning." Herschel felt hopelessly tied down by his aches and pains; the notion dissolved all his desire to do anything.

"I need to take a couple of lamps back up there. Someone else might drive off it."

"It's too cold. Too late at night—"

She looked up at him. Tears sparkled like diamonds in her lashes. "I can do it and be right back. Otherwise I'll worry all night."

"And I'll worry about you."

"I can go and help her," Kate said, the silent girls in their nightshirts standing behind her.

"Both of you be careful."

"Lie down. I have some more medicine the doctor sent. He said for you not to lift anything and let your body heal." She stared close at his face. "I think my stitches may work."

"I'm mending. I'm just not patient enough."

"You'll have to be, Herschel Baker."

Kate brought a big spoon and gave him a dose. "You lie back and rest."

He closed his eyes. Maybe sleep would heal his body. One thing he did know, he needed to get well and fast. On his back again, he watched the fireplace's light dance on the ceiling. *Dear God, please protect my girls.*

He never woke up when they returned later that night. It was morning when he managed to open his lead-weighted eyes and pull on his boots. A task that made his head whirl.

"Coffee?" she asked when he ambled over to the table to take a seat.

He nodded, uncertain for a few seconds where he was and how he got there—Marsha's place and sore as if he'd been rolled on by a horse. He closed his eyes to escape the spasms of pain.

"We hung the lamps last night," she said, bringing him a tin cup of steaming coffee.

"Good. Sorry, I went to sleep." He combed his hair back with his fingers.

"That wasn't a problem. Are you any better?"

"Some. I may not die now."

"Walter's here," Nina announced.

"Mr. Ferguson," Marsha corrected her.

"Oh, no, I beat him at checkers and he said to call him Walter."

"Mr. Ferguson will do."

"Yes, ma'am, but he said—"

A mother's cross face silenced her middle daughter's protest.

"How are you doing this morning, Hersch?" Walter nodded to Marsha coming in the door opened for him by the middle sister. "What happened to the bridge?"

"I about drove over it in the dark last night. Horses balked and saved my life."

"Any idea who done it?"

They both shook their heads.

"Mother said the devil did it," Sarah said aloud.

"Sarah—"

"Aw, she knows the truth, don't get onto her," Walter said. "I better borrow a hammer and some spikes and go put them planks back. I'll look for tracks, too, while I'm up there."

"Do that," Herschel said, feeling worthless in his condition.

"Kate can show you what you need in the shed," Marsha said.

"Won't take long. You any better?" Walter asked Herschel.

"I'm mending."

"Good. I'll be right back." He waved to both of them. Kate wrapped up and followed him out the door.

"Guess he can be the first to sign the new petition," Marsha said, putting it on the table.

Herschel agreed and studied the coffee's vapor. Then he'd only need forty-nine more.

A week later and the first open sunny day, she drove him over in the wagon to check on his place. Heartsick, he kicked through the snow-floured ashes and ruins of his cabin. Charred pieces of the old rocker, scraps of his quilts, the bare bedsprings, cooking gear, his cook stove under a pile of fire blackened rafters. The Hansen boy Toby was busy feeding his stock. Standing in the black circle that failed to ignite the barn, Herschel could see the youth in the distance pitching off fodder to the cattle and horses down in the bottom.

"You can't tell much here, can you?" she asked, wrapped in the blanket against the sharp wind.

He narrowed his eyes and nodded. "No signs left. But I do have that coin button. I ever find the match to it, I think I'll have them back-shooters."

"They ever say anything while they were beating you?"

He sighed trying to recall that evening at the barn. "If they did, I didn't hear them."

"It might have helped you identify them. Are we going to wait for Toby to come back up here?"

"Yes, I want to be sure he doesn't need anything."

She leaned against him. "This must be very hard on you. Coming back to the ruins and all, I mean."

"It only makes me more convinced that Yellowstone County needs some real law."

"I hope it doesn't cost you your life."

He shook his head to dismiss her concern. From that point on, he knew he must never forget to watch his back.

The youth had no problems, so they drove on to Larkin's store. Even the spring seat did not absorb the jarring shock of riding for him. He tried to act all right getting down at the hitch rack, but spasms of fiery pain ran from his jaw up his cheeks. For a long moment, he stood on the ground letting the waves roll away with a final quake of his shoulders under the layers of clothing.

"You all right?" she whispered at his side.

"I will be in a minute."

"Come in out of the cold," Mrs. Larkin said and waved them to the door.

"We're coming," Marsha said. "He isn't up to running races." Her hands on his arm steadied him as they went up the three steps to the porch.

"My Lord, what did they do to you?"

"Don't I look any prettier?" Herschel smiled at her going by.

"You look so beat up—"

"Trust me, he looked much worse a week ago," Marsha assured her.

"Who would do such a thing?"

"Them damn thugs hired by the big outfits," Tam Rielly said, getting up with the others around the stove. "Have a chair, Hersch. How can we help yeh, lad?"

"Marsha has my petition—"

"Sit down, lad. We'll all sign it."

The heat from the stove scorched his windburned face. The beard stubble around his mouth cut his tender lips. Absorbing the heat, his gloves off, he held out his hands to warm them. Seated on the ladder-back chair, he looked around at the others. Faces filled with concern, anger and pity, men he'd known for the three years since he came to the Montana Territory. Texans who came up like he did with the cattle herds and stayed. Iowa folks, Dakota settlers—they all came to south central Montana for a new start and soon found themselves swimming in a sea of longhorns that big money brought up there for a quick profit.

"What're your plans now?" Max asked. "We'll all come and help you rebuild your cabin when you get ready, you know that."

"Thanks, but I'm going to run for sheriff first and clear this county of them that can't live by the law."

The older man nodded his gray head and then spat tobacco in the ash box. "Be a big damn job, I'd say."

"We can either fight them or tuck our tails between our legs like some cur dog and run out of here. The office of sheriff needs a man that knows no sides and investigates every infraction of the law."

"I'll say this, they damn sure didn't gain nothing whupping the hell out of you," Tam said and laughed with the others.

"So that they know it." Herschel stared at the airtight cans on the shelf.

"We better get you home," Marsha said.

"Thanks," he said to the others as they handed him the petition with five more lines filled in. Even Larkin had signed it, Herschel noted, putting it away.

On the wagon seat, she took the reins and clucked to the team. A few hundred feet from the store she looked back over her shoulder, then turned. "I'm sorry for what I said in there. I didn't mean to say go home like that."

"What?" he asked, huddling in his soreness against the wind and regretting he could not hug her.

"That we better go home."

He nodded. "Never bothered me. I wouldn't be alive if you hadn't taken me in."

She shrugged. "Just so you ain't upset."

Confused, he looked off at the faded blue sky. Something, he knew, was unspoken between them—she was upset and he'd have to figure out why.

FIFTEEN

B ACK in the Antelope Saloon, amid a thin fog of cigar smoke and a tinny piano's tune, Buck Palmer rested his elbows on the bar's rim and looked over this part of his empire. Since his visit with the boss, he had figured out the perfect way to eliminate Talbot. He'd have to put his scheme to work before he ever spoke to Walter Sears about becoming the next sheriff. Copelan would be safe enough as the appointed sheriff until after the election. Deep in his thoughts about the way to do it so it never came back to him, a nudge by Earl jarred him to awareness.

"Them two Texans are in the back room," he said, from behind his hand.

"Good enough."

"We're getting low on rye."

"Some freighter's probably stuck in a snowdrift some- where out there. Won't anything arrive dependable until we get that railroad in here."

He took a fifth of the "good-bottle-and-bond" and three

glasses to the back room. When he opened the door, he saw they had their caps and coats off and were seated around the small table.

"Figured you boys could use a little." He held the bottle up high. Both looked up and nodded in approval.

"Word I get's someone beat the shit out of that rustler Baker."

Both men nodded, with their attention centered on the liquor he poured.

"And his cabin caught fire—" He held the bottle as they tossed down the first four fingers of the brown liquid and made big "ah's." With a scowl, he looked at both of them. Still holding the bottle and not moving to pour them some more, he said, "Shame his barn didn't burn, too."

Cooter made a face behind his beard stubble. "Sumbitch was afire when we left."

"Well, no one tracked you down, that's important. " He poured their glasses half-full. Then he looked back at the closed door and lowered his voice. "We need to stage a cattle rustling and have the sheriff discover it."

"Huh?" Denver Smith frowned at him like he'd lost his mind.

"More whiskey, boys?"

They both nodded.

"Yes and blame the rustlers down there for doing it."

"What about Talbot?"

"He won't care."

"How come?" Daws looked suspiciously at him over his glass before taking a drink.

"He'll be dead. Here's the plan . . ." Palmer took a seat between them and began to lay out what they needed to do in the meantime.

"Locate two of the big outfits' steers. And have them ready. Look for a place out of the way that won't point to us. An empty cabin or something where we can ride in and out unseen by most all of them."

"We've got the critters. Hell, they come in every time we feed."

"The place?" He glanced at both his men for that answer.

"I'll find us one," Smith said, looking slant-eyed at him.

"Good, then we need the time and place. That will depend on the weather and when I need to act." Settled back in the chair, he at last felt confident with the two after the beating they'd supposedly given Baker. Word was the Texan had barely lived through it. Hadn't been for that Allen bitch who saved him. She'd get her comeuppance, too, before this was all over.

"Killing a sheriff is dangerous as hell," Smith said, under his breath.

Palmer nodded and then shook his head to dismiss their concern. "It will be for them rustlers down there. Actually it should be worth a hundred apiece for each of you when we finish the deal."

"Good," Daws said and looked at his sullen partner for his approval.

"It'll work. When you sending Lucie across the river to the shack?" Smith gave a head toss to the south.

"Why, is tonight soon enough?" Palmer smiled at them. Those Texans would do until he didn't need them any longer. That day would come, but as long as he could use them, they'd do fine. But they might as well not expect to ever go back south again—they knew way too much. When those two left Montana, it would be in a pine box, not on horseback.

SIXTEEN

"I need to go see more folks," Herschel said, pacing her pegged floor.

"We'll go get more signatures."

"Who will feed your stock?" He looked around the cabin, feeling as if he'd been in prison for days, as much as he loved the company of her and the girls.

"I can get a couple Crows to handle it. And the girls could stay over at the Fergusons' until we get back."

"Oh, Marsh, I hate to ask you. But I don't want the men who beat me up and their bosses to win this fight."

"Neither do the girls and I. I'll hitch the team. You girls each pack a small bag. Help Sarah." She went to the rack by the door and put on her wool coat, then the scarf. "We better go now, before the next storm blows in."

No way he could ride Cob any distance. The buckboard was the only way. Still, involving her in a run for office worried him. But Marsha was a fighter, and maybe they could see enough folks in a few days to complete the petition and file it before his attackers had a second chance at taking it away from him.

An hour later at the Fergusons', they hugged the girls good-bye and left with well wishes to set out to the north. Walter was going to ride down and tell the Indian boys her plans and how to feed. After a brief stop over at Larkin's store, they drove into Billings, arriving after dark at Paschal's stable.

"Man, I heard about the beating," Lem Paschal said, helping her unharness the team. "Good to see you're up and around."

"I need to see some folks. I need some signatures."

"Money wouldn't hurt, would it?" Lem asked, going by with the first set of harness.

"There's a forty-dollar filing fee." He looked off down Main Street. To ask anyone for money to him felt like begging.

Lem came back out in the night. "I've got ten of that."

Herschel blinked in disbelief "But you—"

"I can choose sides. They don't make me afraid. Besides, this winter don't break soon, them big outfits won't have a nickel left."

"I'd hate that even for them. Costs everyone."

"Cattle are dying out here and fast." Lem took the second set of harness away from her and smiled in her face. "I think you've got more gumption than most men, ma'am. He's lucky to have you."

Herschel could have sworn she blushed.

"You two can sleep in the side room. Ain't too warm, but it'll do. Oh, there's two beds in there." The liveryman went off with the harness. "I'll put the ponies up. Get inside."

Herschel stopped. He'd not thought about respectable sleeping arrangements for the two of them. The hotel. Separate rooms. No way did he want to ruin—

"We ain't turning down his generous hospitality," she said as if she knew what was weighing on his mind. Her hand on his coat sleeve, she sent him toward the door. "Plus you have a fourth of that filing fee he promised you."

There were times he felt she belonged to him like his right arm. At the moment even more so, for his healing ribs still made him keep his elbows at his side.

"We need to go eat," he said.

"I've got cheese and crackers in my bag. We can do that in the morning for breakfast. You look jaded."

He chuckled. "If that means tuckered out, I'm jaded."

"It does."

He never slept good. They'd left the door open to the office so some of the potbellied coal stove's heat could reach the side room. The .44 Colt under his covers, several times he felt for the redwood grips when customers came in during the night and stomped around in the office. Some cussed enough to fill a bin full and that, too, disturbed him. In fact, he'd never realized the vocabulary of teamsters was so full of bad words until he had to think about her on the other cot—maybe she wasn't hearing all that. For his part, he certainly hoped she wasn't.

Before sunup, she was sitting and brushing her hair in the lamplight when he raised up on his elbows. "Morning. Better get us some grub and get on our way."

"I was thinking the same thing." She smiled at him, and he felt warm all over despite the chill in the room when he threw his legs over the edge.

Ten minutes later they were in the cafe and he introduced her to Maude Corey.

"Why, Herschel, Marsha and me are old friends. You two want coffee, of course, and I'll get them eggs cooking." Maude hurried off.

"You must be that guy they beat up that I been hearing about." Hersch turned and looked up into a bushy white handlebar mustache. "Name's Lenny Stats. You still running for sheriff?"

"I get enough names on my petition, I am."

"Where's it at?" the cowboy asked.

Marsha fished it from her bag and handed it to him, then bent over for the pencil. "Right here."

"That's the one for sheriff?" another customer asked.

Herschel nodded.

"I'll sign it."

"Me, too. I heard what they done to you."

Marsha grinned big at him as the men lined up to sign the paper. He gave her a nod of approval. The new interest shocked him—from Lem and his ten-dollar contribution to these men willing to sign their lives away—for him.

After breakfast, their team stood all hitched outside the stables. Lem wouldn't take any money. Besides he told them to come back anytime they needed to and stay on him.

On the seat beside her, the pain was less from getting onto the wagon. The horses acted fresh. The buckboard cut northeastward to skirt the steep escarpment north of town.

Smoke from Barley Benton's chimney wafted into a tall column when they crossed the last rolling hill. Some dark specks in an ocean of white stuff, the round pen was visible, too, over the glare.

Barley came to the doorway and blinked at Herschel's dismount from the rig. "Son, you have a horse wreck?"

"Word ain't got up here?" Herschel asked, standing beside the rig.

"Lord, no—"

"Well, they jumped me over a week ago when I got back to my place. Thumped on me awhile and then burned the cabin. Lucky they didn't burn down my barn."

"Aw, the hell you say. Pardon my tongue, ma'am," he said to Marsha and hurried over to assist him.

"I'm fine, I just walk slow."

"Leave them horses. Come inside, I'll get them in a minute. What did they do to you?" He tried to hold Herschel's arm.

"Maybe tell you what they missed—" Herschel forced a smile for the big man.

"They damn sure busted your lip." Barley shook his head. "And she's?"

"Marsha Allen."

"Pleased to meet you, ma'am. Wish it was under better circumstances."

"They never said a word, but they took his petition and money, too," she said, following them.

"Nice folks you deal with." Barley shook his head when they reached the open door. "You could stand some sleep, you look tuckered out."

"Can't do much. . . ."

"Heart, let him lay on the bed."

"Oh my, you do look terrible," the Crow woman said.

Herschel stopped and reached out as far as he dared and hugged her like always. Then he straightened. "I am kinda shaky. Thanks for the bed."

She pulled back the covers. Him seated on the bed, both women jerked off his boots. In seconds he laid down and his world went blank.

In an instant, he was riding in the driving rain at night. Thousands of pounding hooves beside him and cattle bawling that eerie way when they're upset and mad. Stampede. Lightning danced over the nearby hills and cold rain washed his straining eyes, his night horse Coony pounding the ground under him. Twice Coony'd lost his footing, but quickly he'd scrambled underneath him to his feet. But each time, Herschel felt his time had come. The front of the herd—how far ahead in the black night? Could he even turn them when he got there? Shoot the lead steer if he had to—but he must turn them back so they went into a circle and cured this mad race into a black hell. Stupid longhorns anyway.

Maybe when the new grass got taller—and their guts were full—they'd settle down. At the moment, the tumultuous sound of horns knocking, cattle bawling and hooves pounding the wet ground all made an ear-shattering roar.

"Come on, Coony!" He lashed the Texas pony with his reins and set spurs to his sides, knowing full well the mustang was running as hard as his heart would carry him. In the next flash of lightning he reined Coony's chest into the nearest steer, hoping he was close enough to the front to turn the stream. A hazardous risk, but the steer gave to the right and Herschel went to screaming at them. Maybe if he was lucky and Coony didn't fall down in the next few minutes, he'd stemmed the stampede.

At long last they were in a great wad and others came up to join him.

"Seen Travis?" he'd ask each one, and a shake of their head told him, no.

Then another hand would ride up, lighting a roll-your-own and shaking his head over the night's ordeal.

"Seen Travis?" he asked.

"No."

The sound was coming from his own throat as he fought to surface like a man drowning. "Travis is dead!"

"Easy, easy," Marsha said, holding his hand in hers. "Travis died over three years ago, when you were coming up here. Remember, you went back and put a stone on his grave in Colorado."

Herschel blinked and then he saw the room around her. They were at Barley and Heart's place—he felt wet all over like he'd been out there in the rain—chasing them longhorns. Clammy sweat was all.

"You must have been dreaming."

He agreed and laid back. The thoughts of Travis Baker being dead made his throat close and his eyes feel pained with tears. Why, him and his brother had always covered each other. On Saturday in town they took on the bullies and whipped them. Some were even much older than him and his year-younger brother—he'd have to tell Mom about his death. No, she'd died in Texas. No telling where his paw was—he rode off one day to buy more cows and never came back. Comanches might've got him. God only knew about the details of Thurman Baker's demise. He'd left two boys in their teens and a younger sister to help their maw run a couple hundred cows on a west Texas ranch. When Herschel found some paper and pencil, he'd have to write Rosie about Travis's death. She didn't need to know it, but there wasn't much left after a thousand hooves ran over his body. Hersch closed his eyes to the vision of his trammeled corpse.

"Can you hear me?" Marsha said.

"No." He shook his head, sat up too fast and threw his legs over the side of the bed.

"While you were sleeping, Barley went out and got you five more signatures and sent for a dozen more to come sign it. You now have twenty-five dollars and a few coins in your campaign chest."

He rubbed his whiskered face with his callused palms and grinned at her. "I ought to sleep some more."

SEVENTEEN

Buck Palmer hated card playing, but he did it for one reason: the things he could learn from the other players. So that night in the back room of the Antelope, six men sat around the green felt-topped table, playing dealer's choice.

Finished shuffling the deck, Billings Mayor Hugh Whitehall began dealing the cards for five card stud. A large man with white eyebrows and hair like plastered snow, Whitehall dealt the first up card to Snyder Case, who owned a big freighting firm. Case stood five-ten, with a burly build, and had some hard facial features that made him intimidating to look at. He kept the fast eyes of a cornered wolf the entire night.

"Ah, a seven," Whitehall exclaimed, then he dealt Morris Goldberg a red ten.

The Jewish merchant always dressed for Boston, where he came from. Nice gray suit, tailor-cut, large silk tie and diamond stickpin in it, cuff links of silver and a bowler hat made from the finest beaver. If there were two aces in his down cards, the man's dark eyes never flickered.

Lake Denton dealt in wool and hides. With a pencil mustache and pompadoured hair, he was a ladies' man or considered himself as one. Hardly more than a skinny man of forty who'd lost most of his charming looks, to Palmer's notion. If the occasion ever arose, he could be bought off easily by a free sleepover in the bed of one of Palmer's doxies.

Manfred Dugan sat at the end. Palmer dreaded him the most. Despite his fifty winters and threads of silver in his hair, Dugan remained a tough, stocky built man. And by his reputation, he could whip a handful of men in a barroom brawl if he was tired. Dugan was the town's builder and chief contractor.

Goldberg won the hand with a pair of aces and raked in the small pot.

"Who's this Baker running for sheriff?" Whitehall asked as cards came his way. He shuffled for Goldberg, as he usually did, and handed them to the man to deal.

"Small rancher," Lake Denton said. "That Horse Creek bunch. Damn, Goldberg, ain't you got any better cards than that to deal me?"

"All I've got. He won't beat Talbot, will he?" The merchant looked around when no one answered him.

Manfred Dugan raised a quarter, cleared his throat and looked over the table. "Talbot ain't that popular. Got him some airs in the past few years. Looks more like a tycoon than a sheriff walking down the street. He may not be so hard to knock off that pedestal."

"He may be fixing to run for governor when they make us a state," Whitehall said.

"And beat you out of that job." Palmer laughed and winked at the mayor.

"He sure might." Whitehall folded in disgust.

Palmer leaned back. Rupart MacDavis knew more about Billings sitting out at that ranch than Palmer did working in town. But thinking back, he envisioned the times that Talbot had come in the Antelope like some English lord on his way to the opera and paying some mind to the lower class along the way. He laughed aloud at the picture of the windbag doing that very thing.

"You in or out?" Case asked with a frown at him as the dealer. "Raise's fifty cents."

"Oh, I'm in," Palmer said, peeking at his three deuce down cards. "Make it fifty cents more."

Later, when they broke up for the evening, Synder Case, putting on his coat, asked Palmer outright, "What do you think about this Baker getting elected? Everyone else had some words on it."

"Those small ranchers are clannish. I feel a man from Billings would be better for the job than one of them."

"Those rustlers?" Whitehall said under his breath, with a grin.

"Some folks call 'em that."

"I've heard several of the big outfits call them that." Whitehall whipped the plaid scarf around his neck and left by the back door.

"We'll have to see," Palmer said, walking the rest of them to the back way out. "We'll just have to see."

A few minutes later, Palmer stood behind the bar in the thick smoke and sour smell of the barroom. Damn, some of his customers must not wipe their backsides—it smelled bad in there.

"You lose much at poker?" Earl asked, going by him with drinks.

"No. Why?"

"You don't look happy."

"I'll be fine." Even better when Talbot was out of the way.

EIGHTEEN

T HE weather let up some. A chinook blew in, and the horses trotted in mush headed for Wynn Creek and two more stops for him and Marsha. For the first time in ten days, and their third day on the campaign, he felt he might live.

"You probably want to go home and see about the girls," he said, seated beside her in the too bright sun.

She nodded, but never answered.

"You know, despite our success so far, we may not win this race."

A sharp glance at him then back to the road and her driving. "I don't know about you, but I came on this trip for one reason—to get you elected."

He laughed. "I bet you did. Lord, you set your mind to something, you do it."

"I run a ranch. Make it pay."

"You do a great job. Fact a better one than I do."

"I'm still a woman."

He frowned at her. "I never thought anything else."

She sawed the horses down and turned to him. The wet-ness in her lashes flashed in the sunbeams when she turned and clutched his coat. "Oh, Herschel, I've worried so much about you and the beating they gave you and—"

"Hey, hey . . ." He held his head up high and rocked her in his arms. "Please don't cry or I will, too."

"No, we're going to win." She reared up and kissed him on the mouth. "There, Mr. Baker." On the side of her glove, she wiped the tears away. "You will be Yellowstone County's next sheriff."

"If you have anything to do with it. McIntoshes live west of here about five miles." He was gathering up his di-rections that Barley gave him, looking over the rolling country lined with ridges crested in jack pines. "We should be there by dark."

"Yes, we should." Reins in her hands again, she drove on.

The thing made him the sickest was all the dark humps blown off by the shifting winds and thaw everywhere they went. Body counts, he called them. Not hundreds, but thousands of dead cattle were all over—stock lost in the bitter cold winter. It wasn't over either. Even his heavy wool-lined coat didn't keep out the chill he felt time and again over the losses—it made goose bumps on his arms. The disastrous situation would break men, big and small.

Teddy McIntosh greeted them when they drove into his well-kept place, coming out in his shirtsleeves. A burly Scotsman with a brogue that took charge. His plump wife Eve and their four children all acted excited over the com-pany.

At the Wynn Schoolhouse later that night, they col-lected over twenty dollars and the well wishes of two dozen more ranchers and farmers.

"Send that fancy Talbot packing. He ain't no good for

nothing," one man said and laughed. "And I believe you'll do it."

"I'm going to try," Herschel promised the man.

"Well, we have plenty of signatures and filing money," Marsha reported. "Should we head in tomorrow and file them?"

He looked at her and nodded. At the start, things like being proper, deciding where to sleep, and the private things a man and a woman not married must shield from each other in such situations had been painfully uncomfortable. But he no longer felt self-conscious in her company, and he found himself more and more turning to her for an answer, for directions on what to do next. Going back home and being separate from her would not be what he looked forward to.

"Let's go see the clerk and get this over."

"Wonderful," she said and nodded.

He knew by her look that if they'd been alone she'd have hugged him. He wanted to do the same to her, but the restraint of the dissipating crowd in the school building held them apart.

"You're going to file then?" McIntosh asked.

"Yes, tomorrow."

"Good, then you can really go to campaigning. We need yeh in office."

"Thanks, we're going to try."

"No, tell him, Ted," Marsha said. "He's going to be elected."

"Ah, the missus is right. You'll be a shoo-in."

The missus? Surely McIntosh only said that—but what did he mean? Herschel's thoughts were interrupted by another well-wisher shaking his hand as the man prepared to leave the schoolhouse.

"Come November, we'll have us a real sheriff," the rancher named Randle said and went out the door.

NINETEEN

Palmer stood studying the melting snow dripping off the eaves and viewed Billings's main street from the Antelope's front porch. The thoroughfare was turning into a quagmire. Crossing it was a challenge.

Not time yet. His plan to eliminate Talbot needed to be set up perfectly. So all the blame pointed at the rustlers up on Horse Creek.

Two hard-looking men strode up the boardwalk. He knew them. Texans who worked for the Crown Cattle Company—Lem Squires and Salty Conroy.

"We need to talk to you," Squires said, casting looks around to be certain they were alone. A tall, hunch-shouldered man with Injun eyes that could bore holes in thick wood.

"Out here, all right to talk?"

"Yeah. This rustler running for sheriff. Where's he live?"

"Horse Creek. South across the Yellowstone. Why?"

Palmer forced himself not to smile. It wasn't only thawing outside, but these two rannies had no doubt been sent to settle the issue of Baker for him.

Salty Conroy made a sign with the side of his hand across his throat like a knife.

"We heard he had one wreck and never learned anything from it," Squires said and spat tobacco off the side. He used the back of his hand to wipe his beard-stubbled face.

With his gaze fixed across the street at the pert-looking woman striding the boardwalk going for her grocery shopping, Palmer smiled slow-like. "I understand he got beat up."

"Well, we won't make no mistake about it. He can go feet first for our money."

"How's Farrel?" Palmer asked about the Crown Land and Cattle Company ramrod. The man hadn't been in the Antelope in several weeks.

"You know how bald-headed that sumbitch is without a hat?" Squires asked.

Palmer nodded.

"He's done pulled the last of it out over all this damn winter kill." He looked over at Conroy, who agreed with him.

"So have lots of others. I'll treat you two to a drink inside." Palmer gave a head toss toward the doors.

"I don't ever turn down a free drink." Squires hitched his pants up, and the two hired guns went inside ahead of Palmer, who showed them the way. After Earl poured them each four fingers in a tumbler, Palmer left them at the bar with his best wishes for their success.

Maybe those two could eliminate his biggest problem. Too much talk going on in the bar about Baker's candidacy for him to be comfortable about it. Whiskey loosened tongues, and they were wagging about him. He lit the lamp over his desk—better get this bookkeeping finished. And he needed to work more on his "exit fund." There might be a day he needed to shag his ass out of Billings, and he'd need the money right then. Lots of it. Not only the law would want him after that, but MacDavis would send his dogs.

He dipped the pen in the inkwell. How did he get in these traps?

TWENTY

Herschel watched the fiery orange glow of the sun spearing across the snowy landscape. He'd saddled up Cob early and was headed for his place even before dawn was more than a purple promise in the east. Still reminded of Marsha's concern about him riding all that way alone, he smiled. Temperatures were above freezing this early—the old chinook was going to be a lifesaver. If there was any more to save.

He kept Cob, who acted frisky after his long layover eating oats in her corral, in a long trot. When he topped the last rise and could see the blackened ruins of his cabin, some of his heart left him. Lots of his work, sweat and money had gone into that structure. He'd also need to be able to solve crimes like that if he ever made sheriff. But the evidence was all snowed under and the trail way too cold. Still, someone knew something, and they might talk one day. He sure owed the arsons a good pasting with his fists.

He rode Cob through his cow herd. They looked good for the winter they'd come through so far. Most of his stock carried British blood, Hereford or Shorthorn, so they had thick hair—those Mexican cattle they brought up anymore came from so deep down there they'd never seen a frost, let alone a blizzard. Even in a normal year they had trouble wintering up here.

Toby Hansen was doing a good job caring for the cattle. They acted contented, and many of the cows were beginning to spring. Another month, they'd start calving. He might need to set up a tent for headquarters then. Someone needed to be around at calving time.

His horses were all there, and one stray had wandered in to join them. A big dun horse with saddle marks on his withers. Wore a 7T on his right shoulder. Someone would claim him, or he'd advertise and keep him for the feed bill. Toby had done a good job of holding the drifting cattle out of the herd or there wouldn't be any hay left. Several white-capped haystacks were left in the hay yard as a reserve. His tall rail-and-post fencing had helped too.

Mid-morning he found Nels and Toby haying their own herd.

"How's things going?" Nels asked, taking off his glove and sticking out his hand to shake.

"Going to go into Billings and file tomorrow." He stepped off Cob and his legs were under him fine. That gave him confidence after three weeks of layoff.

"Wonderful. We'll all be glad to see you on the ballot."

"Toby, thanks, my stock looks great."

The sixteen-year-old beamed back at him. "See the dun?"

"Whose is he?"

"He just showed up."

"We'll share any reward or proceeds."

"Thanks," Toby said and went back to pitching hay.

"Where you headed?"

"Larkin's. Marsha needs some baking soda."

"You won't buy any hard candy for them girls, now, will you?" Nels asked.

"Oh, I might." Both men cracked up and laughed so hard it hurt Herschel's sides.

In a shortcut for Larkin's store, he cut across Pine Ridge. Still in the bull pines, he noticed two riders coming from the west like they were avoiding the main road. He set back in the timber and studied them. Was he becoming jumpy? Probably some chuck line riders, out of work and looking for their next meal. Lots of them around—they used to pop in on him when he batched. Sort of like a magnet for the out of work and moving on. They'd split stove wood or help do chores for their keep, then in a few days sugar-foot on.

Drops of melted snow began to pelt his cap and the shoulders of his canvas coat. Those two obviously weren't headed for Larkin's. Deliberate-like, they were swinging north of the store, he decided, from his high perch observing the two specks on the white blanket. They could even be headed for his place. Must not know his cabin had been torched.

Why were his guts roiling? Could that be the two who beat him up? More than a coincidence, two cowboys passing a store—deliberate-like, too. Not natural. He pulled off his glove and rubbed the itchy beard stubble around his mouth, checked Cob, who grew tired of standing in the pines. Maybe he better trail them dudes and see what they were up to. Might be nothing more than drifters—still they didn't act like he expected.

When they went over the rise, he sent Cob downhill. They were on a course to his place. Toby would be up there feeding by this time. He best see. On the flat, he short loped Cob, and the snow had begun to turn to mush. A good quarter mile farther he'd hit the rise and could probably see them again. He undid his jacket so the Colt .44 on his waist was handy. He'd not go anywhere without it.

Reining Cob up short, he scanned the still, white scene of his bottoms. He could see the sled filled with hay and Toby coming to feed the bawling cattle. Then he saw the two riders and they'd stopped him.

He booted Cob off the hillside. Whatever they were up to, he needed to see about it. They'd stopped the boy from his hay feeding and were pushing him around. He set spurs to Cob. They wanted someone to beat on, he was coming. Even at the distance, he saw them jerk around and look surprised at his approach. The small mushroom blast of the one's pistol at him told Herschel enough. It was them, the pair that beat him, and they'd come back for more.

Beyond any pistol range, he narrowed the distance, as the one fought with his head-slinging horse, no doubt upset by the shot. The other figure fired two more rounds. Too far. Herschel's fingers closed on the wooden grips, and he jerked his own pistol free. His left hand guided the cow pony directly at them.

He faced the post-and-rail fence in his path a hundred feet ahead. Cob could clear it when there wasn't snow—his footing on the slush might be bad. There were lots of questions in Herschel's mind. But he wanted those two—for his own beating and for shoving around Toby Hansen.

Cob took wing. The gelding flew over the fence, landed in good shape and gathered himself up in a hard run immediately. The shocked looks on their faces was something; Herschel figured he'd never forget it.

The shorter of the two had his horse under control and was fumbling for his gun. In the rocking gait of the horse, Herschel knew any shot hitting a mark would be lucky. He aimed and fired. The shorter man whirled holding his right arm. His bug-eyed bay horse left the country bucking and kicking higher than the sky. The tall one's black horse shied, too, and forced him to shoot wild.

The wounded one on the ground dropped to his knees and took aim. His revolver misfired, and a split second later, Herschel fired three shots that struck him like a rag doll in the leg, chest and shoulder. In a cartwheel-like action, he sprawled on the ground screaming, "You've kilt me!"

"Shuck that gun or die!" Herschel shouted at the taller one.

He obeyed and stepped off his horse with his hands high.

"Good," Herschel said, stepping off the skidding Cob and looking for the boy. "Toby?"

"I'm fine," the youth said, looking flush-faced, appearing from around the sled and carrying a pitchfork like a bayonet.

Herschel kicked aside the one's handgun, ignoring his blubbering, and kept the tall one in his vision. He still had one shot left, if he needed it.

"Who're you?" Herschel demanded of the wounded one lying on his back.

"None of your damn business."

Herschel jammed the Colt in his coat side pocket and jerked him off the ground. "Mister, I'm making it my business and you better go to talking and fast or I'm beating the dog shit out of you."

He held the man's face so close to his own he could smell his tobacco breath. "What's your name?"

"Salty Conroy."

"His?"

"Lem Squires."

"Who do you work for?"

"Nobody."

Herschel drew back and popped him in the face with the back of his hand. Then he drew him up hard. "Who do you work for?"

Conroy shook his head and tried to draw back. "Crown Land and Cattle."

"I owe you a beating." He shoved Conroy hard backward so he sprawled on his back in the snow.

"No, no, it wasn't us." Squires held up his hands in defense. "Honest, we didn't do that."

"Who in the hell did it then?" He scowled at Conroy on the ground.

"Mister, I don't know. I'm bleeding to death."

"Bleed to death, damn you. You better come up with the names of who in the hell beat me up."

"We can't, we only heard about it."

"Why were you here then?" Herschel jerked Squires's coat open and looked at his vest. He didn't have any silver buttons on his vest either.

"To convince you was all."

"Convince me of what?"

"Not to run for sheriff."

"Holy cow," Toby said.

"I'm taking them to jail in Billings this afternoon, but Marsha's going to worry. Can you ride down there after you feed and tell her what happened and that I'll be along?"

"Sure. You need any help?"

"Catch their horses. I'll tie them on behind the buckboard," he said, looking around. Then he took out his Colt, ejected the empties and reloaded it.

"You want the big team?" Toby asked, tossing his hand at the big mares.

"But you—"

"I can catch the other, and when I'm through feeding I'll go over and tell her."

"Good."

After hitching the mares to the buckboard and them doing a few circles to let off steam, Toby helped Herschel load the moaning Conroy, then the sullen Squires with his wrists and feet bound.

"One trick out of either of you and you'll be wolf bait. Savvy?" Herschel threatened them.

Conroy nodded, hugging his wounded arm. Blood had saturated his coat sleeve and dripped off his fingers, Herschel noted, as he hitched their saddle horses to the tailgate. He didn't personally care if the two lived or died. It was a damn big inconvenience for him to have to take them into jail.

Long past dark, he crossed on the ferry, drove the team up the landing and started down Main Street. Sore and tired, he'd be grateful for a hot meal and a bunk at the livery.

At the jail, he drew a small crowd of the curious.

"What did they do?" one whiskered old man shouted at Herschel when he stepped down.

"Came to convince me not to run for sheriff, they said."

"The one looks pretty shot up to me," another announced.

Herschel nodded. "I ain't sure who's convinced."

"You are running for sheriff, ain't yeh?"

"I am," he said over his shoulder. "Watch them. I'm going in and find a jailer."

"Why not string them up and save all that?"

Herschel held his hands up; he wanted no part of a lynching. "We need to let the law handle it."

"What's going on here?" Mayor Whitehall asked, pushing his way to the front.

"Them two tried to convince Baker not to run for sheriff," the bearded man said and then cackled. "They lost."

"I should say so. That one needs medical aid. How long ago were you wounded?"

"Hours ago."

"Let's get him to the doctor," Whitehall said and pushed closer.

"He doesn't deserve a doctor. Let him be," another man said and confronted the mayor. "They work for you?"

"No, but I am—"

"Whitehall, you act like you got a big interest in them two criminals."

"Well, I am the mayor and it's my job—to see that things are done civilized here."

"Hang the sonsabitches!" A roar of approval followed.

Herschel was back with two armed jailers. He helped them get Conroy down, then they carried Squires by his arms between them. They locked the courthouse door behind them. When Herschel turned back, he could see that someone wearing a fine topcoat and a high crown hat was getting on his buckboard.

"Now, boys, hold everything. I don't know all the particulars of this matter, but we need law and order in Montana. As sheriff of Yellowstone County—"

"You won't be for long!" some heckler shouted.

"Better meet your replacement. You're on his buggy, Talbot."

The sheriff looked around with a scowl. "You bring them in?" He glared at Herschel.

"I sure did, and I signed the warrants charging them with attempted murder, too."

"A misunderstanding I am sure."

Herschel shook his head and folded his arms over his chest. "I charge by the hour for the use of my buckboard, too."

"Your word against theirs," Talbot said under his breath when someone helped him down.

"No, I have a witness."

"You don't understand about the law."

Herschel nodded quickly. "Yes, I do. And when I get elected sheriff, I won't be taking sides with the big outfits when they do something wrong."

"Why, you—"

Herschel felt his cheeks heat with anger and narrowed his eyes. "Are you threatening me, too?"

"You'll see about this," Talbot said, red-faced in the street lamplight. Out of nowhere, his chief deputy, Copelan, herded him toward the front door, talking under his breath to control the man.

"Baker for sheriff!" went up the cry.

Herschel nodded thanks, waved to them and drove off to the livery. He still needed to put up the horses and get some supper and a good night's sleep.

TWENTY-ONE

P ALMER saw the whole thing unfolding. Filled with disgust, he plowed through the barroom and went into his
office to kick the wall. Pacing back and forth, he pounded
his fist in his palm. There had to be a way to handle this
mess. Somehow Baker had managed to turn the tables on
those two toughs. He'd underestimated that man—he
wasn't some simple Texas cowboy turned squatter. Conroy
was all shot up, too, from what he could find out. Damn,
and they'd point their finger right back to the Crown. He'd
better get word up to Farrel Goldby.

Shame he hadn't let his Texans kill Baker. He hadn't
learned much from that beating. Maybe he needed to
threaten her—that Allen widow. Women were always more
vulnerable than men. Of course, she had pulled a gun on
Copelan—but he wasn't tough. The most important thing
at the moment, he needed those two out of jail before
morning—and gone.

An hour later, after being sure he wasn't followed, Palmer knocked on the jailhouse door.

"Who's there?" some sleepy-sounding jailer asked.

"I need to talk to Copelan." He looked all around the dark, deserted street. Nothing—must have been some alley cats he heard.

The guard cracked the door with a rifle barrel sticking out. "He expecting you?"

"He should be."

"Any more of that mob out there?"

"Naw, they went home."

The guard stretched and put the rifle on the desk. "Good, I'm tired of this crap."

Palmer nodded and went up the stairs. He found Copelan in his office, and the man looked up. The lamp's reflection glared off his reading glasses. He unhooked them from behind his ears and put them in a case.

"Glad you're here. Those damn supposed toughs must have told Baker everything." Copelan shook his head. "They'll probably get on the stand and scream like eagles."

Palmer took a chair, then put his boots on top of the desk and leaned back. "They ain't going to be no trial."

"How're we going to—"

"They're going to try to escape this jail tonight."

Copelan batted his weak eyes at him. "How?"

"Overpower the guard and make it into the alley, when you're going to cut them down."

"Me?" He swallowed with obvious difficulty.

"You ain't ever shot anybody, have you, Copelan?" Palmer looked hard at him.

"No."

"First time for everything. Just so they're dead and can't talk." Palmer fetched out a cigar from his vest and offered it to Copelan. He refused the offer with a dull head shake.

"I don't think Conroy can even walk. He's shot up so bad."

"Have Squires pack him."

"What if he won't take the bait?"

Palmer shook his head in disgust—who was this Herschel Baker any way? Some kinda gun sharp?

"I don't care if you dump both of them in the alley and shoot them full of holes. I want them out of this jail or all hell's going to break loose around here."

"Jesus, I wish they could walk anyway." Copelan hugged his arms like he was cold and shook his head as if to clear it. "I've never done—"

"A lot of our future welfare—yours and mine—depends on silencing those two."

"I'll do it."

"See that you do it right, too."

"Oh, yeah."

With a small jackknife, Palmer trimmed off the end of the cigar, stuck it in his mouth, ripped alive a gopher match and began to puff on his smoke. Then he smiled at Copelan. "There's at least a hundred bucks in doing this right. I'll see you get the money, too."

"Good, I'll send the rest of the guards home, all but Harker; he'll keep his mouth shut."

"I can cut him in for fifty."

"Hell, he'd choke his own mother to death for that much."

Both men laughed, and Copelan broke out a bottle of whiskey and two glasses from his desk drawer. "How about a good drink before we part?"

"Ain't a better way in the world to seal a good business deal." Palmer put his boots down and scooted up to the edge of his chair.

Minutes later, Harker, a big man with a wide, tough face, let him out the back way.

"Night."

"Night," Palmer said, wondering how that goon would work out for Copelan. No matter, as he grimaced over the mud he was getting on his good boots walking in the dark alley—he knew this episode was about to be handled. MacDavis expected him to take care of things for all the big outfits.

He paused at the street, checked to be certain he was not being observed, and tried to scrape the mud off his boots. Damn mess anyway. Then he went via the various business porches back to the Antelope.

Eleven-thirty on the schoolhouse clock. The crack of shots silenced everyone in the Antelope. Must have been ten or so shots fired, Palmer decided. *Be sure—they are dead.* His last orders.

The barroom crowd poured out into the street looking for the source.

"Where did the shots come from?" someone shouted as Palmer made the front doors.

"Jailbreak," someone shouted.

"What happened?"

"Don't know, but something's going on in the alley back of the jail."

TWENTY-TWO

J AILBREAK!" Someone stuck his head in the cafe to report the latest happening.

The words slapped Herschel in the face like a wet rag. How in hell's name could those two escape—so soon and Conroy all shot up. They had no weapons—he'd searched them good at the ranch. Unless they had help inside—he rose, dug in his vest and threw down some money to pay for his meal, putting on his coat to leave. When he reached the crowd, he made his way through them, wondering, as he listened to their words, what was the truth.

"Both dead," a man said, shouldering him hard in the alley's darkness and leaving as if satisfied he'd seen enough.

Herschel tried to see the two downed men. The other, a bull-dog-looking guard holding a double-barreled sawed-off shotgun, was surveying the crowd.

"You don't need a doctor here, Copelan," the short man

who'd been examining the bodies said. He was rising to his feet. "You need an undertaker. They're both dead."

"Someone get Peabody over here," Copelan said.

"What happened?" someone shouted.

"They had a derringer, pulled it on Harker and made it down here before I stopped 'em."

"Damn handy, wasn't it?" one older man said under his breath to Herschel.

He half smiled and then shook his head in disbelief. "Since they carried Conroy in, he must have got well real fast."

"Guess we've got to take their word for it."

"I guess," Herschel said and turned to leave. He noticed a face in the half-light. Buck Palmer, who owned the Antelope Saloon. A man he considered worth watching. He'd heard that Palmer had bought the Diehl Place after the sheriff's auction. Be damn nice to know whose side he was on. Buck's signature had been on the first petition for office. Maybe he'd known that one would never be delivered and that's why he signed it. He'd sure do to watch.

There'd be no trial of those two. No finger-pointing at their employer or any of the other big outfits. Neither of the pair had on jackets, nor were their hats on the ground anywhere—strange for Texas cowboys to leave them behind. They'd no doubt dragged Conroy down there to the alley, dumped him in the mud facedown, then shot him and Squires both full of holes. End of the issue. But the two dead ones worked for Farrel Goldby, and they all were on the payroll of a big corporation, Crown Land and Cattle.

He knew one thing for certain, the dead ones weren't the same ones beat him up—it made for two others to watch out for, and one wore a vest missing a coin button. So his enemies both big and small were still out there. Why did his thoughts about Buck Palmer keep niggling him? He'd never wear a vest with coin buttons. That hammered coin spelled Texas; probably some Mexican silversmith made it. But over half the cattle folks in Montana like himself sprung from the Lone Star State. Like Herschel they'd come up the trail with the herds—the good, the bad and the treacherous.

After his walk back, he found an empty bunk at Pascal's yard and slept a few hours. Before the sun even tried to peek over the waning snow scene, he had dressed and hitched the horses. In the cafe, there was lots of talk about the night before's jailbreak. More grumbles about how they needed a grand jury to look into it.

"You brought them in?" Gab Frazier asked. "What do you say?" The older man looked right into Herschel's eyes. "There ain't no tears over them two rannies in our heart, is there?"

"No."

"Let the county bury 'em, I say." Frazier paused at the doorway. "Good riddance we need some more like it."

"Suits me," Herschel said, knowing they'd somehow cover up the jail break and shooting regardless.

"The world won't miss them either."

Herschel looked up from his eggs, ham and German fried potatoes. Buster came hobbling out and joined him, sitting down on an empty chair. Looking around suspiciously, at last he began making a roll-your-own in his knotty fingers. "They get to yeh?"

"Na." Herschel shook his head. "They just rode over I guess to kill me."

"Lots of hard cases in this country, drawing double wages."

"You ever see a match to this, let me know." He drew the silver button out and put it on the table.

Buster picked it up and examined it. Then, "No" escaped his sun-bleached, white lips, before he licked the rolled cylinder shut and stuck one end in them. Fumbling under his white apron for a match, he leaned forward when Herschel struck one for him. Slow-like he made little puffs out the corner of his mouth and then drew the roll-your-own away.

"But I'll watch real close."

"Don't mess with 'im if you do find out who it is. Let me handle them if you find one of them."

"Good enough."

"I better get back. I'm a day late getting there."

"Why, hell, it'll all wait," Buster said and rose with pain written on his face.

"Take care of yourself."

"I will. You do the same."

By ten o'clock, he was unhitching his team when he looked up and saw her coming hard toward him. Wheels flinging mud, she slid to a halt and tied off the reins. She bolted out of the buckboard and ran to hug him.

"Oh, thank God, you're all right." She buried her face in his coat.

"Toby told you what I was doing, didn't he?"

"Yes, but I still worried all night." She smoothed back her hair from the wind and looked up at him.

He kissed her. Like it was the thing he most wanted to do at that exact moment. Not just some kiss, but a hard one, a real one. It wasn't she hadn't been on his mind; she had been. But in the fresh air and all—he wanted to taste her mouth, her neck, her whole body. He felt pretty heady holding her to his body.

"W-we can go file the petition. The girls are at the Fergusons' and two Crow boys are feeding my stock until I get back."

"Let me turn out my team and we'll go."

"What happened up there last night?"

"I turned them in to the jailer, signed the warrants and an hour later they shot them escaping."

"Escaping?"

He shook his head in disgust. "They're both dead."

She looked at the thawing ground and chewed on her lower lip. "Is there no justice?"

He stopped and said, "No." Then he finished unhooking the first set of harness, grateful he had something to do in her presence. Hard for him not to just hug and kiss her. First set hung on the tack room wall, he went back for the other ones. Then leading the pair to the gate, he smiled at her.

"We have few more that'll vote for us," he said. "They talked that way in town last night."

"Good, so they don't kill you first. You think they were the pair—"

He shook his head, knowing what she wanted, and grimaced. "No, the button never fit."

"What did these two want?"

"To convince me not to run, and kill me if they couldn't, I guess." He boosted her onto the buckboards. "Let's go file."

"Yes, then at least they can't stop that."

"What I'm thinking."

"You all right to drive?" she asked, snuggled close to him on the spring seat.

"I sure ain't over healing, but I'm fine. I been thinking some. I've put you through a lot—taking me all over and everything. I don't want you to feel—"

"Yes?"

"Good," he said, relieved she wasn't upset about his imposition on her. He clucked to the team.

"What were you getting at?"

The horses moving, he felt better and nodded. "Maybe while we're there at the courthouse and all—we ought to get married." He had it out.

"Today?"

He glanced over at her, then he reined the team to a stop.

"I thought today might be okay."

She threw her arms around her neck and kissed him, "Today is wonderful, 'cept I don't have my best dress on."

"It won't matter. We'll have each other."

"Yes, we will."

Her eyelashes were wet and she looked ready to cry out loud and he didn't know what to do next so he hugged her hard. "Oh, for heaven sakes, Marsha, don't cry on me."

"I'm trying not to—but I'm so happy you asked me." She snuffed her nose and shook her head.

Damn, this was going to be some day. File for sheriff, get married and go on a honeymoon. That part scared him. Why? They belonged to each other. Somehow it would all work out—for the best.

Her hugging him, he drove several miles.

"Guess if I'd bought a ring—"

"Herschel Baker, I don't need a ring to belong to you."

"Hmm," he snorted. "I guess I haven't been thinking enough lately."

"How's that?"

"I don't mean about us, but other things in my life. Here I am about to file for sheriff. I know they gunned down them two last night, but dead men don't talk and I can't prove it."

"You'll figure it all out."

"Wish I had your faith."

"You will. You'll have all of me in a few hours."

His face in the wind he felt it heat up. Sure enough he would.

Inside the courthouse, Opal Johnson smiled and got up from her desk when they came into her office. "Guess you came to file for office?"

"Yes, ma'am." He put the petition on the countertop.

Mrs. Johnson began counting the signatures, repeating names aloud as she went down the list.

"They're all here. And this is your filing fee."

She nodded to the money he'd laid on the counter, then reached underneath and produced a receipt book.

Then Herschel recalled what else he needed. "We need a marriage license, too."

"Hmm," she said and looked at the clock. It was two-fifteen. "The judge could marry you, I guess, at three-thirty."

He glanced at Marsha and she agreed with a smile.

"That's fine with us."

"Be one dollar."

"Oh, yes," he said and fished in his pocket for the money.

"The judge will charge you two for the ceremony," Mrs. Johnson said.

"We can afford it."

"Oh, I just wanted you to know that." She looked around, then satisfied they were alone, she spoke softly. "You know this petition ain't going to set well with some folks."

"We know that," Herschel said.

"I simply wanted to warn you."

"He's learning more and more every day about that," Marsha said as they started to leave the office for the judge's.

"Good luck," she said after them.

"We sure may need it," he said and followed Marsha out.

An hour and a half later, the judge pronounced them man and wife. He smiled big and told Herschel to kiss the bride. The whole world tilted. It was sure something he'd never expected to happen to him. He had a wife—family—three girls. And the woman in his arms was his very own. Whew.

They swept out of the judge's office into the hallway. Herschel was still in a trance, and when he looked up, he saw a shotgun pointed at him. Someone took his six-gun and he faced Talbot.

"What's going on here?"

"You're under arrest for the shooting of Jack Diehl," Talbot said.

"What—"

"You can't arrest him for that." Marsha's face turned angry surrounded by Talbot's men.

"Easy," Herschel said to her, seeing the fury in her look. He turned back to face Talbot. "You have no evidence."

"The hell I don't, I have three eyewitnesses say you shot him in the back." Talbot gave a head toss, and a deputy on each arm, they herded him for the stairs.

"They won't keep you long!" she shouted in a hoarse voice.

"I'll be fine," Herschel said over his shoulder. A large rock formed in his stomach. That no-account Talbot did this to him on his wedding day, too. One more reason to toss him out of office. Before this was all over there'd sure be hell to pay.

TWENTY-THREE

MARSHA Baker had one thing in mind when she burst into the judge's office. Getting her man freed.

"Mrs. Baker? Back so soon?"

"That no-account sheriff just arrested my husband on trumped-up charges." Her breath roared through her nostrils, and she threw her arm back pointing toward the door, looking through half-closed lids at the man. "I want him out of that jail."

"I-I know nothing."

"You set the bail—what is it?"

"But the charges haven't been filed."

"I don't care what the charges are. They've been trumped up."

"That's for a court of law to decide."

"You and I are going up there, and you're going to find out right now or I'll have a mob up here and lynch the whole bunch of you."

"Easy. This can be worked out in a few days. I'm certain it's a misunderstanding."

"Yes, and very convenient isn't it, since Herschel just filed for sheriff?"

"He did. I mean he did?"

"Get up there and find out what they're up to."

"I am—"

"I know who you are. But you better find out and quick what they're up to."

"I will go see, but you best remain here."

"No funny business."

"None whatsoever," Jones promised and left her seated in a chair in his office.

In ten long minutes, he returned. "I am sorry. Sheriff Talbot has filed charges of murder against your husband."

"He's never murdered anyone. Least of all Jack Diehl. The sheriff never even came down there and investigated the case."

"He has two eyewitnesses."

"What's the bail?"

"In a murder case—"

"He is innocent until proven guilty, right?"

"Of course."

"Then what is his bond?"

"Five hundred," the man said quickly.

"I have a ranch—"

"No, that would have to be cash."

For ten cents she'd have pounded the silver-sideburned face before her to a bloody pulp. Instead she clenched and reclenched her fist. "Write that out on paper about his bond. I want no arguments from Talbot when I get the money."

"The banks are already closed."

She waved him on. "Give me that paper."

"This is highly out of the ordinary."

"So is arresting an innocent man."

"There," he said, blowing on the form he had filled out.

Armed with his order, Marsha left the courthouse and started down Main Street. She headed for the diner first. Inside, several early supper customers looked up at the sound of the bell and her entry.

"My name's Marsha Baker. I'm Herschel Baker's wife. They're holding him in jail for a murder he didn't do. Those crooks at the courthouse want five hundred dollars for his bail. Anyone in here want to help me?"

"Yes," said the gray-headed man on the end stool as he turned to face her. "I'll give forty dollars. How can I help you?"

"I don't really know yet." She turned her lips inward when the man gave her three twenties instead of two. "I'll have to see. Thank you."

"Hey me, too. Who's he supposed to have kilt?"

"They say his best friend, Jack Diehl. But the sheriff never even investigated Jack's death."

"Spencer, let's go down to the Antelope. There's a bunch down there that will pitch in."

"We can't— I mean, they won't let her in there."

"They damn sure will if we raise a ruckus."

Inside the Antelope? She swallowed hard. They were talking about the big saloon and her going in there. This was her honeymoon day and Talbot had tried to ruin it. Yes, she'd go in there with them if it meant getting Hersch out of jail.

In minutes, there was a groundswell of men with her and she was swept up Main Street in the flood, joined by more. The talk was all about them holding Herschel Baker on false charges in the county jail. But the anger of the participants also grew, and made her wonder if she had stirred up a hornet's nest.

When they herded her inside the Antelope Saloon, she

saw the big moose first, his stuffed head positioned over the center of the back bar. Two women she considered shady ladies looked her over and curled their lips as if they considered her less than themselves. The man behind the bar with a great mustache looked at her first in shock, then in rage.

"Get her out of here!"

"Not till we've done what we came for, Earl. Stay right there. Boys, listen. Them no-accounts at the courthouse have this lady's husband in jail. We all know what happened to their last prisoners—they shot them in the back. Herschel Baker is running for sheriff, so you can see why they arrested him."

The older man, Spencer, stood on a chair and looked down at her. "My lady, you want to say something?"

"He filed—my husband filed for the office of sheriff a few hours ago. Sheriff Talbot arrested him in the hall of the courthouse on these trumped-up charges. I'm . . . afraid . . . afraid if we leave him there they'll kill him like they did those men he brought in last night."

"Now, sign up with Ed or Seymour," Spencer said. "They'll get your money back to you if you need it, when they turn him loose. We've got to raise five hundred dollars."

"Have a chair, ma'am," Spencer said. "It'll take a little while."

"Yes, thanks," she said as the men milled around the two cashiers. They dug deep in their pockets to help, she could tell, and the pile on both tables was growing—but five hundred was lots of money.

"Earl give us some money sacks," someone shouted.

"Ain't got none."

"Like hell you don't." The accuser's words drew a growl from the men.

"All right, all right, I'll have to get some from in back."

"That's better."

"You need to help us count it," Spencer said to her.

She heard Earl warning them when he returned with the money bags. "The courthouse's closed. They won't take it tonight."

"We'll damn sure see about that. If that's the case, we might even open the courthouse."

Seated at the first table, she flattened crumpled paper money and made stacks. The whole situation was hard to believe. In her own way she had command of an entire tough army. More men came rushing into the Antelope to help. Light-headed, she began to realize that her desperate call for help in the cafe had launched a stampede.

She counted three hundred dollars at her table and looked at Spencer and a man with a monocle counting at the other one.

"Two ninety here." Spencer held his hands up. "We've got enough." He put down the cash and held his hands up again. "We have enough money. Now some of us are going down there and support her at the courthouse."

"That's more—" she started to protest.

"You may need it," Spencer said quietly to her. "Besides I just learned you and Herschel were also married this afternoon."

She felt her face grow red as she nodded. They'd have found out sooner or later.

"Boys, we're going down there to bail him out. If we need to do more then that, we will. But no one is getting out of line till Herschel Baker is out of there. Hold your peace!"

"We'll hold for a little while, that's all, Spencer."

"Hold it long enough so he's clear of that jail," he said and guided her out of the cigar- and whiskey-smelling barroom and into the cold night. The sun had set while they were in the Antelope, she discovered, buttoning up her coat and walking with the shorter man at the head of the procession.

When she tried the front door of the courthouse—it was locked. A loud complaint went up from her army.

Spencer stepped up and rapped hard on the door. "Open up in there!"

"Courthouse is closed for business. Come back tomorrow."

"You either open these doors or we'll batter them down." A roar went up to reinforce his words.

"That's against the law."

"Talbot in there?" Spencer asked, looking hard, as if trying to see something beyond the two closed doors.

"No."

"Copelan?"

"He's here."

"Go get him, and be fast or we're coming in."

"You won't change his mind—"

"You used up one minute already." Spencer turned to her. "Ma'am, you might step back. This may be bloody."

"No, I came to bail my husband out." She drew a deep breath and hugged her arms against the creeping cold. Nothing would stop her; she would see that he was released—unharmed.

The right door finally opened, and putting on his coat, the chief deputy looked over the large crowd in the street. Then he saw her and spoke. "Come back in the morning, ma'am."

She lowered her voice. "Do you want me to tell this crowd what you said to me in the hall that day?" Her intense glare was frozen at him.

He chewed on his lip under the small mustache as if considering her threat. "No need to be hasty. Perhaps we can work out something."

"I have Judge Jones's order in this hand. I have the cash

bond required. Now, Mr. Copelan, I want my husband out here or this jail won't ever be the same." She considered for a split second what this mob would do to the building. Devastate it.

"Everyone can't come in," Copelan finally said. Like those of a cornered rat, his eyes searched the faces of the angry crowd under the lamplight. At last, he pointed at Marsha. "Only her and two more."

"Spencer," she said, feeling confident in the man who was also the key to her success thus far. "You pick another."

"Come on, Hoot," Spencer said to a tall man in the crowd she was unfamiliar with, but he looked Herschel's age and dressed like a cowboy.

Once inside, Copelan's shrill-sounding voice echoed in the empty building. "No need for gunplay or anything like that in here."

"Just get Baker out here and be quick about it," Spencer said.

"You're trying my patience, mister." Copelan gave him a tough look over his shoulder.

"Patience be damned. One shot goes off and this jail will be flattened. Quit stalling." Spencer waved him on with his eyes slitted in a cold stare that moved the deputy into taking the stairs.

Why was Copelan stalling? If anything was wrong.... Her heart pounded so hard she hurt under her rib cage. She felt weak climbing the stairs with Spencer at her side and the cowboy, Hoot, right behind her, taking in everything about the building. Her breathing felt constricted. Air short in her lungs. The railing helped her make each step. Dizziness became a consuming prairie fire she fought. So close, but what if . . . ? No, he would be all right. He had to be. They were only married a few hours before.

Then she realized she was seated in a captain's chair and Spencer was looking intently in her face.

"You all right?" he asked.

She clamped her lips and nodded hard. Had she fainted?

"They've gone to get him."

"No tricks?"

Spencer glanced up at Hoot, and the two men shook their heads to dismiss her concern.

"What happened?"

"Guess you got a little dizzy." For the first time Spencer smiled at her. He grinned like her father had when she was a girl. She wanted to hug him.

"I never get dizzy."

"You're fine now. I can hear iron doors clanging back there." Spencer tossed his head toward the cell block.

Hoot agreed, and about that moment, the handsome, chiseled face of her new husband appeared and looked them over. She leaped up and ran to hug him around the waist.

Filled with new excitement, she threw her head back and looked up at him, making sure he was in one piece. "You all right?"

"I'm fine. I don't know who's responsible for this, but thanks."

"No problem," Spencer said as he and Hoot shook his hand.

"Sign here," Copelan said to Herschel, bent over his desk. "You leave the county, you forfeit the bond."

"How much is it?" he asked.

"Five hundred cash," Copelan said.

"Make him a receipt for that, too," Spencer said, waving his hand at the deputy.

Copelan gave him a scowl and then made one out. "You'll be notified when your trial date is." He handed it and the release papers to Herschel. "You better enjoy your time in the open air. They don't get much of that at Deer Lodge Prison."

A long silence filled the room. Herschel cleared his throat. "If someone needs to worry about prison, you might think on that a little. Murdering prisoners in cold blood is a serious crime, too."

Copelan's face flushed red and his eyes glared like hot coals looking back at Herschel. "Get out of here—all of you."

Tucked under his arm, Marsha left the office with her "man." Oh, the next months to the election she dreaded, but somehow, somehow she knew things would work out—and she had him. She had him, and nothing would separate them for long.

Outside in the dull street lamplight, she closed her eyes for a moment when the roar went up from the excited crowd at the sight of him. Herschel let go of her, stepped forward and spoke. "Thanks, everyone. I'll find a way to pay you all back for your generosity. Come November, we're going to change the brand of law in Yellowstone County with your support."

They shouted and threw hats in the air. On the top of the steps beside the three men, Marsha felt the cold creeping into her body, but also pride in him filled her. Herschel spoke with authority to them and they saw it, too. She closed her eyes and thanked God for bringing him to her. Amen.

TWENTY-FOUR

WHY did he have to deal with such incompetent fools? Why in the name of creation didn't Copelan stop Talbot from arresting Baker? How stupid could those two get? His callused palm had scrubbed his mouth until it felt raw, with him seated at the desk in his small office. When MacDavis found out—heads would roll. No, he had to get Talbot out of the picture and the new acting sheriff, Copelan, under his thumb long before the doors ever opened on Election Day.

What made it worse was they'd even raised the five hundred dollars for Baker's bond in his own saloon. That had unnerved him as much as anything. He better send word and get the two Texans up to the river shack and lay his plans. Talbot needed to be removed from office and the quicker the better.

The next afternoon, with plenty of whiskey, a ham, two crates of foodstuffs and Lucille wrapped in a blanket on the spring seat beside him, he drove to the ferry and then the shack.

"Good," she said, looking around before climbing down off the seat by herself. "Them two damn Texans ain't here yet."

A crate of food in his arms, he laughed. "You won't have to wait long for them."

She wrinkled her nose at him. "Why do I always have to entertain them?" Then, loaded with a basket, she followed him in the shack.

" 'Cause I trust you, Lucille."

"You can quit any day. Those two think they're lovers—" Then she laughed out loud.

"You just make them believe they're the best in the West." He was on his knees starting a fire in the stove. "Get some wood."

She put the basket on a chair. "I know, I know, you pay me well for doing it, too." She went out the door grumbling to herself.

Palmer laughed lighting the kindling. That girl was a kicker. Came to him from a church orphanage in Illinois, two years before. When he'd first laid eyes on her—the day she got off the stage and reported to him—he'd never expected her to make it, but he knew by now that she was a survivor. Two or three years in the prostitution business and most girls like her were either smoking Chinese pipe, had committed suicide, been murdered or run off with a "lover." That meant some smooth-talking loser who'd either become her pimp or abandoned her down the road when she no longer suited him.

In minutes, she was back with an armload and dumped it unceremoniously on the floor. Then she took a seat on a chair, crossed her black-stockinged legs and leaned an elbow on the table. "This sure is boring and cold in here."

"Come here," Palmer said, after he had the fire started

and had straightened. When she stood in front him, he reached down and pulled the ribbon that held the wool cape on her shoulders. A sly smile cracked his mouth. "Let's you and me build us a fire in that bunk."

"Sure," she said. Her blue eyes never flickered, but her lips made a hungry movement.

A while later, Palmer was up, re-dressing when Cooter Daws and Denver Smith rode up. She sat on the edge of the bed pulling on her black stockings.

"Ah, Texas is here at last," she said.

"Remember, your job is to entertain them."

She stuck her other shapely white leg out and pulled on that stocking. "I know."

"If you do a good job with them, might be a new dress in this for you."

"Oh, Boss, I'll do a dandy one."

Palmer nodded and hitched his gunbelt at his waist when the door cracked open and the pair walked in.

"Well, Buck, see you made it," Daws said and nodded to Lucille. "You, too, darling."

Smith set a Winchester by the door and then pulled off his gloves. "Damn, you two even have a fire built." The tall one acted impressed and held his hands out to the stove.

"What's up?" Daws asked.

"Having you boys a little party. Lucille's here for the night."

Smith glanced over at her and nodded his approval.

"Wrap up in some blankets and go sit in the wagon," Palmer said to her with a head toss. "We've got business to discuss."

"I won't—"

Palmer's frown was enough. She took two blankets and headed for the door, gathering them up as she went, closing the door behind herself.

"Well?" Daws asked.

"I want an isolated place we can do this. I want two steers that belong to the big outfits tied up and a branding fire going."

"That old Crib place?" Daws looked at Smith.

His partner nodded. "No one goes over there. That should work."

"What are we exactly doing?"

"Getting rid of a problem I have and putting the blame on some rustlers."

Daws swallowed hard. "That's why you sent her outside?"

Palmer frowned at him. "She don't need to know shit about this. This is Wednesday. Friday, I'm bringing the problem after lunch to that old place on Lacy Fork."

"Yeah, the Cribs' place. What else?"

"We need to steal a saddle horse from one of them rustlers down there, and when it's over, hit him on the rump and send him home."

"Why?" Daws made a face.

"'Cause the posse is going to track him to that place."

"How are you so sure?"

"'Cause horses always go home. Let me worry about the rest."

Daws went over the items. "Two steers tied up, a branding fire, a running iron, and a stolen horse."

"Can you remember all that?" Palmer asked.

They both nodded.

"Things go sour, stay low. I'll know it didn't work when I get there with him and I'll pull back."

"Who's 'him'?"

"You don't need to know," Palmer said, convinced they might back out if they knew his importance. "It works, you'll find out."

"We've got you," Daws said, and Smith agreed with a nod.

"You boys can have your little party now. I have to get back." He rose.

"Hey," Daws called out when he reached the door. "Don't forget to send Lucille back in."

Palmer turned and nodded. "She's all yours. Just don't hurt the merchandise—and I mean it."

"Not us." Daws looked at Smith, and he quickly agreed.

The sun was getting low in the west and spread a bloody light over the hills. Palmer lifted her by the waist off the seat and set her down on her feet.

"Have fun."

"Aw, hell—"

He caught her by the arm and swung her around, his index finger laid on her nose, with a stern look on his face. "I said have fun with them two."

"I will."

"See that you do, if you want that new dress."

"Whoopee," she said in his face and went to doing some kind of sand hill crane dance headed for the shack, waving blankets, petticoats and skirt. Hopping around and kicking her black-stockinged legs as high as her head, she was singing some dirty ditty about the lady from France.

Caught up in her wild, abandoned ways, Daws and Smith came out the doorway and went to waving their hats and dancing around her. Palmer shook his head at their frolicking and clucked to Chester—he had lots still to do for his plan to work.

As soon as he got back to Billings, he needed to find Talbot. At the ferry, the gray-bearded old man looked at him with a frown. "You lose her?"

"Who?"

"That blue-eyed dove you took over with you. Did yeh lose her?"

"You sumbitch." Palmer's hand struck out, gathered him by the gallowses and pulled him close to his face.

"You get nosey in my business and you'll be fish bait in that damn river. Hear me?"

"Wasn't being—I ain't—mister—didn't mean nothing."

When Palmer released him, the man shrunk away and went to the windlass. Palmer would have to be more careful and not cross the river with Talbot when they went south to catch the rustlers. That old man might talk about him coming back alone after that was over, too.

The rope started to creak under the strain, and the Yellowstone's current began to slap the side of the barge. During the crossing, the old man never looked at him again, but kept busy reeling the boat for the north shore. Docked, Palmer drove Chester off and headed for the stables, busy constructing his story for convincing Talbot.

TWENTY-FIVE

I F a man ever got drunk on pure pleasure, Herschel Baker was intoxicated. Curled around his wife's bare back in the hotel bed, he feared the dream would burst any moment. Then he'd wake up in some soggy set of blankets and facing another day on the cattle trail, his eyes burned to the core by the sun, wind and dust. Be eating Corey McKim's long-gone-bad fried pork and gluey oatmeal without sugar and facing another day in the saddle moving cattle north. Ooh, the coffee would be bad, too. All Corey could ever find was gyp water. It must be a dream for there were no stars over him, only the embossed tin ceiling tiles he could make out in the light coming from the street lamp below.

He thought about lots of things that had happened in his life. How he'd brought a hundred heifers of his own north with the main herd in '78. Lost a few of them. All those steers—rode them to death when they cycled. But he struck his homestead on Horse Creek, late that summer—

been easier if his brother had made it. They'd planned to build a ranch together in Montana. Herschel'd broke horses and teams for his eating money. Did some freighting. Built the shack after his first winter in a tent (near froze to death, too), then with neighbors put up the barn, traded his own labor and swapped horses. But while he had no cabin left, thanks to that worthless pair he was looking for—he did have a gorgeous wife and three sweet little girls. More, much more than he ever dreamed about in his wildest fantasies slumped in the saddle and his ears full of cattle bawling. *Thank you, Lord.*

The next morning, Herschel and his bride had breakfast in the cafe. Word was out about their wedding. Maude fawned over them. Across the table, Marsha looked very fresh to him as he considered his eggs and pancakes—no gluey, sugarless oatmeal for him. He wanted to laugh out loud.

"What's so funny?" Marsha asked, under her breath.

"I was thinking about the trail drive up here. We had this old man Corey McKim who was our cook. Hey, he could burn water." They both laughed. "Bad food was McKim's specialty."

"He ain't lying either, ma'am." Buster stood beside the table. In his hands was a carved horse. "This is your wedding present. Couldn't figure out a thing to get ya two."

"Oh, he's gorgeous," Marsha said, holding him up.

"Why Buster, you must have worked months on that."

The older man nodded. "But I wanted you two to have him."

Herschel stood up and shook his hand.

"That McKim was the worst excuse for a camp cook ever came up the trail," Buster said. "I'm sure glad you found a good one." Then he laughed, wiped his whisker-stubbled mouth with his palm and smiled at her. "You've got a good man. He got me up here."

"Well—thanks for the lovely horse," she said and shook his hand. Buster ambled off back toward the kitchen, and Maude came by with the coffeepot.

"That'll be his last horse—" She looked to be certain he was out of hearing. "Arthritis in his fingers is too bad for him to even carve anymore."

Marsha looked up and gave a sad nod that she understood. "He's so real, even the windswept tail. You can sure tell he's a Montana horse."

"Better check the brand. He may be stolen."

Marsha scrambled to turn his other side toward her. "No, he's got an H Bar B on him."

Herschel smiled. "Reckon he's one of ours. If you're through, I'll pay Maude—"

"No way," Maude said. "I can't carve horses, but I can sure feed you on your honeymoon."

The sides of his cheeks felt on fire as he thanked her and helped Marsha into her coat. They moved to the front, hearing from well-wishers among the diners. At the stables, he and Paschal hitched the team up.

"Well, the campaign really starts." Paschal straightened from hitching the belly band on his side.

"Yes, it will." Hersch turned to her and said, "I better go by and see that lawyer Emerson Sparks before we leave town, about the murder charges."

"Fine," she agreed, and threaded the lines back when they'd finished.

Paschal grinned big. "You are going to have to get used to having a man to do that for you, Mrs. Baker."

"Marsha," she quietly corrected him. "He won't mind a little help."

"No, and he's a fine one. You got the pick of the litter."

She wrinkled her nose. "I think so, too."

"Here, I'll help you up before that stable guy steals you," Herschel teased.

"Well, you better or I'd take her away in the shake of a lamb's tail."

Herschel dismissed his chiding and laughed. "You been a bachelor so long you'd not know what you was getting into." He lifted the reins to drive off. "Thanks."

"I ain't dumb and I'd love to try," Paschal shouted after them.

Marsha turned to smile and wave at him. When she turned back and settled in beside Herschel, she said, "I think he was jealous."

"Could have been," Herschel said. "He ain't no fool." His mind was on all the work ahead. They'd sure need to either add on at her place or build new at his.

"I was thinking," he said aloud. "We kinda need a bedroom by ourselves."

"You have me convinced." She clung to his arm. "But if you get elected, you'll need a place in Billings. No need fixing up two places."

"Guess you're right."

"Aw, we'll just have to wait till they're asleep."

He laughed aloud. "Them three ornery girls may never sleep again."

She closed her eyes and laughed. "They may not, curious as they are."

Herschel squinted against the glare coming off the remaining snow and smiled. Lot more fun thinking about being her husband than worrying about them two-legged coyotes trying to harm him.

TWENTY-SIX

U NDER a brass oil-lamp light, Buck Palmer was seated across from Sam Talbot at the back-room table. He poured more good whiskey into the sheriff's glass. The big man used the web of his hand to smooth down his heavy mustache, then raised the glass.

"Here's to yeh."

Palmer nodded. "You know them rustlers are even working this winter, don't you?"

"Cold as it is?" Talbot frowned in disbelief at him.

"Right, stealing steers every day. Cattle are winter-weak, easy to catch."

"Yeah, but they ain't easy to catch at it."

"What's it worth to you to catch a couple of them red-handed?"

Talbot collapsed in the chair. "Couple hundred, I guess. Sure would discredit Baker as being one of them. Yeah, two hundred bucks."

Palmer leaned over the table and clasped his hands together on the top. "I can't be too involved. It could hurt my business if things didn't, say, go right, but I'll get you there and help you arrest them."

"When?"

"Friday."

"I'll get a posse."

"No!" Palmer fell back in his chair and shook his head. "If we don't do this careful, you'll never catch them doing it."

"All right, how do we do it?"

Leaned back, Palmer dried his palms on his pant legs. "You and I can't ride out together. You need to meet me above Horse Creek. Say you leave at nine a.m. I'll be ahead of you. From there we can use some back trails, snows melted some, and sneak up on them." He sat back, letting that take effect.

"You and me are going to take them?"

"Right. It'll look good in the paper. Sheriff Talbot captures rustlers red-handed."

A gleam in the lawman's brown eyes was signal enough to Palmer that his plan might work. "I need some good publicity. That damn Emerson had the murder charges dismissed against Baker this morning."

"Screw Baker. He ain't no problem. You get two of that Horse Creek bunch in jail and them caught red-handed, you'll be reelected by a landslide."

"Cost me two hundred bucks, huh?" Talbot cast a suspicious look across the table at him.

"Bring it along. If we don't get them, you don't owe me a damn anything."

"How do you know so much about this deal that I don't?"

Palmer held up his glass, ready to take a drink. "Oh, whiskey makes some talk in here, and I do some looking around. I was a scout in the damn war."

"Johnny Reb, hissself?" Talbot gave him a scoffing look.

A cold wave like a bucket of ice water swept over Palmer's face at the man's words, but he smiled in time to control it. "That's me."

"Funny, ain't it?" Talbot looked at the whiskey left in his glass like he was assaying it.

"How's that?"

"You and me fought against each other in that war."

Palmer agreed. "New war. New army."

"I been thinking, we get statehood and all, how I'd run for governor. Maybe you'd like a job up there." Talbot smoothed out his mustache again.

Set back in the chair, Palmer acted as if he was considering the man's offer. Then he nodded in agreement like that would be all right. *Maybe in the next world you'll do that, Talbot—but after Friday, you'll be running from the fires of hell, you conceited horse's ass.*

TWENTY-SEVEN

Baker and his bride reached Larkin's store before noon-time. Marsha wanted to get some supplies to bake a special cake, so they and the girls could celebrate.

"Come in," Larkin shouted. "Mrs. Allen and the next sheriff of Yellowstone County's here."

"No, Mr. Larkin, you're wrong," Marsha said.

His face dropped. "I thought you went to file that petition yesterday."

The four men around the stove stood up to learn what they could.

"Oh, we did that," Marsha said and winked wickedly at Herschel. "Got married, too."

"Get out that jew's harp in your pocket," Larkin said. "And go to playing it. I want to dance with the bride."

"It's a harmonica."

"Play it anyway." Larkin waved him off and held out his hand for her to take.

"I don't know." She looked taken back by his idea.

"I do. We're going to dance," Larkin said and took her gracefully whirling between the counters when Herschel hit the waltz tune. The rest of them stood like buzzards watching a cow die, licking their chops to be her next dance partner.

"Come on, Hansen, we ain't going to be left out of this little deal," Mrs. Larkin said to the tall onlooker as she came around the counter, shedding her apron. They soon joined the other pair on the floor.

Behind his mouth harp, Herschel sawed away on the tune. What a wedding celebration—six guys and only two gals to dance with. Worse yet, he was the band for his own party.

"I think it's wonderful you married her, but I lost ten cents on it," Mrs. Larkin said when Hansen swept her past him. "I bet you'd tie the knot after spring roundup. Claris won that one." And she was gone.

Before they left the store, plans were laid for a gathering at the schoolhouse on Friday night for the real dance and celebration.

"Keep an eye out for Joe Duffy's roan horse," Nels told him. "He came by this morning and said it was gone. Strange, unless he was stolen, why a horse would ever leave good hay at home for the damn snowbanks. Might have been stolen."

Herschel agreed. "I'll watch for it."

The big man clapped him on the shoulder and walked him to the door. "You got enough to worry about the next few weeks. New bride and all. We'll find his old horse."

"Thanks. See you Friday."

"Yes. Hey, best of luck to both of you," Nels said, taking Marsha's hand and holding it in his. "Couldn't've happened to nicer folks."

She beamed back at him. "I thought so, too."

When they picked them up at the Fergusons', the girls were so excited they couldn't sit down in the wagon.

"Can we call him Daddy now?" Kate asked her.

She looked over at him. "That's for him to say."

"Why, I'd be pleased as lemonade punch to be called that if you girls want to do that."

Nina squeezed him around the neck so hard from behind that his cap flew off, with her screaming, "Yes, yes, no more, Mr. Baker. You're our daddy!"

He reined up the team and she let go, ducking her head.

"He may quit us and run away," Marsha was waving her finger at them, "if you all are going to choke him to death and make him lose his cap."

He picked up the cap and beat it against his leg, and came back to the buggy grinning at them. "Aw, Mom, I'm as excited as they are. Never had four women of my own. One time before my mom died, I had two—her and my sister, Rosie. Who would love all of you."

"Will she come to see us?" Kate asked.

He paused undoing the reins. "I guess I'll have to write and ask her. She lives in Texas."

"You never mentioned your father," Marsha said. "Is he alive?"

Herschel shook his head. "We don't know. He went off one day to buy cattle when I was fifteen and never came back."

"You think he died?"

Herschel shook his head and set the horses on their way. "I'm not sure. In the back of my mind, I guess I'll always wonder."

"Must have been hard on you the way you act."

He nodded. "For years before I came up here I kept looking hard every time I saw a rider coming over the horizon. Was it Paw, finally returning home or someone with a message from him?"

Marsha squeezed his arm. "I'm sorry."

He shook his head and swallowed hard. Even after all those years, it was still tough to talk about his father's disappearance.

TWENTY-EIGHT

Palmer leaned over the bar and whispered, "Wednesday afternoon, get some things for an overnight stay."

"Those damn—" Her blue eyes narrowed.

He shook his head. "You like that new yellow dress you got on, don't you?"

"I love it." She reached up and ran her hand down his shaven cheek.

"Could be another in this one."

Her face lightened and she smiled. "I'll be ready. What time?"

"After lunch."

"Sure thing." She winked mischievously at him, then went sashaying off to look around the barroom for another customer.

Straightened, Palmer turned back to Earl. "What's it doing outside?"

"Snowing some the last half hour."

He looked over the green half curtains and could see the white stuff coming down out there. More winter. Damn.

The snowstorm left four to six inches and covered the ground again. Temperatures dropped hard and made Palmer wonder how well his plan would work. He took Chester and his saddle horse, Custer, out of the stable. Custer tied to the tailgate, he drove up the alley behind William's Mercantile and picked up the crate of groceries he'd ordered earlier. When he drove up, a boy brought the box out and loaded it. He tipped him a nickel and drove over behind the Antelope.

Lucille jumped up from her chair when he came in the back door. "Wondered where you were," she said with a frown.

"Getting ready," he said, and took up a roll of blankets and other things. His rifle was concealed in the bedding.

"We going for a week?" she asked, looking over all he'd brought out as she climbed onto the seat.

"We might." He checked over everything; then as if satisfied, he climbed up on the seat.

"Damn, it turned cold as all get out," she said, using a blanket to huddle under.

"It may be the worst winter Montana ever had."

"It's sure worse than Nebraska," she said.

"Hell, it's further north, bound to be." He clucked to Chester and swung him out of the alley, then went the back street to the ferry.

The old man was off that afternoon and Palmer felt pleased, paying a new boy two dimes to cross.

"You said you once lived on the Gulf. How much does it snow down there?" she asked.

"Never snows. Never freezes even."

She looked at him hard. "I don't believe that."

He looked up the Yellowstone, at the jagged, icy banks

and swift flow. His ice house wasn't quite full, so he hoped it refroze. He'd need lots of it in the summertime.

"Well, why did you ever leave down there?"

"Why did you leave Omaha?"

"Hell, I was eighteen and they don't keep you past then. You told Reverend Carr I could have a job as a housekeeper in your Billings hotel and you'd pay my passage."

"And two hundred fifty bucks to him."

"He never mentioned that money. Or that I'd have to repay that and my passage back to you."

"Oh, did that preacher lie to you?"

"He never told me the truth." She looked away in a pout.

"You reckon he really knew what he was doing?"

Her eyes narrowed and she pursed her lips. "Hell, yes, he did. He fondled the other girls all the time. I never let him catch me alone in a room after he did it once."

Palmer laughed and laughed.

"It wasn't funny."

He finally turned up the lane to the shack. "He sure is a righteous old bastard in them letters."

"Has to be. He must have kept all that money you paid him. The orphanage paid my railroad tickets to Cheyenne and the stage up here. Plus they gave me ten dollars for meals."

Palmer halted Chester and dismounted. "Come here, baby." His arms held up, he lifted her off the wagon and then kissed her hard on the mouth. Her eyes flew open in shock.

"No Texans this time. All you got to entertain is me."

Her arms flew around him. "Aw, Buck, how sweet of you. Why didn't you tell me—I mean—" She looked up at him and tears filled her lashes.

He looked at her, bobbing his head three times. "Well, I kinda thought you and me needed a little time to ourselves."

"We do. We do."

"Good, 'cause we're going to be up here till Friday."

"You and me and a case of champagne and all this food!"

"Going to have us a real party."

She hugged him again. "You're the best boss in the whole world."

He used his gloved hand to raise her face up and kissed her on the soft lips. "We're going to have a real good time, baby."

Before dawn the next morning, he left her sound asleep in the bed and put a note on the tablet: "STAY HERE. I'LL BE BACK IN THE AFTERNOON. MAY KILL A BUCK MULE DEER. LOVE, BUCK."

He saddled Custer and, carrying the Winchester .44/40 over his lap, headed south. He wanted to be certain that the boys were set up and everything was going as planned, then meet Talbot and take him in to arrest those "rustlers."

He reached the Crib place and could see the strange roan horse in the lot with their horses, along with four steers that belonged to Crown.

"You're early," Daws said, from the doorway, as the sun came up over the snowy scene.

"I want this place cleaned out when you leave here. Nothing can point to you two, right?"

"Right, we'll do that. When's the guy supposed to get there?"

"Be ready by ten."

"Who's he?" Smith asked, coming outside half-asleep and combing his hair with his fingers. He got busy closing the silver coin buttons on his leather vest to shut out some of the cold. "Shit fire," he swore looking around on the ground. "Lost another damn button."

"We'll find it," Daws said.

"Never found the last one I lost," Smith grumbled.

"Be sure you have the whole set going and two steers tied and down. Drive them steers around in the pen after you get the horses out, to cover the tracks."

"We will. Never seen you ride a horse before," Daws said. "Good-looking one."

"He'll do. This needs to come off right today."

"It will," Smith said, going around the shack with a candle looking at the floor.

"You hungry, Boss?" Daws asked.

"Naw, I had some jerky and raisins."

"Good enough. We'll be ready."

Palmer made a last look at Smith and shook his head. "He might not be."

"I'll find it for him." Daws dismissed Palmer's concern.

"Don't mess up." He climbed on his horse and rode back the way he came. The way a posse would ride in.

Two hours later, he met Talbot and they circled west.

"You think they're rustling today?" Talbot asked.

"They rustle some every day."

"Damn, how did you find out about it?"

"I listen to them guys talking in the bar." He motioned for Talbot to ride more west. He didn't need to be there until ten-thirty.

"Where in hell are we going?" Talbot's big bay floundered for a moment in a drift and then found his way.

"This is the only way we can get up close on them doing it and not spook them off. They've got lookouts on all the roads."

"That's why I've never caught them at it."

Palmer turned in the saddle and nodded. "Exactly why."

He checked the sun, time to head that way. "Down this wash about a mile."

"I can smell some smoke," Talbot said.

"Wind's coming our way."

The sheriff opened his coat and from a shoulder holster

pulled out his silver-plated six-gun with a steer head carved in the ivory handles. He checked the cylinder and then nodded in approval and reholstered it.

Expensive hardware—damn gun must have cost a fortune. Palmer rode in close to him.

"No worry. I've got the repeater. You won't need a gun."

Talbot nodded. "Yeah, you're earning your two fifty, I forgot."

"Keep the shack between us and the corral, so they can't see us until it's too late. I can hear a steer bawling, so they must be branding."

"Gawdamn, I want them bastards," Talbot said, under his breath. "You sure are a good friend to get me here for this."

Palmer nodded. "Get your hands in the air."

"Huh?"

"One damn move and a bullet from this rifle goes through your heart." He rode up, jerked open the coat and took out the fancy Colt, then reined Custer back. "Now keep moving."

"What the hell's going on—you said—"

"Talbot, you've outlived your usefulness."

"I'll pull out—do anything." His voice took on a whining plead.

"Shut up."

"Ain't he the sheriff?" Smith asked when they rode around the shack.

"Yellowstone County's finest. Get down," Palmer told the lawman and motioned to his two speechless men. "Drill him if he tries anything."

He handed Smith the rifle and walked over to Talbot. He unbuttoned the coat and saw the hatred in the man's eyes. It amused him—that look on Talbot's face as he filched the envelope with the two fifty in it.

"Well, ain't you going to count it?" Talbot demanded.

"Naw, I don't figure you'd try to double-cross me. Let's go to the corral." He gave a head toss in that direction.

"What the hell for?" Talbot asked.

"So you can see what the rustling operation looked like you came to surprise."

"You bastard. These two work for you?"

"You're getting smarter. When that posse finds you, they're going to think that you surprised some real rustlers."

"Huh?" Talbot's eyes had the shocked look of a trapped animal.

Palmer shoved him inside the corral and held out his hand for Smith's revolver. "See, you caught them rustlers fixing those two steers brands. 'Get your hands up,' you ordered, but they went for their guns, like this—"

Talbot began gurgling. "Don't shoot me."

Palmer shot Talbot twice, low in the guts. The lawman's knees started to buckle and he fell forward. With his left hand, Palmer shoved him backward, then put two more bullets in his heart, and Talbot fell on his back. Palmer aimed the gun and put the last bullet in his forehead. He gave the blanched-faced Smith his smoking gun back.

Then he drew the fancy six-gun from his waistband and fired three shots across the corral. He handed the smoking revolver to Daws, butt first. "Put that in his right hand and close his fingers on it. I don't want him robbed of anything. This was a case where the law jumped some rustlers and they had a shoot-out. Talbot lost. Turn the roan horse loose now and shoo him towards home."

Smith, still looking dumbfounded and shocked, rubbed his palms on the lower part of his coat. "Cut the steers loose?"

"No. If you'd just shot a sheriff, what would you do?"

"Run like Billy Hell."

"Exactly. Better evidence is leave them tied then."

"Yeah," Daws said, then "Come on" to Smith. "We need to get our asses out of here."

"Oh, yeah, here's the bonus and a little more." Palmer handed the shocked Daws the envelope and went for his horse. "I've still got to find a mule deer." He stepped into the saddle. "Put Talbot's horse in the pen, too, so he can't leave and bring them back here."

"They'll find him though," Smith said with a frown.

"Hell, yes, but the later they find him the colder the trail will be."

"I hope they don't find him for week," Daws said and stepped into the saddle, ready to leave.

"I'll send word when I need you two. Lay low at my place."

"Yeah, boss. Come on, gawdamnit it," Daws swore at his partner.

Palmer short loped for the road. He still had a half day to get a mule deer. One problem down and out of the way, and an election in the fall to go, and he'd be set for a while. He spotted the deer on a hillside and slowed Custer to a walk. He'd need to get closer to ever shoot one of them. They moved away from him, so he pulled up his horse. There would be more.

An hour later, he jumped a fat buck up and took two snap shots. The second bullet dropped him and he rode over. Dismounted, he cut the jugular vein. Scarlet blood rushed out onto the white snow, and when most of the flow had quit, he threw the carcass over the saddle and mounted the nervous Custer. Talking softly to the dancing horse under him and the limp deer draped over his lap, he headed for the shack. Thoughts of him using Lucie's subtle flesh and naked young body drew a smile on his cracked lips. He went to whistling "Dixie."

TWENTY-NINE

COPELAN came through the front door of Larkin's store, accompanied by the tough jailer that Herschel had seen in the alley the night of the jailbreak. Both men looked on the prowl. Herschel felt the two were up to no good, and he shared a nod with Walt and the others around the stove.

"What can I do for you, Deputy?" Larkin asked.

"Anyone in here know anything about the sheriff's whereabouts?"

Herschel shook his head, and the others did the same. "Why?" he asked.

"Yesterday, he left to come down here to check on some reports of rustling."

"Who in the hell would want to rustle cattle in this weather?" Nels Hansen asked in disgust. "Besides who's got the hay left to feed them?"

"Listen, my boss hasn't been seen since yesterday. I'll ask the damn questions."

"Copelan, you can't come down here and run roughshod over folks," Herschel said. "None of us know a damn thing about him. You'd been civilized, some of us might have offered to ride and help you find him if he's lost. But you have kinda burned that bridge."

"Listen, cowboy, you ain't getting elected sheriff, so stop acting like you are."

"Long time till next November." Herschel poured himself a cup of coffee from the pot on the stove. "Good luck, searching." He sat down and ignored the two like they weren't even there. The others followed suit.

"I'll have all of you rustlers in jail by the time the grass greens if one hair on Talbot's head is disturbed!" Copelan said.

"Sounds bad enough," Tam Rielly said, then he spat tobacco in the ash pan and grinned big, behind the hand he used to wipe his mouth. "Wonder if he has a compass."

"Lost, he'd sure need one out here," MacDuffy said.

"Come on, these worthless bastards ain't going to help us." Copelan and his big buffalo of a deputy headed for the front door.

"He's got a half dozen riders with him," Larkin reported, watching them leave from the front window.

"Must suspect something's gone wrong." Herschel said his thoughts out loud. "Why have a posse looking for a man on a mission like catching rustlers? He's only been gone one day according to Copelan."

"Damned if I know," MacDuffy said and they shared rueful looks around the stove.

"We need a shivaree," Rielly said, when Herschel stood up and stretched.

"Aw, you don't have to," Herschel said, knowing full well they planned some wild deal to pull on him over his marriage.

"Oh, yeah, you can just fret and worry about us coming," Hansen teased. "Better have plenty of cigars and candy to pass out."

"My, my, I'll let you all alone to plot the deal. I need to go check on my stock. That poor boy Toby is no doubt tired of being the only one works up there."

"Hey, did I tell you all? My gray mare came home late yesterday."

"Any marks on her?" Herschel asked, recalling Mac-Duffy saying he thought someone stole her.

"No, she came from the north though."

"Maybe she got away from the ones that stole her."

"No saddle marks on her and she had no halter on her."

Herschel nodded. "Strange deal. I've got to run, boys. Any of you find the sheriff, draw him a map back to Billings."

They laughed. He thanked Larkin, took the small items that Marsha wanted and headed for the outdoors. The fresh wind swept his face as he placed the sundries in his saddlebags. He couldn't get the posse business off his mind. In the saddle he set out in a long trot for his place. Something wrong about Copelan and his deal—but what could he do to learn more? Damn.

THIRTY

PALMER met the posse at his new place, the former Diehl's ranch, that evening. He'd told Copelan, his man Starr would put them up and feed them at the Diehl house if they had to spend the night. When he rode off the ridge and saw all the strange horses in the corral, he knew the bunch was there. Obviously they'd not found Talbot's body. All this wind and shifting dry snow would obliterate lots of sign. He could hope the wolves didn't eat too much of the body. They'd probably eat the live steers left tied up for them.

Buttoning up his coat, Copelan came from the house to meet him.

"No sign?" Palmer asked.

"No and that really bothers me," Copelan said. "Had a run-in with that damn Baker over at Larkin's store."

His cinches undone, Palmer removed the saddle. "About what?"

"Aw, him mouthing off like he was the damn sheriff already."

"What did he say?" He put his saddle and pads on the rack.

"Aw, how if we came and kissed his ass he'd helped us look."

"Guess he's in charge up here." Palmer motioned toward the house.

"Yeah. I guess. What the hell do you reckon Talbot got into down here?"

"Damned if I know. But he ain't showed up in town. I checked before I left, and the ferry man ain't seen him since he went south the day before."

"Reckon he rode out of the country?"

"Naw, not Talbot. He ain't never had nothing this good in his whole life." Palmer stopped on the porch and considered the fiery sunset. Maybe they better "find him" in the morning. "We'll find him."

"I sure hope so. I'm beginning to think something bad's happened to him."

"Aw, he may be tracking them rustlers."

"Not like him. He weren't never no cowboy. He ran a damn store in Nebraska."

"What's for supper?"

"Beans and corn bread."

"Oh, good, we can all bunk in the house till it explodes." Palmer laughed. Laughed freer than he could recall in months. A good plan was working; it could only get better.

Dawn peeked across the white blanket at the ranch house and pens. With their mouths issuing clouds of vapor, the grumbling posse members saddled up and rode out. They made a wide circle south and were drawn up on a ridge to rest their hard-breathing horses.

"Who's that coming?" Copelan asked, squinting his

eyes against the glare. He tossed his red scarf over his shoulder. "You all wait here. I'll go see what he wants."

"I'll go, too," Palmer said.

A youth of maybe fourteen rode a big horse up and reined him short. "Sheriff? Paw sent me. They've found his body."

"Whose?" Copelan batted his eyes and shook his head in disbelief.

"The other sheriff. He's dead."

"Who found him, son?" Palmer asked.

"My paw and me. We was backtracking a gray mare that was stolen."

"You telling me that Talbot's dead over a stolen horse?" Copelan acted distressed by the news.

"No," Palmer said. "They were backtacking one."

"That's right. She came home yesterday. Been gone several days and they'd took her out of our corral."

"And Talbot's dead?" Copelan asked, like he couldn't believe the words.

"Been shot to pieces."

"He shoot anyone else?"

"If he did, they ain't there."

Copelan turned in the saddle and waved the posse down the hill. "They've found Talbot and he's dead. Ike, you go get a buckboard. Where's he at?" he asked the boy.

"You know the Crib cabin up on Lacy Creek?"

The man called Ike nodded. "I can borrow one at Larkin's, I think."

"Borrow it. Rent it. My gawd, what'll I tell folks?" Copelan dropped his gaze as if overwhelmed.

"We better get up there before the clues are all gone," Palmer said, hating that the rustlers had found Talbot first. Backtracking a damn horse—something he had not planned on either. But it could still work his way—somehow—he needed to take charge of this deal. Copelan had turned awfully soft with the news of his boss's death. Bad as them two Texans had been the day before when he gunned the sheriff down—he thought they'd upchuck over the deal.

"I'm on my way," Ike said, and rode off in a hard lope for the store.

"Let's go," Copelan said, and waved for the others to follow him.

The hard ride required almost an hour. But Palmer could see the crowd at the old cabin. Must be every jack somebody on Horse Creek had beat them to the scene. Damn, this could turn out tough.

"Where's he at?" Copelan demanded.

"Over under the blanket in the pen where they found him," Herschel said.

"What's been disturbed here?" Copelan asked.

"Not one thing. They found him lying on his back, six-gun in his hand. He'd been shot five times."

"Five times?"

"All we could see. Twice in the lower gut. Two in his chest and one 'n his forehead."

"They damn sure wanted to be sure he was dead," Palmer said, making a face that he was impressed and nodding to Baker.

"What's them steers doing here?" Copelan asked, looking at the two dead ones.

"Had to shoot them. They'd been left tied up for a long while."

"Guess you figure that you're the new sheriff now since you filed for the job and Talbot's dead." Copelan glared at him.

"I don't figure nothing. The man was shot here and we'd all like to know who did it." Herschel tossed his hand toward the ranchers on the outside of the corral.

"Damn convenient he was shot up here, wasn't it?"

"Copelan, you've got a mouth problem. None of us shot him."

"You're a prime suspect."

"This ain't a game. We ain't drawing sides and having no fights," Baker said, and pointed to the shed. "Two men stayed over at that shed for some time. They wore run-over boots. You can go look at the tracks."

"What else did you find?" Copelan asked.

"Whoever shot him reloaded his own gun at a hundred yards west of here."

"How do you know that?"

"Five casings I found alongside his tracks." Herschel poured them into the man's hand.

Copelan shook his head, waved his posse members back to the gate and went to Talbot. He knelt and lifted the edge of the blanket. A pained expression swept his face at the sight of the corpse, and then he stumbled over to the corral fence for support to puke.

Palmer dropped to his haunches, held the sheet up and studied the body. "He has his silver gun in his hand all right. They must have been fast shooters." Palmer reached down and picked up the fancy revolver. He cocked it and spun the cylinder on his coat sleeve. "Three shots gone. Copelan, he may have wounded one of them."

The deputy shook his head and wiped his wet eyes. "I never figured on him being dead. Not like that."

"They never took his wallet. Money's still in it," Palmer announced. "He must have caught them red-handed changing brands on those two dead steers."

Copelan sighed. "He must have. Anyone know anything about this?"

Nothing but the wind.

"You bastards ain't getting by with killing an officer of the law. I'll find you whoever you are and I'll see you hang."

"If you're accusing any of us, better spit it out. We sent word for you. We could have let the damned wolves ate him."

The ranchers nodded and looked slant-eyed at the head deputy.

"Copelan, we did it right. You never went and looked at them tracks he told you to look at," Hansen said from the top corral rail. "Maybe you don't want to find the killer?"

"I won't stop until I do." He shook his fist at Hansen.

"Better save that anger for the killers," Ferguson said and gathered the other ranchers to leave. "Let's go, boys. They don't want to know the truth."

Buck Palmer stood with his back to the fence. Disappointed at the outcome. Not how he wanted this plan to work. Still, at least Talbot was out of the way, and the finger of accusation could still be pointed at the small outfits, Baker included.

Herschel Baker swung into the saddle and curbed Cob's dancing. In his coat pocket was another hammered coin button. It matched the one he'd found at the shed after they gave him the beating. He had no interest in the world in disclosing that piece of evidence to Copelan. More of his own case. But the men who beat him were also prime suspects in the murder of Yellowstone County's sheriff—who in the hell ever they were.

What was Buck Palmer doing up there? Strange, but he'd never known about him riding with posses before. Maybe Palmer had his eye on getting the badge, too. Especially since Talbot was dead. Too many questions to ask and not any answers.

THIRTY-ONE

THAT evening Herschel explained the whole situation to Marsha after the girls were in bed. At the fireside, she was on the small rocker making him a new shirt, and he sat opposite her in a straight-back chair, idly tossing wood shavings into the roaring blaze.

"That could have been a showdown with all those ranchers there and Copelan's posse."

"Everyone ain't a hothead like him." He shook his head to dismiss the notion.

"I guess not. But sounds like you sure ruffled his feathers. He may want to run for sheriff himself."

"Free country." He whittled some more on the stick of firewood.

"You don't sound worried."

"I'm not—" He gazed into the crackling fire. "Somehow, Buck Palmer worries me more, and I don't know why."

"'Cause he took charge up there?"

"Maybe. He acted so familiar with the scene. Like he knew what happened about the steers and all."

"He's not any fool. He's rich enough to buy the Diehl place."

"I need to check on a few things more if it ain't howling cold tomorrow."

"You be careful." She came over, sat in his lap and combed the errant hair back from his forehead. "I'm getting awful spoiled having you around."

He laughed and swept her up in his arms. "Me, too."

Next morning there were no threatening cloud banks on the horizon. He finished feeding her stock early and saddled Cob in the weak sunshine shooting across the snow. He left the gelding chomping on a nose bag of oats and headed for the house for his own breakfast.

The girls were scurrying around to get ready to go to school. Marsha looked up from cooking on the range. "Morning, early bird. I liked to slept in. You feed all ready?"

He nodded, hanging his heavy coat on the peg.

"It's kinda nice you doing that," Kate said, looking up from setting the table. "I don't have alfalfa in my hair all day at school."

"We have lots to be grateful for," she reminded her girls.

"His harmonica," Kate said and grinned big.

"Yes, his music." She delivered the skillet of fried potatoes to the table. Then the ham and eggs on a platter, and the pan of brown biscuits. "Kate, please ask the grace."

They bowed their heads and all said amen at the end.

"What do folks eat in Texas for breakfast?" Nina asked.

"Sometimes fried mush and sometimes grits."

"What's that?"

"Cornmeal dishes," Marsha put in.

"Can we try it?"

"I guess if Herschel will show me how." She looked in his direction.

"Been so long, I may have forgotten, but I'll search my memory."

"What did you cook for breakfast?"

"Nina, eat and stop pestering him."

"Oh, lots of oatmeal."

"Every day?"

He chuckled. "Sometimes twice a day."

"It's a good thing you married mom."

"Nina!"

"She's fine." He laughed. "I am lucky to have her, and you three girls."

"Please now, let him eat. He has things to go see about today."

"If I don't get back by nightfall, I may have to den up somewhere. Just don't worry."

Marsha chewed on her lower lip. Obviously she wanted to say something, but held it because of the girls. "We'll be looking for you to get back."

"I'll be fine," he said, holding out his coffee cup for Kate to refill.

"Next Saturday is the end of the school session up here," Marsha said. "They can't get enough teachers, so we have to share Miss Pruitt. She'll do a four-month term somewhere else in the county after this week."

"Oh, a school program is coming, huh?" Herschel nodded his head.

"Yes."

"I'll be there."

The girls' faces brightened up.

After the meal, he rode north for Billings, checking on Toby and his own place near nine on the weak sun time.

"Going all right?"

"Fine. No one has claimed that horse that showed up here yet."

"I'll check on him in Billings." Herschel prepared to remount, satisfied that the boy was doing a good job.

"Who do you reckon killed the sheriff?"

Herschel looked across the glaring snow and shook his head. "Don't know. But it looked strange to me that Talbot, who never went anywhere without backup, tried to arrest some rustlers on his own."

"Paw said he wanted to get a big story in the newspaper to get reelected."

"Whatever he had in mind did not work. They executed him." Wait. He stopped short and considered the five empty cartridges that he'd found. One man shot Talbot five times at such close range it burned his clothing around the wounds. He wasn't shot by three or four men in a struggle. One man did the killing and close up.

Then the fancy gun was still in Talbot's hand. Been fired three times. Did Palmer check that pistol's cylinder close to learn that or did he already know there were three spent casings in it? He couldn't recall hearing the clicking of the Colt being examined by Palmer for how many shots were spent. Maybe he'd missed him doing that action. No, Palmer knelt down, took the pistol out of Talbot's hand, smelled the muzzle and nodded. *Three shots gone.*

He better keep that information and the two silver buttons to himself for the time being. There was more and more unfolding in the deal to make him wonder.

"Something wrong?" Toby asked.

Herschel shook his head. "Naw, everything's fine. I was just thinking about all I have to do yet today."

Before noon he was at the ferry. Isaac, the operator, was in a bad mood. Herschel stood holding Cob by the bridle as the man winched them for the north shore.

"This ferry's getting to be that Buck Palmer's private ship."

"Really?" Herschel asked absently.

"Yeah, he hauled that whore over there today and came back without her." The old man spat tobacco in the river. "Tomorrow he'll go back and fetch her."

"What's he do with her over there?"

"Danged if I know. Told me to mind my own damn business."

"How often does he do it?"

"Take that little sweetie over there?"

"Yes."

"Oh," the old man scratched his chin whiskers then went back to reeling, "about every week."

"How long is he gone?"

"Oh, maybe an hour. He's in a hurry, he'll be back in thirty minutes."

"Guess he's having fun with her?"

"Naw." Isaac shook his head and spat again. "He don't hardly ever smile. You know that look I'm talking about?"

Herschel nodded. No way Buck Palmer could ride out to his own place or the Diehl outfit in an hour and be back. Wherever Palmer was going was close.

"Thanks," Herschel said when they docked.

"Yeah, guess I shouldn't complain. Palmer pays me. That old cheap-ass sheriff said he was on county business the other day and he didn't have to pay. Well, I gladly gave him a ride back in that buckboard for free—old sumbitch."

"Palmer go over that day?"

"They wasn't together—naw, him and that whore must've went over the day before when the boy was on. He brought her back late that afternoon. Copelan went over."

"The same day that Talbot went south?"

"I'm pretty sure that's how it went. Don't you tell Palmer I said nothing. He might hurt me."

"He won't ever know from me."

Isaac bobbed his head, satisfied, and ambled off for his shack to warm up.

Herschel mounted Cob and rode for town. Palmer
wasn't in the Antelope when Talbot was shot. He was with
some doxie and south of the Yellowstone. But he came
back that afternoon and went back to Billings. Back to
town in time to join the Copelan posse. It didn't match up
too well—none of it. Throw in the stolen horse that went
home. Horses go home—convenient that it went from the
scene of the crime back to its own place. Herschel shook
his head and dismounted at the courthouse. All he could
figure was he was playing with half the cards in the deck;
the rest were still out there—somewhere.

Opal Johnson smiled at him when he entered the
clerk's office. "How's the only sheriff candidate doing
this morning?"

"I didn't intend for him to be out of the race."

"Oh, I know that. What do you need?"

"Are there maps with names of the owners on them?"

"Why, sure. Where you want to look?"

"If I get elected, I may need a small place closer to
town. Maybe someplace across the Yellowstone."

"Here's the map for that land south of the ferry." She
drew out a large map from a drawer and put it on the
counter.

"Good enough. I'll look and see if I know any folks that
own land down there that I might buy."

"Help yourself."

He found the spot where the ferry docked and traced
southward. "B. PALMER" was written on ten acres. The
area was a mile south of the ferry and another mile east of
the road. That would tuck it in a canyon and out of sight in
the cottonwoods. He looked at several other places to cover
his discovery. At last, he thanked Opal and left the office.

When he stepped into the hall, he spotted Copelan
standing in the door to the sheriff's office, glaring after
him. At the head of the stairs he thought he felt darts in his

back that the deputy had thrown at him. Secretly, he'd need to check out Palmer's south-of-town place and learn all he could about the dove and his activities down there, too.

The American flag flapped at half-mast, for Talbot he suspected, and he headed for the cafe. Maybe Buster knew something more. All he had were bits and pieces—nothing strong enough to accuse anyone, and with Copelan in the sheriff's office, there wasn't much he could do.

Why would someone on their side kill their own man? Because he'd outlived his usefulness to them and to point the finger at the small outfits? Maybe Talbot knew too much. No telling. He pushed inside the cafe.

"Hi," Maude said and smiled at him, busy waiting on some men seated at the counter.

"Buster here?"

"In back."

"Thanks."

He found the ex-cowboy straddling a pail, peeling potatoes.

"I've took up tater whittling," Buster said and grinned big up at him.

Herschel checked around to be sure they were alone, then dropped to his haunches. "You hear anything out of Daws and Smith?"

"Said they was feeding Palmer's cattle on that west place he's got."

"They stay out there all the time?"

Buster nodded, put aside the knife and wiped his hands on his soiled apron. "Funny you'd ask. Pete Cantrell met them two on the south road the other day. They was still pretty juiced up and bragging about being with some woman all night." Buster made a V with the paper and poured in the tobacco. "Only thing, they never came to town that day. Pete couldn't figure no woman lived south of Billings close there doing such a thing for them two."

Buster licked the cylinder shut. Then struck a match and put the twisted end in his lips. He coughed on the smoke and then nodded. "Who do you reckon's doing that for them two?"

"I'm not certain. But I've heard some other tales. Thanks, Buster. I'll be back to see you."

"How's the campaign going?"

"Fine, I guess."

Buster nodded and puffed on the cigarette. "Better since Talbot dropped out anyway."

Herschel shook his head at the man's dry humor and went out front to catch some lunch. He had two new cards in the deck. Buck Palmer owned ten acres south of town and those two hard cases could be using the place for their entertainment—complete with some dove that Palmer was delivering to them. Why? Palmer might be afraid they'd talk, so he provided for their hell-raising in a secluded cabin. Most folks didn't treat their hay hands that good. No, the stakes those boys were playing for were much higher.

He ate a bowl of chili and crackers, then went by to see Paschal at the livery.

"Hey," he said, starting to get up. "Just the man I needed to see. Do you want to sell them Belgian mares of yours?"

"They'd be high priced."

"High ain't the issue. Man was in here today. He needs a well-broke pair."

"Five hundred."

"Pay me fifty for making the deal?"

"Sure. He must need them badly."

"He does. When can we get them?"

Herschel took off his cap and scratched his head. He'd have to switch and Toby use the younger horses to feed with. They weren't wild, but sure not as dependable as the big mares, or as stout. The four fifty would sure come in handy. Maybe he could buy Marsha a gold ring. "I'll have them up here in three days, unless we hit a blizzard."

"I understand blizzards."

Herschel looked around to be certain they were alone. "You know anything about a cabin or shack that Buck Palmer owns south of the river?"

"Come to think of it, there's an old trapper's shack down there. East of the road in a canyon. The guy originally built it was a real carpenter. But there isn't any land to farm or garden around it."

"Ten acres shows on the country map."

"What's Buck need that for?"

"He's got a pair of hard cases—" Herschel made a quick search then continued. "They're out at his west ranch. They come up to this shack and party with some doxie he brings out to them."

"I know them. Let's see, one is Smith and the shorter guy is—"

"Daws."

"Yeah. Why do that?"

"Maybe to keep them from blabbing their mouths off."

Paschal nodded. "That could be so. You think they're behind some of this stuff like beating you up and shooting Talbot?"

With a deep, hard look at the cluttered desk, Herschel nodded. "But proving it may be hard as hell."

"How did you learn all that?"

"A bird told me coming up here."

"Someone's coming, I heard the outside door open," Paschal warned and went to the office door and opened it.

A black man appeared, with gray on his temples and a top hat. "You must be Mr. Baker."

"I'm Herschel Baker."

"I's Mr. MacDavis's driver, Washington. He would sure like to talk to you some, sir."

"Where's he at?" He shared a private look with Paschal, wondering what was happening.

"Well, sir, he's in his suite at the Palace Hotel."

"When does he want to talk?"

"Right now, sir, if'n you's got the time."

"Tell Mr. MacDavis I'll be over there in thirty minutes." Washington tipped his hat to him and thanked him.

When Herschel was certain that MacDavis's man was gone, he turned back to Paschal.

"What in the hell does the big man want?"

Paschal shook his head. "Damned if I know."

"How did he know I was even in town?" Herschel felt disturbed by the notion.

"Who knows?" Paschal went to the stove and picked up the small coffeepot. "Made this this morning. It's close to tar. You want some?"

"No, thanks. I better go see what the big man wants."

Paschal filled his stained mug and set the pot back. "Ole Rupart can be pushy."

"That a nice word for bossy?"

"Way I get it, he runs things for the big outfits. They do as he says or else."

"That's good to know. Thanks." He left the stable office after reminding Paschal he'd have the team up there in three days. Dry snow frozen out of the cold air floated about like small chicken feathers, and he could see the three-story Palace down the street. Maybe he'd have more cards in his deck when he finished with MacDavis—he'd have to be on his toes. This man for his part was more dangerous than a Texas sidewinder.

THIRTY-TWO

Washington answered the door and Herschel could see the opulence of the place the minute he swung the door back. A teardrop crystal chandelier overhead, mahogany tables with Chinese painted mats draped over them. A green statue of a great muscled horse rearing atop an embroidered lace cover on the chiffarobe.

Seated in an oversize wood-and-leather chair with a scotch robe over his lap was a man with fluffy sideburns who must have weighed three hundred pounds.

"Mr. Baker." MacDavis nodded at the other like chair. "Excuse me for not getting up, sir. This cold weather really bothers my arthritis."

Baker handed his cap, scarf and coat to Washington. "That's all right."

"Have a chair there."

"Fine." Herschel noted that MacDavis made no offer to shake his hand. Which was fine with him. "What did you have on your mind?"

"Oh, you may well know the railroad is coming to Billings."

"I hear rumors off and on that one's coming."

MacDavis agreed. "But it will come to south central Montana. Next year or the next. Economics and Wall Street are the determinants about that. But you know railroads have avoided places with bad reputations before."

"You are saying they might not come through here if they think it's a hell hole."

"Mr. Baker—"

"Herschel's fine."

"Herschel, railroads build tracks to bring new settlers to the area—transporting them in here, bringing the implements, seed and material they need, then they haul the farm produce away. The town with the railroad is the one that grows."

Herschel flexed his shoulders, feeling stiff from the ride up there. "I'm still listening."

"Yellowstone County and Billings can't afford for the railroad to go around us."

"And?"

"There have been some serious incidents lately that have made national newspapers across the country according to my contacts in the East. These items unfortunately disturb the business community in Billings."

"Disturbs me, too, that they've happened."

"Would you like some whiskey or something else to drink?"

Herschel shook his head. "I'm still listening."

"This murder of the sheriff Sam Talbot comes on the wings of the rest. It will be splashed over the country's front pages." MacDavis rubbed his hands over the top of the plaid robe, and his clear blue eyes bored a hole in Herschel.

"You must have a solution for all this."

MacDavis nodded his head and his jowls shook. "I do.

It may be a sacrifice to you, but it is the best plan for this town and the county."

"What's that?"

"You step down and support our candidate for sheriff for the mutual good of all concerned."

"I haven't heard who that is."

MacDavis made deep exhale. "We haven't told the public. But he's a businessman that can unite us all."

"You don't think I can unite this county?"

"Don't get your back up. Politics is give-and-take, son. We need a man to straddle the middle. You—you definitely represent the small outfits. But wait, you haven't heard my entire offer—" MacDavis held his hands up to settle Herschel, who was on the front edge of the chair, his eyes drawn into slits. "We would give you a voice in the selection of deputies."

Herschel scooted back. "Maybe a good cleanup of this place would delight that railroad you talk about."

"We can do that in time. First we need Talbot buried and the whole thing quieted down."

Herschel laughed out loud. "Sam Talbot was executed out there. Cold-blood executed. There was no shoot-out with rustlers in that corral. The killers lured him down there and shot him at point-blank range. The rest was a setup."

MacDavis cut a startled hard look at him. "You're saying—"

"Talbot was executed. It was made to look like some small ranchers were rustling steers. Any dummy knows hay's so short we'll be lucky to get our own stock to spring. Why steal some skinny steers—and have more bawling mouths to feed?"

"You have proof of this?"

Herschel looked him straight in the eye, used his tongue to loosen a shred of chili in his teeth, and nodded his head.

"They even stole a saddle horse and turned it loose after the killing so the tracks would lead to a family's place."

"I guess you've been to the judge with all this evidence?"

"I will be."

MacDavis folded his arms over his chest like a man taking a new route. "You owe some money at the bank."

"You going to tell them to call my note?"

"I have lots of power in this town."

"Call it and I'll tell everyone why."

"You know you can't win, why don't you be sensible?"

"I can win if you don't stuff the ballot boxes."

"Washington, bring me a scotch and water. My guest want anything?"

Herschel shook his head.

"You're a babe in the woods when it comes to elections," MacDavis said and shook his head.

"You know that messing with the election process is a felony?"

"Of course, I know the laws of this territory." He scowled at Herschel.

"Then be damn sure you don't break them. Or any of your associates either."

MacDavis slammed his palm on the table. "I'll make you one more offer—two thousand dollars cash and you get out of the sheriff's race."

"Six weeks ago, someone shot my best friend, John Diehl, in the back. Before I left his funeral, I promised myself I'd find those killers. Money, threats don't scare me, Rupart MacDavis. Your puppet Talbot wouldn't do a damn thing. Yellowstone County is going to have a new sheriff, and the ones that have been running roughshod over the decent citizens, they'd better saddle up and ride out of here. Their days are numbered."

With a hate-filled scowl, MacDavis shoved his finger at

him like a gun. "You'll rue this day, Herschel Baker. I invited you here for a gentleman's conversation."

Herschel was on his feet. "No, you invited me here to buy me off. I ain't for sale. Get my cap and coat, Washington, before I lose all my temper."

"You're a fool. A gawdamn stupid fool, Baker!"

"Go to hell, you fat sumbitch. We'll see come Election Day who wins this one." His cap on, he pulled down his sleeves as Washington held his coat for him to put his arms in.

"You certainly won't." MacDavis threw back the robe and sprung to his feet.

No signs of arthritis in that move, Herschel decided. "One more thing, you send around your two thugs again to get on me and I'll plant them too."

Still in a huff a block away from the Palace Hotel, Herschel was breathing great clouds of vapor. *Damn you, MacDavis.*

THIRTY-THREE

Buck Palmer went to the back door of the Antelope. Earl said Washington was out there and needed to tell him something. MacDavis never sent his man to deliver any verbal messages. Things must really be bad or he was upset. Damn.

"He wants to see you at the hotel," Washington said, standing back from the door with his top hat in hand.

Palmer looked around to be certain no one else was out there in the alley. "When?"

"Now. Come in de back way."

"What's wrong?"

"He spoke to that Baker about an hour ago. Got real mad."

"What did Baker tell him?"

Washington moved close and leaned toward Palmer. "I hear Baker say they executed Talbot."

Palmer frowned at him. "What did he say?"

"He say Talbot was executed." Washington shrugged. "Then they went to shouting at each other."

"Oh, shit fire, that damn Baker—"

"You better come fast. The boss man, he ain't in no good mood."

"Yeah," Palmer said, wondering what he should do next. Maybe getting close to shuck-and-run time for him. "Tell him I'll be right over."

"Yes, sah, I's tell him you be there."

What did Baker mean saying Talbot had been executed? He couldn't prove a damn thing. Speculation was all that was about. If MacDavis fell for his bullshit— Palmer would have to straighten that man out.

An hour later he slipped up the back stairs into the Palace and knocked softly on the apartment's service door.

"Come on in," Washington said, taking Palmer's hat and coat. He frowned at him, then said in a low voice, "He's still angry."

"Oh, Buck, you made it, did you?" MacDavis stood in the doorway to the living room dressed in a velvet robe.

"What's wrong?"

"Wrong? That son-of-a-bitch Baker was here an hour ago. He's got some kind of evidence that Talbot was executed."

Buck shook his head. "He has nothing. He was only testing you."

MacDavis shook his head. "No, the man said Talbot was shot at close range by his executioner. Not by multiple shots either. And the killer stole a horse to make it look like some rustler had done it."

"Talbot discovered a rustling operation and they shot him."

MacDavis buried his face in his arm on the door facing. "Damnit, Buck Palmer, I know when a man has the goods. Herschel Baker has the goods on the killers. I think he knows those two men of yours beat him up, too."

"Never. They wore masks. He's trying that crap on you for your reaction."

"Well, I tried everything—made no sense with him at all. He wouldn't even quit for a goodly sum of money."

"So we need to convince him."

"You did a piss-poor job of it last time. Talbot's wild murder case against him has been dropped—the prosecutor's already dismissed it."

"I can convince him or else."

"What in the hell did you have to kill Talbot for anyway?"

"You said you wanted for him to step down. Well, he wasn't about to step down. He wanted to be the state's first governor when we made statehood."

"Gods—the nerve of some people. He couldn't find his own ass, how could he expect to do that?"

"Said he had enough on all of us—"

"You better search his office and I mean now. Palmer, we aren't playing this game."

"Playing?"

"Playing. If he had something, it might be uncovered. Can you get Copelan to help you?"

"Yeah, he's all right."

"Do that and then contrive a plan to get rid of Baker. The man's a lunatic." MacDavis shook his head warily.

"I'll handle it."

"You better or your head will roll." MacDavis gave him a cold look.

"I can handle it. Anything else?"

"I have two men on my payroll at the ranch that are tough as any come along. You need them you send me word."

"I will."

"When we meet again you better have the following done: Anything that Talbot had that points a finger at us is destroyed and Baker is no longer a threat to my plans for this county."

"I'll handle it."

"See that you do. I can find a new manager for the Antelope, you know?"

"Yes, sir."

Palmer left the big man's apartment and took the stairs to the alley two at a time. That son-of-a-bitch Talbot was liable to have something written down in his stuff. He'd been bluffing when he told MacDavis about how Talbot had threatened to blackmail them, but it would be just like him to have that written down somewhere—oh hell, what next?

Fifteen minutes later he was in the sheriff's office and found Copelan with his boots on the big desk.

"What's up?" Copelan said, flush-faced and taking his feet down hurriedly.

Palmer closed the door and held his finger to his mouth. "What did Talbot leave?"

"Leave?"

"Yeah, like a log or a diary."

"Hell, half a dozen of them. He wrote in one every day. Why?"

"Where're they at?"

"What're you getting at, Buck?"

"If the sumbitch left a record, I want to see it." He looked around to be certain they were alone. "It might save us some time in the pen."

"Pen? I ain't going to no pen."

"Then start searching. I want all of them."

"Some are out at his house, I know that."

"Go out there and get them."

"Now?"

"Of course now, you idiot." He scowled at Copelan.

"What in the hell are we doing this for?"

"To see if he wrote something bad down about us. Go out to his house and get anything you can find."

"What'll I do with it?"

"Hmm," Palmer snorted out his nose. He hadn't thought about where to go with it. "Put it in crates and take it out to my shack. I'll burn it out there."

He looked in the second drawer and found a logbook. "This one of them?"

"Yeah, he wrote in one of them all the time."

Palmer tossed it on the desk and used his teeth to remove his gloves, wondering what was on the pages. When he glanced up and saw the confused-looking Copelan still there, he exploded at him. "Damn you, get after that stuff!"

Copelan about fell over his own feet running out the door. Palmer glared for a long while after him, then settled in the chair. Talbot had written in a flowery hand, what Palmer expected out of a Nebraska storekeeper turned sheriff.

The entry was January, 3, 1882: "Last night Mayor Hugh Whitehall visited his mistress, Ramona Whitaker. Her husband was conveniently down at the billiard hall. This was the third time in less than two weeks that he's entered the Whitaker residence by the back door, after dark. From where I stood back from their sight, I could see Mrs. Whitaker only wore her underclothing. The mayor being a happily married man with a family, no doubt would not want the knowledge of his indiscretions with this dark-eyed Latin woman spread about town."

Indiscretions? What in the hell was that? Must mean they was making love or something like that. Palmer shook his head at the word. What did Talbot do with all this crap? Worse yet, how much more was there of it?

He might not want to burn all this. He leaned back in the chair and the springs protested. Thank God, he'd found it before someone else had. A man had all this, he could be powerful, too. Stupid Copelan probably couldn't read. Good, he'd saved the day from any competition from Copelan. Talbot should have stuck to being a storekeeper. He'd have lived lots longer. Palmer thumped his knuckle on the hard cover of the log. Talbot, you may have done me a big favor.

A careful search of the entire office and he only found the one log. It was getting dark outside when he finally left the courthouse. What was taking Copelan so long? He should have been back hours before that. Copelan might be pulling a double-cross on him. If that scrawny bastard was, he was dead meat.

Better hike up there to Talbot's house and see about him. Not married, the sheriff lived by himself in a log cabin north of town. When he was a block away, Palmer could see a light on in the window. He better control himself until he had the situation in hand.

When he opened the front door, Copelan bolted up from a chair with another log in his hand. His eyes were big as silver dollars. He looked to Palmer like a sheep-eating dog. "You know what's in these things?"

"Lots of gossip."

"No, no. You know that big rancher Quail—"

"Van Quail. What about him?"

"Says right here he ran off and left a wife and kids in Tennessee."

"That's why we're collecting all this," Palmer said through his teeth. He jerked the log out of Copelan's hands and backhanded Copelan so hard he spun around and fell against the log wall.

"Hell, Buck, you didn't need to do that." Shaken, Copelan rubbed his jaw and pushed himself up.

"Listen, if any word gets out about any of this stuff, we're liable to all swing on some cottonwood tree."

"Not me, Buck, I won't say nothing. You know me."

"How many more are here?" He looked around the room. His shadow was cast like a great bear on the wall.

"I found three. Some are from his days in Nebraska. You ever figure he was that much of a snoop?"

Palmer drew a deep breath up his nose and glared at the lamp. "I never figured he was anything, but a pompous ass."

"Yeah, he was kinda that. Always dressed like he was somebody better than the rest of us."

"He thought he'd be the first governor if and when Montana got statehood."

"Oh, I knew about that. He told me he was practicing making speeches to all them meetings and things."

"That's all there are?" Palmer glanced around the living room. Damn—if he hadn't thought about these diaries, he'd have been in duck soup.

"I think so."

"You come back up here in the morning and recheck the entire cabin."

"Sure, sure. Can't let them fall in the wrong hands."

"Right." He carried the logbooks and went outside in the night. He had lots of reading to do. Talbot must have documented all of it in them.

An hour later in his hotel room, he read the first entries. Not much happened. Then he saw his name . . . "Met saloon owner Buck Palmer today. A big man and tough. Runs the Antelope Saloon and I think must have other ties. Need to use this man for my own goals, he can open doors and for all I can learn, he controls the local vote. I'll need his approval to ever gain office here. With what all I know about Mayor Whitehall's womanizing, he will get me in with Palmer."

His eyes burning, Palmer set down the book on the nightstand and swore aloud. "Damn, it was Whitehall that mentioned Talbot as the man for sheriff."

THIRTY-FOUR

W HAT did MacDavis offer you?" Marsha swept the lock of hair off her face with the back of her hand while busy washing dishes.

"Well, after all his plans to get me out of the race that I told you about didn't work, he offered me twenty-five hundred to get out."

"Twenty-five hundred dollars?" Her blue eyes flew open and her mouth dropped in shock.

"I know I'm a damn fool for not taking it. It would have me out of debt and everything, but I couldn't—"

"No, no." She dried her hands on a towel and rushed over to hug him. "They want power that bad. I can't believe it."

He shifted her back and forth in his arms, his chin on the top of her head, enjoying the intimacy of holding her close. The smell of lilacs in his nose, he closed his eyes. Marsha and her daughters were the finest thing ever happened to him. The girls were at the Fergusons', playing over there. He'd arrived home mid-morning from Billings after stopping by to inform Toby about the sale of the mares.

"I sold Betty and Faye for four hundred and fifty dollars."

"Wow, that's lots of money. What else happened?"

He explained what he knew about Palmer's shack and speculated with her on its importance. After holding her for a few minutes, he wasn't ready to ride back to town and leave his new wife.

"Aw, I'll deliver those horses tomorrow and stay here with you today."

She turned her head sideways to look up at him, as if to be sure he wanted to do that. "That's lots of money."

"The deal's made. Now tell me what's been happening here."

She threw her head back and laughed. "Nothing as exciting as all that. We fed the stock hay. Did some wash. Tommy Blackhat brought me a wagonload of split firewood."

That afternoon he loaded the hay sled for the next day's feeding, and he was up before dawn to deliver the team. She cooked him breakfast while he saddled Cob.

"How cold is it?"

"Close to twenty."

"Maybe you won't freeze riding up there." She smiled and brought him coffee to go with his fried eggs, bacon and biscuits.

"Oh, I'll be fine. But I doubt I get it all done and back with you tonight."

"I understand."

"Good." He winked at her. Lord, he was lucky to have her.

An hour later at his place, he was putting halters on the Belgian mares. The grim reminder of the charred ribs of the cabin roof sticking out of the snow made him grimace. In the next year he'd need to consolidate both herds and have one base. Meanwhile, he needed to find the ones set the fire as well as beat him up. Somehow when he found them, he felt certain he'd have the executioners of Talbot. But to prove it, that would be the real test.

He stopped at Larkin's store and talked to the neighbors.

"We ain't seen as much of you since you got a wife," Rielly teased.

"She's fine," Herschel said.

"I imagine she is." Then they all laughed around the stove.

"Any word on who killed Talbot yet?" Walt asked.

Herschel shook his head. "Might be like Jack's, they don't want to know."

"Ain't been anyone down here since that posse came."

"If they're so well organized they can kill a sheriff and get by with it, how are you going to beat them?" Hansen asked.

"Honesty, and doing the right thing comes to the surface eventually like cream. They'll mess up and then we'll have them."

"What can we do to help?" Rielly asked.

"Tell everyone to vote for me." He smiled at the man.

"We'll do that, but you've got a big job ahead of you."

"I figured that out ten minutes after I told the clerk I was running for sheriff."

Everyone laughed and then wished him well. Past noon, he was in town, warming up at Lem Paschal's office stove.

"Those mares look great," Paschal said. "The buyer'll be pleased."

"He's paying for good horses." Herschel nodded to the offer of coffee.

"There's a guy helped your wife the night they arrested you. Wants to talk to you."

"What's his name?"

"Damned if I can recall it at the minute—Arthur Spencer, that's it. He's a freighter."

"Where's he live at?" He took the cup of steaming brew from Paschal.

"He usually sleeps here when he's in town."

"What do you reckon he knows or wants?"

"I think he wants to help you more than anything."

"I was going to ride back to the ranch this evening since I'd made such good time coming up here."

"Drop by the Antelope and see if he's not in there."

"I will, after I get some food."

"Be careful," Paschal said. "I'll have your money next time you're in town."

"Good. I better get to cutting."

Buster came out of the kitchen and joined him while he ate.

"It got damn quiet around here since Talbot got shot." Buster finished rolling a cigarette and struck a match. "Too quiet. I ain't learned a thing to tell you. 'Cept I heard that Rupart MacDavis was mad as hell at you."

"Who told you that?"

"Clerk over at the hotel. Said the old man was storming. Something about you not listening to him."

"He wanted me out of the race."

Buster's eyes twinkled with amusement. "He don't know you like I do. You set your mind to something, you're hell on wheels to ever change."

"Let him be mad. I've got to run. You know a Spencer that freights?"

Buster nodded. "I like him. He eats in here."

"Good. I need to go find him."

"Probably playing cards at the Antelope."

"I'll find him."

A short while later in the Antelope, he asked Earl which one was Arthur Spencer.

"The short guy over at the middle table."

"Thanks." He walked over and spoke to the man with wavy gray hair and mustache, who was sitting alone.

"Arthur Spencer?"

The man looked up, then smiled. "You must be the next sheriff."

"Anything to drink, gents?" the bar girl asked.

"Two beers," Spencer said and nodded for Herschel to take a seat.

"What can I do for you?"

Spencer looked around, then lowered his voice. "Maybe I can help you."

"Good. I need lots of it."

"Seems that the late sheriff was blackmailing several folks in town. You know anything about it?"

"No. But it could be the reason they wanted him executed."

"Could be—" Spencer stopped and thanked the girl when she delivered the beers. "Put it on my tab."

"I will, darling," she said and sashayed off.

"That's Lucille. She's another part in the puzzle."

"How's that?"

"Buck sends her out to entertain two Texans." Spencer winked at him. "She hates them. Bitches to me about them two every chance I spend a little time with her."

"She meets them at a shack across the river?"

Spencer looked around. "You know about it?"

"I heard a few days ago that there was something going on down there from time to time."

Spencer nodded and sipped his beer. Then he wiped his mustache with a kerchief and sat back.

"These two Texans feed Buck's cattle."

"Daws and Smith."

"That's them. They had a party with Miss Lucie two days before the sheriff was shot."

"Maybe those two need to be asked some questions." Herschel tasted the beer.

"You can't trust any law here. Copelan and that bunch are thick as thieves. But I know a U.S. deputy marshal at Miles City who might come over and help you."

"I could use someone of authority."

"Draw me a map to your place and I'll send him."

"What's his name?" He found a receipt in his coat pocket and drew a sketch with a pencil on the back. "This is Horse Creek." He pointed it out to the man.

"I bet he can find it. Charlie Otter is his name."

"Has anyone started blackmailing those folks that Talbot was working on?"

"No, but they're nervous that whoever killed him will."

"I'll need that blackmailer's name, too." Herschel set back in the chair.

Spencer nodded. "There's quite a conspiracy going on. Miss Lucie probably knows more than she's telling me when I'm in bed with her. But I kinda like her, so go easy on her."

"You've got a deal. All I need is a break."

"Charlie Otter is the man."

"How can I thank you?"

"Get elected sheriff and clean up this mess."

"You're dead serious, aren't you?"

"One night, Talbot for no good reason used his pistol to beat a boy that worked for me. He ain't been right since. Out of his head, lives with his folks over in South Dakota."

"Reason enough."

"How's the lovely bride?" Spencer asked with a grin.

"Fine. Thanks for your help that night. And watch yourself, you've joined my crew, I guess, and that can be dangerous."

"I will, and good luck."

"Give Otter a week or so to get here?" Herschel asked then, finishing his beer.

"Two weeks, more than likely." Spencer waved away his offer to pay. "Tell the missus I love her." Then a big smile broke out. "I'd give anything to find a woman with that much spunk."

"I'm lucky."

Long past sundown, he reached the ranch house and Kate opened the door for him. "We thought you weren't coming back tonight."

"I got lonesome for you girls," he said and hugged her shoulders, then he hugged the other two and smiled at Marsha.

"I met a man that's sure soft on you today."

"Who's that?"

"Arthur Spencer."

"Oh, he helped me that night."

"You sure impressed him," Herschel said, taking off his coat and wraps.

"I didn't mean to flirt with him."

He hugged her. "You didn't. He just admired your spunk, he said."

"Good. What else?" She looked up at him.

"He's sending a U.S. deputy marshal from Miles City down here to help me."

"To do what?"

"Solve the execution of Talbot for one."

She swallowed. "Oh, you've made the big outfits mad. Now taking over the law enforcement—I sure hope you know what you're doing."

"Best I can do." He pulled her close and put his cheek on top of her head. "The best I can do."

THIRTY-FIVE

B<small>UCK</small> Palmer nodded when Earl told him Baker was in and spoke to Spencer earlier.

He grimaced at the news. "What was that all about?"

"Damned if I know. Baker wasn't in here long."

"Spencer helped Baker's wife the night they bailed him out." Palmer shook his head, wondering what else could go wrong.

"You know why, too," Earl said. "Spencer hated Talbot over beating that kid senseless who worked for him."

"Maybe that's all." Palmer looked across the smoke-filled room; he could see the familiar gray head of the teamster in a card game.

Earl shrugged and went off to wait on more customers.

Crap! Palmer gave an exhale. Everyone in the damn place was a potential threat to him. *Executed* was what MacDavis called it. That was Baker's word. The best planned killing in his whole life and somehow it turned against him. No, they couldn't prove nothing.

Who could testify against him? Lucie, maybe she needed to be eliminated. No one missed a whore. All she could say was he went deer hunting that day and got one. Unless those two Texans bragged to her about their part. Damn, she might be the one to talk if they pushed her.

Then he smiled. Who was going to push her? Not Copelan, or any of his thugs in the sheriff's office. Maybe if they got her apart—damn, he was becoming obsessed with all this business about who was doing what. Baker was a dumb Texas drover. He had no authority to do one damn thing.

Vigilantes were what Palmer worried about the most. Montana was the worst place for them to spring up. No word they were even forming, but they could overnight.

"I need to talk to you," Palmer said to Lucille when she came by for drinks. "In the back room as soon as you deliver them drinks."

She frowned and then nodded she would be there.

Palmer sauntered back there. When she stuck her head inside the door, he motioned for her to come in.

"Shut the door."

Her back to the closed door, her eyes looked full of fear. "What's wrong?"

"What's this Spencer up to?"

She blinked her eyes and shook her head. "He freights. Why? Brings in supplies."

"No, I mean with this Baker running for sheriff."

"They talked today is all I know."

He reached out and grasped her by the arm.

"You're hurting me. Honest, they just talked."

"Gawdamnit, you find out what they talked about."

"You're hurting my arm." Tears began to spill off her face.

"Listen, bitch, I'll hurt you more than that if you don't find out what the hell they talked about today."

"Okay. Okay. I'll find out."

"One more thing. You ever talk about that shack, them Texans or me, and I'll cut your damn throat. Hear me?"

Her hand flew protectively to her throat and her eyes widened. "Buck, I do all you ask me to do." She sniffed.

"Well, you better do this, too."

She nodded, numb-like, and fled.

He dropped into a chair and rubbed his mouth and the beard stubble around it. Maybe he'd overstayed his time in this damn cold ice box. He had a few thousand salted back, skimmed off the Antelope's take. California or Washington might be the new ground he needed. Maybe sail around the world. What should he do? Wait, they had nothing on him so far, and if he kept after them, like Lucy, he could cut it off at the bud.

Then there was all that stuff in Talbot's logs. He must have been blackmailing a half dozen people in town. The sumbitch was really down and dirty about the business. No wonder he got so much approval around town—they all feared him. How could Palmer use that to fill up his own treasury?

Maybe if he had Baker out of the way. Maybe he needed to be executed, too. It was an idea. All Palmer needed was the plans. Those two Texas guns about puked over Talbot's killing. They'd be no good unless they back-shot Baker. Pay them five hundred and have them shag off for Texas after they did the job. No, he didn't trust them. Damn, this was getting to be a bitch. He'd do it himself.

Ten o'clock the next morning, Palmer arrived at the Antelope and walked through the bar room, where three grizzly swampers were cleaning up. Earl motioned to him from behind the bar, where he was polishing glasses.

"One of your whores ran off last night."

"Which one?"

"Lucille."

"Where did she go?" He felt like he'd been kicked below the belt. Why her?

Earl shrugged. "I can't find out."

Palmer nodded and rebuttoned his heavy coat. "I've got a notion. I'll be back."

Minutes later, he was in Lem Paschal's office. "Spencer pull out this morning?"

"Yeah, before daylight. You need anything?"

"Naw, I was looking for some guys to play poker tonight."

"Guess you'll have to catch him in Miles City."

Palmer shook his head to dismiss it and left. That damn little bitch. He ought to go ride them down and bring her ass back. She was out of the country. How could she harm him? No way.

He strode the boardwalk back to the Antelope.

"Find out where she went?" Earl asked when he came by the bar.

"Yeah. Miles City with Spencer."

Earl set down a polished glass. "Don't doubt that he was sweet on her."

"Stealing my help . . ." Palmer went off to his office. Her running off niggled him but not enough to go kill her as well as Spencer and a couple of his teamsters. Who'd believe what a whore said anyway?

THIRTY-SIX

H ERSCHEL took a day and scouted the empty shack. No smoke coming out the stovepipe when he surveyed it from a distance. He advanced slow-like and dismounted with caution. Cob hitched at the rack, he looked around, being as wary as he could be. A big wood supply was piled up by the door. The latch was unlocked and he stepped inside. Aside from a row of glass bottles for a window, letting a band of light in the room, it was dark. He struck a match and lighted a candle.

Looked like a typical bachelor's cabin—couple of beds, a table, three chairs, a handful of supplies like flour and baking powder that the cold wouldn't spoil. Some page-worn *Police Gazette*s were about the place. A holey sweater hung on the peg by the door. Not much else. He finally blew out the candle—nothing in this place to help him unless the walls could talk—and went outside. A fresh deer hide was tacked on the back wall. Evidence that it had been butchered remained, and in the shed he found most of the frozen carcass hanging up off the floor. Only the loin on one side had been cut out.

Nothing else, he went out front, mounted Cob and rode home disappointed there wasn't a crumb of evidence in the place. Maybe he'd expected too much. The time would pass slowly waiting for this marshal to come and help him. A quick stop at the store for candy and he checked with Toby at his home, about the stock.

"Fine, except you were right, I really miss them big mares to hay with."

"Well, we need to find another young team to break."

After sundown, he was back at Marsha's and the girls were excited. Had he remembered candy?

"A little," he said and produced a sack he handed to Kate.

"Don't eat it all at once," their mother directed. "Save some for later."

He simply laughed and hugged her shoulders. "That ain't any fun."

"You learn anything today?"

"No, nothing. Just a cabin. Log walls don't talk."

"Supper's ready. You better get washed up. It'll be cold."

"I may ride west tomorrow and check on them two," he said privately.

"Take Walt along."

"Oh, he's got work to do."

She nodded, but did not look satisfied at him. "Wash and eat. We can talk later."

"Yes, ma'am."

After loading her hay sled in the morning, he rode over to check on his own place and helped Toby load and feed. It gave him a chance to see the cattle and horses' condition. They looked good for all the bad weather, and many of his cows were showing the first signs of springing. Six weeks and he sure hoped the weather let up. No house and all, it would be rough to batch over there for calving time.

"How's the sheriff election going?" the youth asked when they finished.

"I'm not sure. I don't have an opponent they've named yet."

"That's good. Sure are lots of starving cattle out on the open range."

Herschel agreed. They were stacked up at the Yellowstone's banks in black piles, with many bloated corpses floating by. "Won't be hard to count the live ones come spring."

"What'll folks do that lose that many?"

"Some will go out of business."

"It's going to be rough."

Herschel agreed. He wished his man would arrive.

THIRTY-SEVEN

Buck Palmer changed his mind and left Billings under the cover of night. Mounted on Custer, he aimed to make lots of miles. He wanted to be in Miles City when Spencer arrived with that slut Lucille. The sooner she was eliminated, the less worries he would have about her spilling anything—no matter what she'd told Spencer. He could be eliminated, too. But he'd thought enough about it—she was the only one that could link him to the murder on that day, save those two Texans, and they'd outlived their usefulness, too. Except he needed them for one more plan—the execution of Herschel Baker.

He stopped at an empty line shack mid-morning the next day. Found some split wood under the snow to stoke a fire with and ate some jerky from his pocket. While the stove heated the dugout log cabin, he fed Custer some oats in a tin pan in the shed. Out of the wind, the horse could rest, too, and Palmer would sleep a couple of hours in the

shack. His breath came in clouds of vapor as he headed
back for the cabin and studied the far sky. Another damn
storm bank was coming out of the northwest. He better
sleep quick—damn the luck.

By sundown, the dry snow was beginning to fall. He
saddled Custer after watering him with some snow thawed
in a pail. He was on the Miles City Road before the sun set.
A couple hours on his way, he discovered sight of a fire
and then the ghostly outline of some freight wagons. He
reined up Custer and led him off the road. There he hob-
bled him, hoping all the time that he'd found Spencer's
wagons.

He came on a bent-over run until he was at last behind
one of the rigs. Then slow like a cat he moved along the
back side of them, the fire casting long shadows of the rigs
beyond him.

"Going to be a bad storm." That was Grimes's, the old
man's, voice.

"Aw, it's just another snow," Lucie said.

A smile crossed Palmer's face—*she's right here*. She'd
have to go off and relieve herself sooner or later. All he had
to do was wait. Then conk her over the head and take her
on his shoulders. Once he was far enough away—he could
shut her up forever.

Time passed. Men sat around the fire and talked about
the snow and the road and the animals. Palmer was about
to give up when at last he saw her coming his way. He
moved slow-like to be right where she exited between
the wagons.

His six-gun drawn, when she came past him, he
smacked her over the head and she went facedown in the
snow. He stuck the revolver in his holster and quickly
shouldered her small body. Then he ran across the road and
started for his horse in the coulee. All her clothes made her
heavy, so he was soon breathing real hard.

"Oh," she moaned.

"Shut up or I'll cut your throat."

"Buck?" she whined.

"Damn right, and you scream you're dead."

"What are you doing with me?"

He set her down and jerked her after him by the arm. "I paid your gawdamn passage out here. You ain't running out on me."

"But you held that out of my money."

"Not the interest. Now, shut up."

"But, Buck, he loves me, he has money, he'll marry me."

"You dumb bitch, no one marries whores. He was going to set you up in Miles City in a crib like he done all those other girls he's promised to marry."

"No, Buck—" She started to pull away.

He slapped her so hard her head snapped back and she staggered. He had no regards for her, so he undid the hobbles and then swung into the saddle. "Get up here behind me."

"Buck, you're ruining my only chance."

"Better than you ruining mine," he said and caught her by the hair.

"No!"

"Then get up behind me and fast."

She took his arm and he tossed her on behind. In minutes, she sobbed at his back and mumbled about his taking her away from the only man ever treated her like a lady. He ignored her and tried to concentrate on his directions in the dark night.

At last, Buck felt certain they were on the Billings to Mile City road, and he held his horse into the wind and snowflakes. In a few hours, the horse stopped.

"Where are we?" she asked in a hoarse voice.

He set her down and then dismounted. "At a line shack. We can wait out the storm here."

"Is there a stove?" She hugged her arms and shivered.

"Yeah. Go build a fire. There's wood in there."

"Okay, just don't hurt me anymore please."

"Go build the damn fire."

"I am. I am."

Alone, Buck arrived back in Billings after dark the next day. He told the boy at the stables to rub down his horse, real good, grain him and then give him two pails of warm water. He walked up through the new snow on his way to check on the Antelope. He stopped at the bar to speak with Earl. The place looked deserted.

"Anything new?"

"The mayor's in your office. Wants to see you bad, he said."

"How long has he been there?"

"I set him up with a bottle and a glass. Oh, a couple of hours."

"*Must* want to see me bad."

When Palmer swung the door open, Hugh Whitehall, who looked limber-necked, pointed a shaky finger at him. "I want those gawdamn books!"

He quickly shut the door. "What books?"

"Those . . . books of his. You know what I mean."

"Who said I had them?"

"C-Copelan did."

"I don't have any books."

Whitehall rose shaky on his feet and started for him. Palmer slammed him back in the chair. "Sober up, stupid. Have you lost your mind, getting drunk in here and shouting at me?"

"I-I want them damn books—"

"Listen, you sober up then we can talk."

Whitehall passed out and fell out of the chair onto his face. Disgusted, Palmer went out and told Earl to have two men carry the mayor upstairs and put him in Lucille's bed. She for damn sure wasn't coming back.

THIRTY-EIGHT

"Two men're coming," Kate announced, looking out the front window.

"Who is it?" Herschel asked, and put Sarah down from his lap. "I better go see who it is."

"Will they hurt you?" Sarah asked

"No, baby, I bet they're friends."

"One's Arthur Spencer," Marsha said. "I'll make coffee."

"Good idea. The other must be the marshal," he said, slipping on his coat. He put on his cap and pulled the door closed after himself.

"Come on in," he said, shaking Arthur's hand and then the thick-set man behind the dark bushy mustache.

"Charlie Otter, Baker, nice to meet you." He turned to the other man. "Why are you here, Arthur? I wasn't expecting you. Not that you aren't welcome."

"Before I left Billings, Lucille, the bar girl you know I told you about? Well, she offered to marry me. Hey, I ain't so old a fool I couldn't resist, so I took her with me. Third night out of Billings in a snowstorm she disappeared. We can't find a trace of her."

"You suspect foul play?"

"It was snowing like blazes and cold. There was no reason for her to walk away."

"Did she know much?"

Spencer nodded. "She said the two of them were at his cabin on the day Talbot was killed. Buck went deer hunting and came in about dark packing a buck."

"What did she think?"

"Well, he acted that night like they were going to stay up there and eat it, but before daybreak he had her packed and was headed for town like his pants were on fire."

"Why?"

"He said that he needed to form a posse to go find Talbot's body."

"But I thought they were going looking for Talbot 'cause he hadn't come in."

"Lucy said he must have made a slip. He frightened her pretty bad. I think that's why she took my offer."

"Now she's gone." Herschel frowned at Spencer and couldn't figure what had happened to her. "We've got a few left. His hired man at the Diehl place and the two gunhands at his other place."

"What do we know about his barkeeper, Earl?" Spencer asked, hitching his and Otter's horses at the rack.

"Bet he's the last one to tell us anything. He's a pretty tight lip." Herschel had not even considered the bartender— but he had to know lots of what went on.

"You're right. Copelan?"

"He might if we scare him enough."

"You think his two ranch hands are the hired ones?" Otter asked.

"Why else would he wine and dine them before and

after the murder? Not because he liked how they fed hay."
Herschel shook his head at the man.

"That's Daws and Smith?"

"Yes. Where should we start?" he asked the lawman.

"I would say in the morning we look them up," Otter
said.

"Fine. Come on in, my wife's fixing coffee. We can put
the horses up later."

Spencer hugged Marsha, and they went off across the
room talking privately. The girls stood back and Herschel
winked at them. "This is Marshal Otter and Mr. Spencer,
girls."

They nodded politely.

"Nice to meet you ladies," Otter said and smiled for
them.

"Get a seat," Herschel said, taking his coat and hat.

"Sure hope we didn't inconvenience you all," Otter
said, sitting on a straight-back chair.

"Heavens, no," Marsha said. "Herschel wanted some
help solving this business. The girls and I can stand company if you three can solve it all."

"We're here to try," Spencer said and took a seat across
from his friend.

"You know unless we can find something they did
against the federal government's laws, I have no authority,"
Otter explained. "But that don't keep me from investigating any crime."

"So if you arrest someone, he needs to have broken the
federal laws?" Herschel asked.

"Like I said, I can still investigate. Governor Howard
sent my boss a telegram to find the source of all this trouble in Yellowstone County. So I am here with the chief
marshal's blessings, too."

"Spencer tell you about my arrests?"

"How they gunned them down in the alley? Yes. So if

we do arrest someone, we will need our guards at the jail, no doubt," Otter agreed.

"If I thought for one minute that Buck Palmer had kidnapped Lucy at my camp, I'd end his days." Spencer's blue eyes turned cold as ice.

"Like the rest, proving anything is tough," Herschel said, then blew on his coffee. "We need someone to talk and that will blow the lid off all of it."

"We ever get one to talk, they'll fall like dominoes," Spencer said.

"I guess our best chance is the men that work for him," Otter said.

"His hay feeders." Herschel grinned. "Marsha, your house may be a little full tonight, but come morning I hope we're after the bad guys."

"No problem. They can stand my cooking, I can sure stand them."

"Ma'am, anyone's cooking beats ours." Otter laughed, and the others joined him.

Before dawn they set out for Buck Palmer's ranch. Spencer knew the man, Joe Starr, on the Diehl place and felt that the drunk was only that—a farmhand. So they rode for the place where the two were supposed to be. A cold fifteen degrees, but the wind was down, so they jig-trotted their vapor-breathing horses northwest through the powdery snow. Close to ten o'clock they drew up above the place in the jack pines.

"That's it," Herschel said. "Belonged to Hank Spears. He sold out and went to Oregon. No one ever heard from him again."

"You don't reckon he met with foul play?" Spencer asked, checking his prancing dun.

"I never thought about it until now. Strange, he never

wrote any of us who knew him a letter about the country out there. He was literate."

Otter nodded his head. "Better get your gun handy. These two might get flighty they figure we're on to them."

Herschel removed his .44 from the holster and put it in his coat's side pocket. Then he stepped off Cob and stretched his legs. Those buildings down there represented to him the source of much of his own problems—he thought about the two buttons. All he needed was a match for them.

"Marshal, I have two silver buttons. One from the night they beat me up and one from the scene of Talbot's execution."

Otter pressed down his mustache with the web of his hand then put his gloves back on. "That may be all we need."

"I checked those two that came gunning for me. It wasn't them."

Otter nodded and was ready to ride in.

They rode three abreast from the gate under the crossbar toward the main cabin with smoke curling out the pipe. Cob sensed the tension and began to single-foot. Herschel spoke to settle him, but inside he was as excited as the gelding. Maybe this would be the day he learned all about what was behind his beating and the execution of Talbot. Somehow these two had to be tied to it.

"Come out!" Otter demanded. "U.S. deputy marshal here."

The three sat their horses. Otter banished his short-barreled Colt. No one came.

"You got two minutes to come out hands high or die!"

Herschel stepped off his horse and kept an eye on the plank doors. His .44 in his hands, he looked across at Otter.

The lawman nodded to both of them. He and Spencer were on the ground, too. The three advanced on the cabin.

"Back way out?" Otter asked under his breath.

Herschel shook his head.

"All right! All right! We ain't armed."

"Get your hands in sight," Otter demanded.

The door opened, and the shorter Daws came out with his hands over his head. "What the hell do you want?"

"We're arresting you for murder—get out here," Otter ordered, and sullen-faced Smith came next.

Spencer checked them for weapons and nodded they were clean. By then Herschel had their horses hitched at the rack. He came across the snow, staring at the leather vest that Smith wore. Glistening in the sun were a few silver buttons.

In two steps, he moved in and jerked the man to his face.

"I've got the proof you beat me up and the proof that you executed Sheriff Talbot."

"Huh? You can't prove nothing."

Herschel smiled. "Oh, yes, I can. You lost a button off that vest at both scenes."

"I did not."

"You carry a .45?"

"No."

"Spencer, go in and find his gun."

"All right, all right, I have a .45. That don't prove I shot Talbot."

"Spencer, go get their pistols." Herschel never took his glare off the Texan.

"Sure thing." Spencer went inside the cabin.

"What are you trying to do to us?" Daws asked.

"Prove that you two killed Sheriff Talbot."

"Why would we do that?" Daws looked around like a trapped coyote.

Herschel nodded. "Because he caught you branding cattle."

"No way you can prove that."

Herschel looked at Spencer coming out of the house with two handguns. He took the first one with rubber grips. "This yours?"

Smith nodded with his fish-eyed look.

The hammer cocked, Herschel fired two shots in a row. Then he spun the cylinder and opened the side gate. He pushed out two smoking cartridges.

"The hammer marks on the center fire are the same as ones we collected at the scene, you boys are looking at a rope."

"What the hell do you mean?"

"Kinda stupid to shuck those shells right there."

"Who hired you to kill Talbot?" Otter asked.

"We never killed him!" Daws screamed, the terror in his eyes. "We never shot him!"

"Then who used that gun?" Otter demanded.

"Oh, geez, he'll kill us if we tell—"

"No need in hanging for someone else. Who killed Talbot?" Otter pressed him.

"Buck—Buck Palmer took Smith's gun and shot him point-blank." Daws was trembling. His eyes wet. "I swear we never done it."

"Palmer hire you to tie up them cattle?" Otter asked.

"Yeah, but he never said what for. Then he brung—" Daws swallowed hard. His face a pasty white under the whisker stubble, he stammered out, "He done it. He grabbed Denver's gun and shot him—oh, we never—"

"No, but you shot Jack Diehl in the back," Herschel said.

"It was us or him," Daws said.

Herschel turned away. He wanted to pistol whip the short Texan until he couldn't talk. The damn worthless outfits shot a good man in the back. Wearing masks, they had beat him up. What else had they done?

"Who does Buck Palmer work for?" Otter asked, taking charge while Herschel stepped away deep in his own thoughts and trying to get some control of his feelings. He considered how those two had been the root of all his troubles—them and Buck Palmer. And he had two of them in his custody.

It would be easy to simply lynch them and save the territory all the expense of a trial, but he was running for sheriff, not head of the vigilantes. He couldn't be a part of the lawlessness and at the same time ask for the job to uphold the law.

"What's Copelan's part?" Herschel asked, turning on his heels and looking back at the pair.

"We don't know."

"He executed the last two I brought in. You boys better be telling us all you know about him."

"Nothing. We don't know anything. We stay out here at the ranch. He won't even let us go into town."

"You know what he did with Lucy?" Spencer asked.

Both men shook their heads. "She gone?" Daws asked.

Spencer bobbed his head that she was gone and walked over to Herschel, who was standing apart. "It's a hard two days' drive to Miles City. But we could jail them there. Right, Otter?"

The lawman agreed. "I can get the sheriff up there to hold them."

"We bring them into Billings and all hell might break loose," Herschel said. "Plus we need them to testify against Palmer."

"I can take them to Miles City," Spencer said. "You two can go do what you need to in Billings."

"We need to arrest Palmer before he gets word we have these two," Otter said to Herschel.

"I hate to leave Spencer with these two."

"I have some leg and cuff irons in my saddlebags."

"No, too dangerous, Charlie, you better go with him. I don't want anything to happen to these two. They'll testify to save their own necks. It's the only way we'll ever get Buck Palmer."

"You aren't going to try to take Palmer alone?"

"No, I'm first going to the prosecutor, and if he don't cooperate, I'll wire the governor."

Spencer made a pained face of disapproval. "Palmer has killed lots of folks before. He won't back off from killing you either."

"I need to know some things inside that courthouse. It will take me a day or so digging and I may have some answers. Takes you guys two days, he won't know anything until after I have my talk with the prosecutor and look at some records. I never saw who really owns this place here."

"You mean you think in the records it will show who Palmer works for?" Otter said, folding his arms over his chest.

"Good chance of that. Let's put them in your cuffs and fix us something to eat. They must have food in there." Herschel tossed his head at the shack.

"Good idea," the lawman said. "Maybe keep them out here instead of hauling them to Miles City—then he won't know till we're ready to spring the trap."

"We can look at the food supply," Herschel said, going along with Spencer after the cuffs. "I can even send some if we need more."

"I never knew you could tell a hammer's mark on a bullet."

Herschel glanced back and then held back his grin. "They didn't either."

Spencer clapped him on the shoulder. "Well, it worked good enough."

Herschel looked across the snow at the white-capped

hills. He'd found the two who had murdered Jack Diehl, yet somehow it wasn't over—wasn't through, wasn't re-solved. Ever since the funeral, deep inside his mind, he'd thought when he finally found them it could be laid to rest. But instead it had opened up a bigger sore. Buck Palmer was the man behind it all—but why?

THIRTY-NINE

I knowed it looked all wrong down there."

Buck Palmer was listening to Hiram Spokes. He sat in his swivel chair. Hiram had come boiling back from the ranch without delivering the supplies he'd sent him to deliver.

"I seed them all out in front of the cabin and reined up. Three guys putting them two Texans in irons. I set my horse and the two packhorses up there in the jack pines and used my spyglass. Came close to riding in on the deal."

"Who were the three?"

"I recognized that cap that Herschel Baker wears. The second guy was short. He's a freighter from Miles City. I see him often."

"Spencer?"

"Yeah, he's in the Antelope all the time."

"Who was number three?"

"I ain't sure, but he looked official, like a damn lawman."

"But why were they putting irons on those two? Daws and Smith?"

"I ain't sure, but even at the distance, I knowed what they was doing."

Palmer tented his fingertips. "You're sure Herschel Baker was one of them?"

"Hell, as sure as I know who I am. That's why I high-tailed it right back here to tell you."

Palmer held up his hand to settle the indignant old geezer. "I know, Hiram, and I'm going to pay you for doing it. Pay you well, but not a word to anyone."

"I always work for the man who pays me."

"Good. Could you tell if they were bringing them into Billings?"

"No. But I figure so. They arrested them."

Palmer squeezed his forehead between his thumb and forefinger. The headache raging inside his skull was threatening to explode out both ears. That damn Baker! Should have let them kill him instead of beating him up. All it did was spur him on. Those two sorry Texans would talk and talk a lot. They'd have to try to escape jail—he better warn Copelan he'd soon have two more to execute—that was what the sumbitch Baker called it. So Daws and Smith weren't around to spill any beans—he might have to do that himself.

He better get out to the ranch and learn all he could about the deal. But they'd be bringing them in shortly. Best if he went to the jail. He dug in his pants pockets and came out with two twenty-dollar gold pieces. "Here's for your trouble."

"What about the supplies?"

"Guess you can eat them, can't you?"

"Oh, sure." Hiram's rheumy eyes lit up.

"Take 'em, but be quiet."

"Thank you kindly, sir." Hiram pocketed the money and left whistling.

Palmer slammed his fist on the table. Baker! He needed him eliminated. Somehow, some way that didn't point at him. Those Texans had to be silenced. They were the only ones that could implicate him. And this Spencer needed it—messing where he didn't belong. He'd do the same thing to him he did to that whore—slit his throat. Number three was a mystery man—Hiram felt he was law—but who? Not county law; he knew them. Was Baker in with the governor on some undercover business?

Copelan first. He took his coat off the rack and his scarf. The acting sheriff had as much to lose as he did. Dressed, he slapped on a felt hat and went out the back way. He mushed through the snow to the courthouse and went up the stairs two at a time. A young man sat at the front desk where Copelan worked when Sam Talbot was sheriff.

"Copelan in there?" He tossed his head toward the door and started past the kid.

"Wait! You can't go in there."

When Palmer reached for the doorknob, he discovered it was locked. The notion flew all over him, and before he kicked in the frosted glass, a voice shouted, "One minute."

One minute? Then he heard the whispers of a woman in distress. He stepped back and Copelan stuck his head out. His black hair in his face, his shirt partially buttoned, he slipped out in the office and looked at Palmer.

"What do you need?"

"Talk and in private."

Copelan pointed to the small office to the side. He herded Palmer into the room, looking back several times toward the frosted door marked "Sam Talbot, Sheriff of Yellowstone County, Montana Territory."

"We've got some problems," Palmer said.

"What kind?" Copelan asked, finishing dressing.

"Baker has arrested my two cowboys."

"What the hell for? He ain't the sheriff."

"I know you're the sheriff, but this morning Hiram was delivering supplies and caught sight of Baker and two others putting Smith and Daws in irons."

"Where are they now?"

"I guess bringing them in."

"What do I have to do?"

"Make damn sure they don't talk."

"Not another jailbreak."

"Hang them like they did it themselves in their cells."

"Aw, I didn't—"

Palmer drove his forefinger into the man's chest—hard. "Listen! You are in this as deep as I am. Them Texans blabber and we can all swing on a vigilante's rope."

Copelan clutched his throat. "I never—"

"Who's in that office?" A smile crossed Palmer's lips.

Copelan reset his tie. "You don't know her."

"It ain't Ramona Whitaker, is it?"

"No—"

"Don't lie to me. I don't care who you're dilly-dallying with, you've got to be damn certain them two don't talk."

"But what if—"

"That prison at Deer Lodge ain't nice this time of the year."

"All right. All right. They'll die somehow when they get here."

"Good."

"What're you going to do next?"

"Execute that damn Herschel Baker."

Copelan collapsed on a chair. "Oh, God."

"It won't reflect on you."

"How many more have we got to kill?"

"Whoever gets in the damn way." Palmer reached out

and grasped him by a fistful of his shirt. "You're in this now. It's do or die. Do you understand?"

"Yes, yes."

Palmer left the courthouse uncertain that even Copelan could be trusted for long. He would make one try to clean out Herschel and his posse at the ranch if they didn't come in. Why wouldn't they come in? No reason. Even if they mistrusted Copelan, this was where county prisoners were incarcerated. No telling what Baker was up to—if they weren't in Billings by dark, he was riding down there and eliminating the whole bunch of them. Damn, he might need to get all his money and special things gathered and have them ready in case his plan didn't work.

Sundown came and no prisoners showed up. Maybe the old man was mistaken about what he'd seen happen. But Palmer held no real doubts about him telling the truth. It was a trap set out there for him. He checked on the money in the office safe. Several thousand he'd skimmed off the take over the past two years. Enough to make himself a new way of life in a new place. California. He'd heard it never snowed down there.

He told Earl he had business to attend to and to close up later for him. Outside in the night, on his way to get Custer, he thought about Arthur Spencer, who must be in on the deal over Lucille's disappearance. He'd damn sure never find her. She was three feet under in the dirt floor of an abandoned homesteader's shack. That's where that sawed-off freighter should be, and who was the big man with them? Hiram thought he was the law. What law?

The horse saddled and himself bundled up for the cold, he put the .50-caliber Sharp's rifle in the boot. If he needed long-range, the Sharp's would do it. Two dozen of the heavy cartridges in his saddlebags, he felt set to pick them off at long distance. And he hoped Herschel Baker was the first one in his sights.

He crossed on the ferry, and by nine o'clock was at the Diehl place. His sleepy man Starr came to the door and blinked in disbelief.

"What do you need?"

"You seen Herschel Baker and some others tramping around here?"

"Naw." Starr set the candle lamp on the table.

"You know anything about him?"

"I seen him last week at Larkin's store."

His coat unbuttoned, Palmer paced the floor. "Him and two more guys arrested my men at the ranch today."

"Arrested? He, the damn law, now Talbot's dead?"

"No. Copelan is. He's taking the law in his own hands."

"Why?"

"Meddling is all."

"What did he arrest them two for?"

"God only knows." Palmer still did not have a good plan devised yet to take the prisoners. He needed to either shut them up or kill the other three. He should have fed those two to the Yellowstone, instead of treating them to Lucie, like when he had Talbot out of the way. Damn lots of things he should have done—now he was left with the pieces.

"Whatcha going to do, Boss?"

"Go see what they're up to."

"Be careful," Starr said, walking him to the door.

"I will, and you keep your mouth shut. I wasn't here tonight if anyone asks."

"I ain't seen you in weeks."

"Good." He rebuttoned his coat and went back outside. In minutes, he was riding for his place under the stars. When the sun came up, he intended to pick them off. One by one like a buffalo hunter. If he didn't freeze to death first.

On a rise where the sun would be at his back, he set the

Sharp's in a V formed by a branch in a pine tree. Full view of the cabin's front door and the rifle's sights set, he waited. Weaker men would have frozen already—he was determined. Stomping his feet for circulation, he saw someone bareheaded look around, and next the two Texans in irons came out. Behind them with a rifle he recognized— Arthur Spencer.

Round one roared off and slammed Denver Smith against the side of the cabin. In a fluid move, Palmer ejected the casing and poked in cartridge number two. He took aim on the ashen face of Cooter Daws turning slowly for the doorway. The muzzle roared and the bitter gun-smoke came back in Palmer's eyes. Daws threw his mana-cled hands in the air and fell facedown.

The mushroom-looking blasts of Spencer's rifle would fall far short of him. He reloaded and searched through the sights. The cabin door was closed and Spencer was gone from his view. A grin crossed Palmer's face. He had the upper hand. Only one way out of that cabin and he had it covered whenever they wanted to come out. Confident of his situation, he took aim at the row of bottles in a frame that made the east window and fired. That would ventilate the cabin some plus make them duck.

He laughed aloud. The whole deal had warmed him some. Next he needed to shoot their horses in the corral. Where was the roan that Baker rode? Not among the four head in the corral. Shame—he intended to kill him next.

"You listening out there?" someone shouted.

He set the rifle down and cupped his hands. "Yeah, I'm listening."

"I'm U.S. Deputy Marshal Charles Otter, and you bet-ter drop that gun and put your hands up."

Palmer's raucous laughter echoed off the barn. "Go to hell, Otter. You two better come out unarmed and hands in the air."

"Palmer?"

"Yeah?"

"What did you do with Lucille?" Spencer shouted.

"Wouldn't you like to know." He began laughing again. He had them like ducks in a pond. "I'm through talking, boys." He raised the rifle and sent another heavy bullet at the window, knocking off more of the bottles and making it look like a broken-toothed mouth.

Twenty minutes later, one by one, taking his time for effect, he shot the four panicked saddle horses. There would be no escaping on them come dark. He needed to sneak down there, set the cabin on fire and drive them two out. Maybe he'd do that later.

To fill his empty stomach, he chewed on some jerky he kept wrapped in oilcloth in his pocket. After this was over and those two dead, he needed to cut and run. Get his money out of the safe in the office and get the hell out of Billings and Montana. But he wanted one more thing— Herschel Baker in his gun sights. That worthless Texan was the cause of all of this trouble. If he'd handled Baker himself and not used Daws and Smith—well, they were eliminated anyway.

MacDavis wouldn't like any of it. More bad headlines. He hated them. Too bad, you fat bastard, just too bad. In twenty-four hours, he'd be gone from Montana and they'd never find him. Palmer smiled and rested his cheek on the walnut stock of the Sharp's. *Show yourself, Spencer.*

FORTY

H ERSCHEL kissed his wife good-bye and rode for Billings before dawn. Her soft words, *Be careful*, echoed in his ears as he short-loped Cob through the powdery snow. This day he needed to find out many things. Who really owned the Antelope? If he could learn that, maybe he could find out who was Palmer's boss. A saloon-keeper had nothing to gain by hiring thugs to beat Herschel up—but whoever was behind him might—might want to run things like who was elected sheriff.

By the time the courthouse opened, he had stabled Cob at Paschal's and was headed up Main for the clerk's office. The U.S. flag popped in the wind on the staff, and inside he took the stairs two at a time, unbuttoning his coat.

"Good morning," Mrs. Johnson said, looking up.

"I need to learn about some more land ownership."

"Fine. What township and section?"

Herschel was pulling off his gloves, and looked around

to be certain they were alone before he spoke. "The Ante-lope Saloon, for one thing."

"That's easy," she said, drawing out a map and placing it on the counter. The edges overlapped the counter. She moved it around until he could read the narrow name on the property.

"Yellowstone Investments?" He blinked and looked up at her. "Who's that?"

"Rupart MacDavis," she whispered.

"He's the man I need to see next."

She wet her lips and then with sadness in her eyes said, "You be careful, Herschel Baker. He's a mean man."

"I've met him before."

"Still, when you step on his toes or get into his business, he'll send his tough hands after you."

"Thanks."

"That's all?"

"That's enough for now." Herschel decided he'd better go and check on Spencer, Charlie and the prisoners. He knew MacDavis would be a hard nut to crack—but if they leaned hard enough on Palmer, he might spill the beans, when his options to get away from hanging were taken away.

In the hallway, he went past Copelan, who whirled and demanded that he stop.

"Did you bring some prisoners in here?"

"You mean Daws and Smith?" Herschel was amazed that the man even knew about the situation. How had he found out? If he knew, Palmer knew.

"Yeah. They in my jail?"

"No, not yet."

Copelan's face reddened. "Why, I'll—" His hand on his gun butt, he was inches from Herschel.

Gripping Copelan's forearm tight in his grasp, Herschel whispered in the man's ear. "I'm not escaping jail—don't try to shoot me. And by the way, mark a cell for yourself. The next grand jury will want you housed there."

"What grand jury?"

"The one that's going to be set up to investigate the execution of those two I brought in from the Crown."

"Your life ain't worth ten cents—" Copelan clenched his teeth so tight his head rocked on his shoulders.

"Don't threaten me. You're the one they'll hang that one on."

"You ain't sheriff yet and you won't ever be either."

"I guess the power man told you that you could run for sheriff now that Talbot was executed?" Herschel stepped back, after seeing that the tension in the man had gone down some.

Copelan blinked. "Power man—what are you talking about?"

"Rupart MacDavis. The one who runs things around here, including you."

"Baker—you're meddling where you don't belong—"

"Tell the grand jury that—they'll love to hear all about you and MacDavis."

Herschel turned on his heels and left Copelan cursing him and his ancestry as he went down the stairs. More distinctly, he was wondering how they'd found out about the prisoners. Damn, he better go see about them and his helpers.

He short-loped out of Billings to the ferry, and after the crossing, he rode south hard for Palmer's place. It was long past sundown when he rode up on the place. Strange to him there was no obvious light on in the shack. He reined the hard-breathing Cob up in the starlight and searched.

"Spencer! Charlie?"

"Be careful!" Spencer shouted back. "He's got a long shooting rifle."

Herschel bailed off his horse, trying to make out anything in the gray-white night that offered him any threat.

"Where was he?" he shouted, undoing his coat and drawing his Colt as he ran for the barn.

"East of us."

Behind the security of the barn, he shouted back. "How long since you heard from him?"

"About an hour."

"He may have taken off— Sumbitch." Herschel swore at the sight of the dead horses in the pen when he came around the side of the barn.

Spencer and Otter joined him.

"He was waiting at sunrise for me to take the prisoners out to relieve themselves," Spencer said as all three searched in the night. "He dropped Smith then Daws and I barely got in the cabin. Then he shot out the window bottles and kept us pinned inside while he shot the horses."

"Who was he?"

"Buck Palmer," Charlie said.

"Well, I think I learned who he works for today."

"Who?"

"Rupart MacDavis. I also had a run-in with Copelan in the courthouse. He thought I'd brought the prisoners in this morning."

"How did he know about them?" Charlie asked, shaking his head.

"Damned if I know, but I expect that Palmer knew first and told Copelan, then headed down here to eliminate us."

"He did a damn good job of trying," Charlie said. "We need to take these two bodies in and have an investigation held."

"I can get Walt Ferguson to bring his wagon over and haul you two and the bodies into town in the morning."

"I guess he's gone," Spencer said, looking around in the night. "We'll be fine until Walt gets here."

A wolf howled off in the night and Herschel nodded. "If Walt can't, I will."

"This Palmer is a bad killer. You be careful," Charlie said.

"I'll meet you in Billings or leave word where I am at Paschal's Livery." Herschel took off running for his horse.

An hour later he reined up at Walt's and the man came out. "Need you to pick up Arthur Spencer, Charlie Otter and two bodies over at Palmer's ranch."

"The Diehl place?"

"No, Palmer's west place."

"Get down and come in."

"No, I don't have time. Buck Palmer killed Daws and Smith, tried to kill Spencer and Charlie. They can explain more about the deal. Oh, yeah, Palmer shot their saddle horses, too."

"I guess then Buck's been behind all this whole thing."

"I got more to tell you, but it can wait."

"That'll be good. I'll be over there before sunrise and take them to town."

"Thanks," Herschel said and reined Cob around. He wanted to check on Marsha and the girls before he went back to Billings to look for Palmer. On the fly, he left Walt Ferguson and headed for home.

Sight of the light in the window warmed him coming off the far hillside. At the shed, he put a feed bag of oats over Cob's head and his out-of-breath wife tackled him from behind.

"I've been so worried about you all day. What did you learn today?" She threw her face up at him and tossed back the wave that threatened her eye.

"Somehow Buck Palmer learned about the prisoners." He undid the cinches and jerked the saddle off his horse's back. "So early this morning he shot the two Texans at long range and kept Spencer and Charlie in the cabin all day. Oh, and he shot their horses, too."

"I never trusted him. How are they?"

"Unscathed. Walt's going to haul them and the bodies into Billings in the morning."

"And you?"

"Get something to eat, sleep a few hours and go see if I can find Buck Palmer."

"Won't he run?"

"Maybe—" He used his fist to cover his yawn. "But he won't get far."

"What have you eaten today?" she asked, trailing along beside him hugging his arm.

"Breakfast."

"Oh, heavens, you must be starved."

"Starved to see you," he said and hugged her shoulder as they went on.

"I'd almost believe you," she said and then laughed. "I'd never imagined all the fun I've missed not having you."

"Didn't you and Mel have fun?" he asked, referring to her first husband.

She turned her head sideways to look at him. "Yes, but somehow I feel so free with you. You ask so little of me and treat me like a queen."

The door flew open as he said, "I'll try to keep doing that."

"You back, Herschel?" the girls asked.

"I guess for a short while."

They hugged him and he kissed each one on the forehead, getting on his knees to kiss Sarah.

"We missed you all day."

"I missed you girls, too," he said, unbuttoning his coat, grateful for the warmth of the fireplace.

Across the room, Marsha was stoking the range. "Girls,

don't wear him out. He'll be back when he gets this all set-tled and have time for us."

"Will that be soon?" Nina asked.

"I hope real soon."

"Good," Kate said over her shoulder, off to help her mother cook.

After supper, Marsha promised to get him up by two a.m.

Getting awake proved hard for him at the early hour, but she thrust a cup of steaming coffee into his hands when he realized she'd not been in their bed for some time. Break-fast was fixed and on the table after he dressed.

Seated, he looked at her in the flickering lamplight. "Sure beats my oatmeal."

She laughed. "Really, did you eat lots of it?"

"I wintered on it the first year I was up here."

"Oh, my, how can you still eat it?"

He wrinkled his nose. "I've ate worse things."

"But oatmeal for all your meals?"

"I was low on funds and determined to stay up here."

She went over, smothered his face to her apron and rocked him back and forth. "I'm sure glad that you did."

"Wrap a string around your finger. I'm going to buy you a ring when I get that horse money."

"I don't need a ring."

"Yes, you do. A woman needs one to twist around her finger when she's worried and to show off when she's proud."

"For a bachelor, you sure have noticed things."

"My maw did that. I just watched her ring a lot when he went off and didn't come back."

"I guess I'd wear it out over you."

"No, cut me that string. I'll be coming back." He went to eating his breakfast of eggs, ham and pan-fried potatoes along with hot biscuits, butter and huckleberry jam. Kings didn't eat that good.

Hours before sunup, he left her place for Billings. Lots on his mind, he short-loped his roan horse across the sea of white. A shroud for the thousands of head of dead cattle lying under it. Come spring, it might be easier to count the living than all the dead ones piled up in draws and creek beds waiting for the thaw. In fact, he'd not seen or heard any wandering loose cattle in the past thirty days.

The ferry ride across at dawn, then he rode up Main Street. Billings bustled with merchants receiving goods. A man was carrying in a beer keg on his shoulder, into the Antelope, when Herschel dismounted at the rack. A quick check around and he followed the man inside.

Earl was behind the bar getting ready for the delivery of the keg. He nodded to Herschel.

"Buck in?"

Earl shook his head.

"You expect him?"

Earl shook his head again, helping the man set the keg down. "I'll go back and show you something in a minute."

"Sure." Herschel wondered what Earl felt he needed to see about Buck being gone. But since Palmer obviously wasn't there, he needed to take the time and see whatever.

Headed for the back, Earl waved for him to follow. In the small office, the bartender pointed to the mess of papers on the floor and the open safe door.

"He do that?" Herschel dropped to haunches.

"He had the combination. I locked it after I closed last night."

"Sure wasn't busted open. What was in there?"

"I put eight hundred and forty-two dollars in there when I closed it."

"Was there more in there than that?"

"Could've been. I don't know when he made the last deposit at the bank."

"Where did he sleep?"

"Hotel across the street."

"Guess I better go wake him."

Earl wrinkled his nose. "Want my notion?"

"Sure." Herschel looked up at the man.

"Buck's left the county for good."

"We'll see."

At the hotel, they had not seen him. Herschel asked to be shown the room. The clerk told him no.

"I want to see the manager," Herschel said, checking around to see if anyone else was in the lobby.

"He's—"

Herschel held his hand out. "The key."

"Mr. Palmer will be mad." Reluctantly the boy delivered him a key. "201."

"Thanks." Herschel headed up the staircase. He put the key in the hole and quietly turned it and the knob. With an easy push, the door gave and opened as the sunlight spilled on the unmade bed. The smudged window was etched in frost. No Buck Palmer. Herschel went to the nightstand and opened the log.

He began to read about the mayor and his indiscretions. This wasn't the work of Palmer, he quickly decided, but it must be the work of a blackmailer that fell into Palmer's hands. There were others on the bureau. Nothing in the room looked like Palmer had taken a hasty powder. But somehow after seeing the open safe, Herschel felt certain the man had fled.

He'd silenced the two who could testify against him, then run. But which way should he go look for him? Buck Palmer was the man behind Jack Diehl's death. He needed to be brought back and face the consequences. Herschel

took the four logs he'd found and went out of the room.
Then he locked the door and went downstairs.

"I understand you have a safe," he said to the clerk.

"Yes, we do."

"Fine. Place these in the safe and hold them for the
grand jury. If they get away, you will answer for them.
Make me a receipt."

"A receipt?" the boy asked.

"Yes, a receipt for the court."

The whiskerless youth swallowed hard. "Yes, sir."

"Fine," Herschel said, taking the paper. He left the
hotel. Palmer must have kept his horse at Kime's Livery,
the other one in town. He headed for there next.

"I want to know what time that Buck Palmer left last
night," Herschel told the man in charge.

"How the hell would I know?" the man said, looking all
over his desk piled with papers for something. "I wasn't
here. Go wake that boy up in the bunk room. He was on."

"Thanks," Herschel said and went into the back room.
Becoming the law sure was tedious at times. He awoke the
boy, who looked at him out of unfocused eyes.

"Which way did Buck go last night?"

"Took the buggy and went east." The boy shook his
head.

That could mean Miles City or Wyoming. How would
he know? Wire Miles City and tell them to be on the lookout and he'd ride south. In a little while he'd know which
way Palmer went.

"Thanks," he said and left the youth to go back to sleep.

The town marshal, Joe Gates, was in the Antelope when
he went back. Earl had shown him the safe and he in turn
had sent word for Copelan to come down.

"I don't want anyone accusing me of stealing the
money," Earl said defensively to Herschel.

"You must be Baker," the lawman said.

"I'm him. You Joe Gates?"

"Yeah." Gates looked up when Copelan walked in.

"What're you doing here?" Copelan demanded when he came in, looked up and saw Herschel.

"Helping the grand jury."

"What grand jury?"

"The one that's going to get to the bottom of this business."

"You better mind your own damn business—"

"Don't threaten me, Copelan. I don't scare. See you, Earl, Joe."

Outside, he felt pleased and checked the cinch. Palmer had taken a powder. Copelan might be next. He'd better round up Palmer, he decided, and swung a leg over Cob. In a short lope, he headed east.

It was dark when he reached Fort Custer. He left Cob at the livery and walked the block up to the sutler's place. Some soldiers were inside the stale-smelling room, washing down their insides with beer. A slovenly woman waddled over and asked him what he wanted.

"What's for supper?"

"Stew."

"Beef?"

"I think so. Whatcha going to drink?"

"A beer." He figured the water was unfit or short from the smell of her. She hadn't had a bath since the past spring, if then even.

When she brought his beer back, he asked her, "I'm looking for a big man—was he in here late last night or this morning?"

"Lots of big men come in here."

"No, you'd know this man. Blond hair, blue eyes."

Her brown eyes met Herschel's. "He was here about ten. Drove a fine buggy."

"Say where he was going?"

She nodded and then swept the stringy hair back from her face. "Yeah, he did."

"Where?"

"To Hell. He was a no-good mean sumbitch."

"Guess he hurt you?"

"Slapped me hard when I told him we were closing."

"Anything else?" Herschel asked, hoisting the foamy mug for a sip.

"We fed him, but I'd poisoned his food if I'd had any."

Herschel took a swig of the beer and nodded thanks to her. Cob would catch him in another day. He better get a few hours' sleep or he'd fall out of the saddle. He felt confident that Palmer wasn't many miles ahead and had no idea about his pursuit. Maybe he'd catch him at Hardin or the Crow Reservation headquarters.

But the next day he found nothing at either place but word that a big man with a fine horse had driven through there. He passed the Little Big Horn battlefield, site of Custer's defeat, and went over the pass into Wyoming. Dayton was a sleepy small village on the Tongue where he paused. He overslept in a boardinghouse and was late getting Cob saddled and on his way next morning.

It was at the stage stop fifteen miles south that he spotted a rig parked in front he felt might be Palmer's. He dismounted Cob, swept his coat back and placed the .45 in his side pocket. Cob hitched to the corral, he began to slip toward the main building, a low sod-roofed cabin. A man came out and stood on the porch—not Palmer.

Was his man inside?

"Howdy." the man dressed in buckskin said.

"Howdy. That your rig?" Herschel indicated the buggy.

"No, it belongs to the missus."

"You seen a man driving a rig like that on the road south of here?"

The man sucked on his eyetooth. "Couple of hours ago, we did."

"He say where he was going?"

"Never talked to him."

"Thanks."

"Guess you're after him, huh?"

"Yeah," Herschel said, and went for his horse.

"He kill somebody?" the guy shouted after him.

Herschel nodded when he rode past the man. "My best friend."

FORTY-ONE

B UCK Palmer felt certain it was only a dozen miles more to Sheridan. From there he could take the stage to Cheyenne and catch a train for California. Palmer felt confident as he clucked to Chester and kept him in a jog trot. Every time he twisted around and looked back, he expected to see pursuit. Nothing. They might not even know he was gone yet.

No, but it made no difference. He had plenty of funds in his pocket and intended to enjoy himself some before he settled into working again. MacDavis would put out a reward on his head. Let that fat slob do that—no one was catching him. He beat Alabama at that game. Why, them overstuffed big ranchers wouldn't have a shirt left on their backs come spring with the huge losses of cattle they were having—time to find some new fertile ground.

He came down on Goose Creek and smiled. In a few hours, he'd have Chester sold and be on his way to Cheyenne. Shame the deal got rushed. He could have sold the ranch and other things. No need to look back; he had his whole life ahead of him since he shook the dust of Billings and Montana.

They'd had a melting down there. Still, things were locked up tight. He'd seen plenty of dark forms—dead cattle. He was going where it never snowed, where an old boy from the South belonged. Only white thing he wanted to see was cotton bolls. He twisted on the seat—nothing back there.

In the sunshine in front of the Maddox Stables, the liveryman checked out Chester. He checked his teeth for his age, his shins for splints. He walked around him several times squeezing his chin whiskers, appraising the horse.

"He's all there," Palmer said, growing anxious to get the deal over. What was he feeling so damn sentimental about? It was only a horse. Best one he ever owned, but simply a horse. Why didn't this tobacco-spitting bastard say something?

The man spat aside then wiped his mouth on the back of his hand. "You got a bill of sale on him?"

"Right here."

The man hooked some wire frames behind his ears and peered through the glasses at the paper that Palmer handed over. "Hmm. Looks good enough. I don't know if I can find a customer for a horse this good."

"What would you give? I need to catch the stage."

"Why, I'm liable to insult you."

Palmer looked at the sky for help, then the man. "What would you give?"

"A hundred fifty for him and the buggy."

His eyes closed, Palmer held out his hand. "Pay me."

"I know it ain't enough, but hay's high and lots of these fancy horse buyers ain't got any money left after their winter losses."

"I know all about it," Palmer said and jammed the

money in his pocket. He'd have to leave the buffalo robe and horse blanket, get his valise and head for the stage depot. Sooner he was out of this place the better. He wasn't sure why, but he had a cold feeling. Somehow his skin under all the clothes he wore was chilled and felt ready to shiver.

Catch the stage, get to Cheyenne and then he should be free again. He drew a deep breath and went around a double freight wagon going up the street with three teams. He wished he'd shot that damn Herschel Baker like he did those worthless Texans. Didn't matter anymore . . .

FORTY-TWO

Herschel could barely keep his eyes open. He'd followed those thin buggy tracks for days. It was Palmer's rig all right, and he'd only been hours ahead according to the stage depot hustler at Dayton. The man on the seat answered to Buck Palmer's description. When Herschel dropped off the last ridge for Goose Creek, he wondered if this would be the place he at last would confront the killer. Lots of things danced in his mind. How was Marsha doing? The girls? They'd become a vital part of his life. And Toby left to feed his cows with a green team.

But he also thought about Jack Diehl lying in the cold ground—his death at the hands of Palmer's men, a total waste. His widow left in poverty, her and the children gone home to her folks. Worthless bunch of crap—Palmer acting like he was their friend, all the time the kingpin of the trouble.

Herschel rode up the ruts called a street, dodging freight

wagons and rigs. Then when he saw it, he reined up Cob. The topless buggy sat before the Maddox Stables, without the horse. He looked over everything—on the boardwalk, the people crossing the street. Then he booted Cob on. A sense of wariness clutched his chest and restricted his throat. If Palmer was there, Herschel needed eyes in the back of his head.

He unbuttoned his coat to get at his gun. At the livery, he dismounted and, looking around, noticed the man come out, spit tobacco and nod to him.

"Want to stable him?"

"Yeah. The man drove that buggy in—he around?"

"Buck Palmer?"

Busy searching for sight of him, Herschel nodded.

"Sold me that rig and his horse. Why? You the law?"

Herschel nodded, still wondering where Palmer went. In all the traffic and commerce going on in the business district, it would not be easy to pick him out before Palmer spotted him.

"He didn't steal that outfit, did he?"

"No, he murdered some men."

"Well, he said he was going to catch the stage."

"Where would he do that at?" Herschel felt a wave of anxiety sweep over his body and denied part of his strength for the task ahead. Buck Palmer was a cold-blooded killer. Herschel had never killed anyone. If he gave Palmer one chance, he'd be dead. A notion that rode deep inside him.

Maddox pointed to the north. "Stage line office is a block down and around the corner."

"Feed my horse some oats and water him when he cools down. The name's Baker, Herschel Baker," he said quickly and took off.

"Adolph Maddox," the man said after him. "You be careful. He looks mean to me."

Looks mean. Heavens, he's the angel of death. Herschel

crossed the slushy mud thoroughfare and stomped his boots on the boardwalk. Two blocks of businesses fronted the main street, an assortment of saloons, dives, gun and harness repair places, and general mercantile, along with professional offices of lawyers and several banks. Obviously, from the freight business and commerce, Sheridan was booming.

He rounded the corner and saw the fresh teams being held for the switch. The stage couldn't be far away. If he only could—he wet his lips, considering the reflection of the waiting horses in the glass window. Hand on the wooden grips of his Colt, he loosened it in the holster— Buck Palmer would never give him a chance. Fair play in this case could mean his death. It was no time to consider anything but Palmer or himself. He dropped back into the open double doors of the stage line's stables.

Patience could be the virtue, his mother often said when he itched to dive into something as a boy. In the shadows where he stood, the sun's radiation couldn't reach him. The sharp wind cut his face. He waited. If Palmer was inside, there remained a good chance he'd not seen him. Ready to get on the stage, he might be off his guard enough to jump him.

The safety of the others, if there were other passengers, must be a consideration, too. It wouldn't be Palmer alone. His guts roiling, Herschel waited. The stage rattled around the corner with two teams of hard-breathing horses gagging on their bits. Some kid shouted, "She's here!" in the front door of the office and rushed off to help the hostlers change teams.

"Be here ten minutes, folks," the driver shouted and helped a lady depart the coach. "Be ready to roll or be left!" he said in a booming voice.

They brought the first team by Herschel, the sweat-soaked animals still wild and stomping high from the excitement of the drive up there. The youth leading them was too busy to notice Herschel and went back in the barn, holding the leads and shouting "Whoa" at them.

He dried his palm on his canvas pants and drew the six-gun, holding it close by his leg to not be obvious. Where was Palmer? A couple of derby hat drummers with carpet-bags were out on the boardwalk. The driver was soon back and putting their luggage in the boot.

Herschel turned and checked the alleyway to be certain no one was coming up behind him. Nothing. The second team went past him on the half run. The pistol beside his leg felt like an anchor on his right arm.

"Mister, if you're going, get your valise out here. We ain't got room in that coach for it today."

Palmer stepped outside the office, the bag in his right hand. His face turned to one of shock when he looked at the gun in Herschel's hand advancing toward him. A woman screamed and ran inside holding her hands over her mouth.

"Buck Palmer, you're under arrest for the murder of Smith and Daws."

"You ain't got any authority—"

"Let the bag down easy and raise your hands. I'll put a bullet in your heart if you so much as flinch."

A grin broke over Palmer's face. "You've got the wrong man. Who do you think I am?"

Herschel spun him around and removed the small-caliber pistol from his coat pocket. When he reached for the gun on his waist, Palmer moved. Not quick enough. Herschel busted him over the head with his pistol and drove him to his knees.

"What's going on here?" A constable arrived with his club drawn.

"I'm arresting a murderer from Montana," Palmer said, jerking the six-gun out of Palmer's holster as he stayed on his knees.

"What are you, mister, a bounty hunter?"

"A citizen making an arrest of a killer."

"Everyone stand back. Where are you from?"

"Get up." Herschel jerked him by the collar. "You try that again and you're dead."

Palmer set his high-priced hat back on his head, the crown crushed from the blow. "You won't ever get me back to Billings."

The constable looked at him with a frown. "He ain't done bad so far. What we need to do—"

"You got some handcuffs I can borrow?" Herschel asked the man, checking the gathering crowd for any sign of someone coming to Palmer's aid.

"Yes." The man reached behind his back and produced them. "Put them on tight so he don't slip out of 'em."

Herschel holstered his own gun, clamped the handcuffs on Palmer's left wrist, then spun him around and did the right one behind his back. Palmer contained—Herschel's breathing began to slow down and his rapid heart rate declined. He licked his lips and dried his wet palms on his britches.

"We need to go to the jail and clear all of this with the head marshal."

Herschel nodded and took the valise from the driver. "Get walking."

"Everyone on board for Cheyenne. The fun's over and we're leaving," the driver shouted behind him. Walking toward Main Street in a line led by the constable, and behind the sullen Palmer, Herschel drew a deep breath. He no longer felt cold—something had crept in and warmed him to the center of his body. *Marsha,* he thought, *I'm headed home.*

In the county courthouse, the chief marshal looked over Buck Palmer and stuck a hand out to Herschel. "My name's Flanagan. Good to meet you, Mr. Baker. You trailed him all the way from Montana?"

"Yes, sir."

"What can we do for you?"

"Jail him. I need about six hours' sleep and I'll head back."

"I'd advise you take him back by public conveyance."

"Stage?"

"Yes, sir. You'll be back up there in twenty-four to thirty-six hours, depends on the weather, of course."

"When's the next stage north?"

"I think about eight or nine in the morning. Give you plenty of time to get some sleep and then go back."

"Lock him up. I'll need to buy some cuffs and some leg irons."

Flanagan nodded. "We can sell you some of those. John, take him back and lock him up tight." The jailer hustled Palmer out of the room.

"Good. Now I need to make arrangements to get my horse back home, some hot food and a bed."

"I still can't get over how you trailed him down here."

Herschel shook his head. "I owed a man he killed that much."

"Must have been a real friend."

"He was." And Palmer's valise in his hand, he left and went to the livery. Walking the boardwalk he felt the tight muscles in his back. He never realized how coiled up he had been.

"I want that horse delivered to Paschal's Livery in Billings. There someone here will do that?"

"Cost you big bucks."

"How much?"

"Thirty bucks."

"Make sure he don't ride him into the ground getting there."

Maddox agreed and took the money that Herschel handed him. "It'll be a day or two before I can get some-one."

"Fine, so he takes good care of the pony."

"He will. Ain't you the guy they're all talking about that arrested some outlaw at the stage line? Pleasure to meet you. We need more men like you. Damn outlaws are ruin-ing this country."

"Thanks," Herschel said and went off to find a meal to cure his gnawing guts.

Hours later, he lit a lamp in the hotel room and opened the valise. What did Palmer have in— Currency spilled out on the bed. One-hundred-dollar bills, fifties and twenties— there must be a fortune. But it wasn't Herschel's money. Good question: Whose was it?

He sat down in a chair and pulled off his boots, consid-ering his find. Not his money. The pile of bills on the quilt looked like a fortune to him in the yellow light. Ill-gotten gain—but not his. He would pay his expenses out of it. Cost of getting Cob back home, the cuffs and irons to hold Palmer, and their stage line tickets—the rest he'd turn in when he got back. Should make Palmer happy to know he was paying his own way back.

Herschel clasped his hands behind his head and leaned back in the chair. He wiggled his free toes in his wool socks and smiled. He might make a lawman after all.

FORTY-THREE

Hᴵˢ telegram to Paschal must have set things off, 'cause a crowd was gathered at the stage office in Billings when the Sheridan coach arrived. No idea who was in charge of the jail, he wondered how he'd ever keep Palmer in the cell and not shot in the back.

A roar went up from the crowd when he stuck his head out the door of the stage. He spotted his wife's beaming face and was about to get choked up.

"He's back!" someone shouted and he saw Charlie Otter and Spencer. "And he's got that killer."

On the ground, he turned back and helped Palmer down.

"Got news for you. Governor Howard has made you acting sheriff," Spencer shouted above the roar of the mob wanting to lynch his prisoner. Herschel nodded he had heard him.

"No!" he shouted to the crowd, holding his arms up to silence them. "They tell me I am the new sheriff of Yellowstone County. I don't hold with lynching. Palmer will get his day in court. All of you are good citizens. We all chose Montana as our home. I want to make it a home for all of us, big and small. Let me handle this, please?"

"Handle it!" someone shouted and the crowd wilted into a good-natured, head-bobbing mob.

"Where's Copelan and Harker?"

"They lit a shuck," Spencer said.

"Been gone long?"

"Since the governor's telegram said you'd be the acting sheriff."

He shook Charlie's hand. "You must have helped me get that."

The lawman nodded. "Want some help getting the rest of them?"

"Yes, I do. This job won't be over until I have them, too." He glanced down at the woman on his arm and smiled. "I sure missed you."

"The same for me, but you're all right."

"No scratches." He wanted to kiss her, but the crowd all round held him back.

"Here's your valise," the driver said and handed it to Herschel.

"Spencer," he said, under his breath. "You and Charlie take this over to the First National Bank and count it with them. I want it deposited in an account for me until I know how to dispose of it."

"How much is in here?" he asked, taking the bag.

"Thousands."

"Oh—" The shorter man smiled and, with the deputy, moved through the dispersing crowd. Satisfied that would be done right, Herschel turned back to his prisoner. "Palmer, get hiking. You know where the jail is."

"I can't walk in these damn leg irons."

"Then crawl." He gave him a shove in the direction of the jail.

"The girls were really worried about you until Paschal sent me word that you had him and were coming back."

"Sorry to worry them and you."

"Oh, Herschel, I figure your girls will worry a lot about you in this new job."

He looked at the open sky over head. Maybe they would . . .

FORTY-FOUR

V ERN Simmons, the prosecuting attorney for eastern
Montana, sat in the chair opposite Herschel before the
roaring fireplace in the sheriff's office.

"You want a grand jury?"

"I want one."

Simmons twisted the end of his mustache. "It might be
painful."

"I don't give a damn. There have been some bad things
happen. An innocent man was shot—Jack Diehl. A woman
with young children lost her ranch and is penniless. I was
beaten up. Two Texans were gunned down. A sheriff was
executed and two prisoners were shot in cold blood,
supposedly escaping. And a prostitute called Lucille is
missing."

"You want all that investigated?"

"I don't care whose tail gets caught in the door. Palmer
is sitting up there in his cell; he knows who hired him to do
all this. He ever talks, we'll know more."

"That lawyer Crane from Helena wants him out on bail."

"I checked on that. We don't have to let him post bail under murder charges. He's a risk to run, plus they'd kill him if he ever stepped out of the courthouse door."

A scowl crossed Simmon's face "You think that's why they want him out?"

"Yes."

"You'll have to round up the people they want to testify—"

"I have three deputies I trust."

"Can you find this Copelan and Harker?"

"One of my deputies is out looking for them right now."

"I'd've thought they'd left the country." Simmons shook his head as if he didn't understand. "I will ask the judge for the order, and you should be in grand jury business in three days."

"Good." Herschel sat back and considered his efforts. He wished he would get word from his deputy Barley Benton on the two that were on the loose—Copelan and Harker. He sure wanted them to talk to the grand jury. Copelan might know enough about Palmer to sing.

He shook Simmons's hand and walked the man to the door.

Simmons nodded to Marsha as he went past her in the outer office.

"Mrs. Baker," Herschel said and bowed at the waist. "Come in my office."

"Oh, did your business go well with Simmons?"

"Went very well," he said, removing her coat and hanging it on the tree with her scarf. "How are the girls?"

"Anxious for you to come home."

He looked out the window at the nearby building. "Going to be a while."

"Looks like we'll have to move up here then."

"But the ranch and all—"

"We can find good help to care for it. I don't like us split apart." Alone with him in the office, she fussed with his shirt.

"Well. I'm sure we can find a house in town."

"How far out is this shack of Palmer's you spoke about?"

"Why out there?"

"We could have a milk cow and chickens and fatten some pigs."

"I see I need a small farm."

"Exactly. To spoil your wife." Her face beamed and she swept back the lock of hair from her forehead.

He kissed her. "I'll see what I can do. Maybe trade my place for one."

"Oh, that sounds wonderful—" They both turned at the knock on the door.

"Yes?"

"Deputy Benton is back, sir," his new clerk, Sam Davis, said.

Herschel nodded his approval to her and hurried to the door. "Come in, Barley. What did you learn?"

He stripped off his fringed gloves and nodded to Marsha. "Howdy, ma'am." Then he turned back to Herschel. "I think I've located them up near the Milk River. Got word from Sioux I know that they were up there hiding out on a ranch owned by Miles Anthony."

"We'll ride up in the morning," Herschel said. "I'll have Charlie and Spencer watch the office."

"Come by my place and get me on the way up," Barley said and nodded to Marsha. "Good to see you, ma'am. Sorry, we're so on the run."

"Maybe one day things will settle down." Marsha smiled at him at as he took his leave.

Herschel agreed, closing the door after Barley.

She tackled him around the waist. "Oh, I guess I hate to share you with everyone."

He rocked her back and forth. "After we get those two. Things should slow down."

She peeked up at him and laughed. "There won't ever be an unbusy moment in your life, Herschel Baker. I'll just savor the ones I get."

Before dawn, he left Marsha at the hotel room, after her giving him a sleepy good-bye kiss. An hour later, he rode out of Billings on a stout bay horse Paschal had provided him. The boy had not brought Cob up from Sheridan yet, but Mattox had warned him they were busy.

Paschal called the gelding Bear Paw, Paw for short. Herschel found he had a smooth long trot and stepped out well in the cold. Herschel pushed him, and he was at his deputy's house by nine. Heart opened the door and welcomed him before he could knock. He was relieved to be inside her warm house, if only for a short while. She hurried after some coffee for him.

Barley turned from warming himself at the fireplace. "Morning. Reckon this arrest business could wait until spring?"

"I never had a sheriff in my house before," Heart said, handing him the cup.

"I've never been a sheriff before."

Barley nodded and looked back at the flames licking the wood. "I was shocked the governor appointed you. But I guess the big guys decided if they put a man in and this went sour for them, they really would look bad."

"You think they're cutting their losses?"

"Exactly. We better get in the saddle, if we're going to find these birds."

Herschel downed his coffee, thanked Heart and rebuttoned his coat going outside. This sure wasn't Texas. The Texas he knew in the hill country, it hardly ever frosted in the winter. His breath coming out in vapor clouds, he checked the cinch and mounted up. Barley led his pony out of the shed already saddled and they headed north.

Mid-afternoon they reined up in the jack pines and scouted the Anthony ranch. Barley used his brass telescope to scan the place, hardly more than a hay camp in the creek bottoms.

"There's horses in the corral. They still may be here."

"They've got a fire. Maybe we can warm up."

"I don't figure they'll go in without a fight."

Herschel agreed. "Guess we better come in from the back side. I bet there's only that south set of bottles for a window in the place."

"We can ride up this ridge and come down the bottoms on their blind side."

They found a gate and came through the hay fields. Herschel put his Colt in the large side pocket of his coat. Barley unlimbered a .44/40 Winchester and levered a shell into it.

Back of the shed, they dismounted and hitched their horses.

"One word of caution," Barley said. "When you knock, don't stand in front of the door. They're liable to fill it full of bullets."

"Thanks," Hersch said. Feeling tense and stiff from the long ride, he hoped to get this over quickly. His soles crunched on the crusted snow that had melted on top and refroze. At the side of a small shack he decided might be a store room, he paused and studied the main cabin.

The two he sought might not be in there. The six-gun held close to his face, he sure didn't want innocent folks killed. No telling—

"Damn it's cold out here—" Someone in gray long handles was getting wood off the stack. His startled look and lantern jaw sagged.

"Hands in the air!" Herschel ordered, aiming the Colt at him.

Harker swore, but obeyed, straightening with his arms in the air. Barley went by like an Indian, staying close to side of the house, rifle ready. He made the big man move aside.

"What the hell?" Copelan's eyes widened as Barley shoved the gun barrel in his gut.

"Get out here. Anyone else in there?"

"No-o."

"Get out here and don't try anything," Barley ordered, moving him aside and then peeking in the door. "Looks clear. Let's warm up some in here."

Harker's eyes narrowed and Herschel knew the man was about to explode. He shoved his gun hand forward. "Stop right there."

But it never was to happen. Harker swept up a large piece of firewood and, screaming at the top of his lungs, charged Herschel with his weapon. The Colt barked in his hand and Harker stopped, dropped the stick, stepped back in the haze of the gunsmoke. He looked down dumbfounded at where the gunpowder had burned a hole in his underwear. Like a wooden puppet, he clutched the wound in his chest with a large hairy hand, gurgled something inaudible, sunk to his knees and at last pitched facedown in the snow.

"Nothing else you could have done."

Barley's words brought him out of the trance. There hadn't been any options; still he felt remorseful. A man was dead who didn't need to die, but he chose the way he went.

"Come inside," Barley said and herded Copelan through the doorway.

"I want to make a deal," Copelan said, once they were in the cabin. "I want to make a deal."

"You can talk to Simmons. He's the prosecutor."

"You—you know they'll storm the damn jail and hang us."

"They've got to come over me."

"What about Buck Palmer?" Copelan asked, looking at the two of them like a wild man.

"He's behind bars."

"You know he set up all this."

"I suspect he did."

"No—no, he—"

"Shut up," Barley said, shaking his head in disapproval. "Or I'm putting a gag in your mouth."

"Good idea," Herschel said, warming himself at the red-hot stove. He wasn't over the shooting, but he wondered what Marsha was doing. She was going back to her place and check on the girls staying at the Fergusons'. He better find that place close to town for them.

FORTY-FIVE

His main force was gathered in the office, all sitting in a circle facing the roaring fireplace: Spencer, Barley and Otter.

"What's the plan?" Spencer asked.

"Obviously Palmer ain't going to talk. Maybe they bought him off," Herschel said.

"The grand jury indicted him for murder of them two," Spencer said, cutting a wary look at Herschel.

"He's tough. But I have a plan called my truce plan."

"What's that?" Charlie asked.

"I want to ride out and speak to every big outfit and tell them I'm willing to let this drop, if they send their gun-hands packing."

"You reckon that'll work?" Barley asked, raising his elbows off his knees.

"They've all lost lots of cattle. They don't need any more range. None of them want to be named in a grand jury indictment."

Barley nodded as if satisfied. "What do we do?"

"Ride along."

"When do we start?" Spencer asked.

"I made a list. I want to ride out to the Crown in the morning."

Charlie chuckled. "This may be interesting."

"I think it may be. Better dress warm, they won't invite us inside," Herschel warned them. "Now I have to go with an agent and look at a place for my family. Meet everyone at Paschal's at dawn."

He met Abner Brown, the land agent, in the courthouse lobby and they took his horse and buggy three blocks north of the courthouse. The house was painted white, with lap siding and a nice front porch. A matronly woman opened the door.

"Mrs. Kary." Brown introduced her, and she showed them the spacious house with the upstairs finished and suitable for the girls.

There was a small barn to keep horses and a cow, chicken coop and pigsty. Mrs. Kary told him about the garden spot and the pasture. Ten acres. That should suit his wife.

"And you are moving where?" Herschel asked, after peering in the hand-dug well.

"Oregon. My husband is already up there. He sold the business here two months ago. But if the railroad comes, land here will skyrocket."

"Yes, ma'am, if it ever gets here. I will discuss this with Mr. Brown and let you know my offer."

"Thank you, sir." She did a small dip and then went back in the house.

"Will it do?" Brown asked when he drove Herschel back to the office.

"Fine. I can pay them four hundred down, the balance of the fifteen hundred over three years."

"Mr. Kary wanted all cash."

"Obviously he hasn't found that rich man yet. I am considering selling my place on Horse Creek and pay this off, but I haven't sold it yet."

"I'll see what I can do."

"Fine," Herschel said and got out of the buggy at the courthouse. Lots to check on. A boy had finally rode Cob up there from Sheridan. So he'd be glad to have his horse to ride in the morning. He hoped the moderate weather of the day lasted while they went and saw the big outfits. His plan might flop—but he had nothing to lose. A good truce and the hired guns out, and things might calm down in his county.

Good thing that Marsha was at her place—he might have been tempted to tell her about the Kary place. He sure hoped it suited her and they accepted his offer. Time would tell.

His posse left early the next morning. The less obvious the four men carrying rifles were, the better Herschel felt about it. The day threatened to warm, and the strong south wind made high-crown-hat-wearing serious business.

They reached the big house and the spreading ranch headquarters of the Crown in mid-morning. His posse two by two came up the long lane, balancing Winchesters on their legs. The horse stock across the rail fences looked winter-weary and drawn. Herschel saw no evidence of haystacks remaining.

A hatless, balding man with gray hair came out on the porch.

"You Goldby?" Herschel asked.

"Yeah. I guess you're that new sheriff."

"I am sir. My name's Herschel Baker and I came to talk."

The man hugged his arms. "Well, talk."

Herschel looked around. Obviously Goldby had no intention of inviting him inside. "We've got a new regime in Yellowstone County. Send your gunhands packing."

"And if I don't?"

"Then I'll hold you responsible for anything they do."

"You may be the law, but you ain't bossing me around about who I can hire—"

Herschel held up his hand to silence the man. "I've not made myself clear. Fire the gunhands, Goldby, or I'll find a place for you up at Deer Lodge."

"I've got lawyers—"

"I've got juries ain't going to smile and turn their head at you big outfits running over the small ones."

"You're calling this a truce."

"Mister, I'm calling this a promise. Don't try me."

Charlie booted his horse up beside him. "You know harboring known criminals is a federal violation. I've got a notion I can find some posters fit a few of them boys."

Goldby nodded and looked away. "All right, it's a damn truce."

"I knew you'd understand. Good day." Herschel touched his hat brim and swung Cob around.

"Baker?" Goldby called after him.

He reined up and half-turned to listen.

"Bet you don't get MacDavis to agree."

Herschel ran his tongue over his back molar and spun Cob around. "He will or he better have himself a good suit to be buried in."

"We'll see."

"Mind the truce, Goldby. Come spring, you may not have a job anyway from the looks of the losses we've seen coming up here."

They rode out and didn't say a word until the end of the long driveway.

"Will he or won't he?" Spencer asked.

"You got him backed to the wall. He can't spend the

company's money on lawyers. Hell, they won't have any money when they count the dead cattle," Charlie said.

Barley agreed. "He won't need them gunfighters then for sure."

"Whatcha going to do about MacDavis?" Spencer asked

"I figured ride up there today." Rupart MacDavis remained a thorn in his side. The unsettled part of this whole effort to bring all of Jack's killers to justice. The entire time he'd spent bringing Buck Palmer back, he never once got him to admit MacDavis was behind it all. There had to be a way to squeeze that out.

"We better hustle then. Daylight's burning," Barley said.

Past mid-afternoon, they rode into the MC ranch basin. Barley saw the rider first and pointed him out as he angled across the open country toward them. He came with a rifle in his arms and everyone but Herschel drew his out of the scabbard.

"We'll try to talk sense into him first," he said. "But be ready."

The rider reined up a hundred feet from them and leveled the rifle at them. "Far as you go. This is MC land."

"I'm the sheriff of Yellowstone County and I'm here to talk to your boss."

"He ain't having no visitors. Turn around and ride back."

"You know you're going to die if you squeeze that trigger," Charlie said. "One shot and we'll all cut you down. It won't be nice dying on this cold mushy ground. We ain't going to bury you or take you to no doctor if you don't die natural-like at first."

"I . . . I'll get one of you."

The rifle in Barley's hand swung around and smoked

death. Hard hit, the guard's gun went off in the air as he spilled out of the saddle. His horse left, pitching high for the ranch. Barley spurred his horse over and cleared the long gun from the guard's hand, and jammed it in his scabbard. "Sorry, guess we warned them we were coming."

"He wasn't listening," Herschel said and spurred Cob for the distant ranch buildings.

Standing in the stirrups, short-loping, he wondered if they faced a firefight or what. It was time, time to face the man who no doubt ran all the undercover things for the big outfits.

A fury of activity was apparent around the big house as the four abreast riders drew closer. Armed men ran about as if looking for a place to get behind to ambush them.

"Ho!" Herschel halted his posse. "No need in any more dying. I'll take a truce flag and ride in there and talk to the man."

"They may gun you down," Spencer said.

"They do, you boys can have them." He booted Cob forward, tying a white kerchief on his rifle barrel.

His stomach felt queasy and he dried his palms on his pants. How did that psalms go—*Yea, though I ride in the valley of death . . .* No matter, he intended to arrest the big man—he was as guilty for Jack's death as Palmer and the rest of them. Today was the day. This was the time. A new resolve set in. So it caused a big stir—maybe folks would realize. He could make out hats and gun barrels behind the wagons and everything in front of the house. Then the front door opened and the massive form of MacDavis came outside, under a Scottish wool shawl. Bareheaded, he flipped back the thick, graying hair the wind upset.

"What are you doing here, Baker? This is private land."

"I'm the sheriff of Yellowstone County. I've come to arrest you for the murder of Jack Diehl."

"Ha, that's funny." MacDavis folded his arms. "All I have to do is snap my fingers and you'll be riddled full of holes."

Herschel shook his head. "They murder a sheriff, they won't get out of this county. That U.S. marshal and my two deputies will get them." He twisted in the saddle and indicated the three men down the driveway. "Word gets out, they'll be strung up in every cottonwood along the river."

"Get ready to shoot him!" MacDavis ordered.

"Not me. I ain't shooting no damn law." The man put down his riffle and started for the bunkhouse.

"Me either."

"Me either."

Then his hired hands began to melt away, leaving their rifles and holding their hands up in surrender.

"Be kinda dumb," a tough-looking kid said, tossed his rifle in the brown grass and got up from behind a buckboard.

"Wait for me," another said after him.

"You'll not get paid!" MacDavis shouted after them.

"Looks to me like you're under arrest."

"The hell I am." He drew a small-caliber pistol from the pocket of his coat and cocked it.

"Put the gun down."

Herschel could see the shotgun in Washington's hands, stuck in the big man's back.

"You's ain't shooting no one."

"Washington! You ungrateful sumbitch!"

"I's ain't ungrateful. I's not letting you shoot him."

Herschel dismounted and was up the stairs. He took the gun from MacDavis's fingers.

"You can't make any murder charges stick on me. I'll have you out of that office in days."

Herschel searched him for any more weapons, then

started him down the steps. "Buck Palmer sees you getting off with murder I think he'll tell us who ran this outfit."

"You won't—"

"Shut up—Washington, go hitch up the carriage. I'll take him in to Billings."

"You won't—"

"Meet my deputies, Rupart. You'll get to know them well before this is over."

"What happened?" Spencer asked, looking around for sight of any opposition.

"I arrested Rupart MacDavis for the murder of John Diehl."

"He can't prove that. You there, Otter, you're a U.S. marshal, have him release me."

"Oh, I couldn't go against the duly appointed sheriff."

Herschel put the cuffs on his wrists—tight. He still needed to prove a case, but somehow he was going to tie MacDavis to that crime.

"It'll be long past dark before we get him to jail," Barley said.

Washington drove the team up. "Mr. Baker, may I's drive it to town. I'm through here and needs a way."

"Sure." He climbed aboard Cob and looked at the setting sun casting a bloody red light over the shrinking white blanket, exposing hundreds of dead cattle carcasses. Be a helluva spring. But the rejected Rupart MacDavis sitting handcuffed in his own carriage convinced him he'd carried out his promise to Jack Diehl.

Two weeks later, they were sleeping for the first night in their new house in Billings. The furniture had not been even moved, but the girls were so excited, Marsha agreed to go up there and sleep one night.

Herschel and her were asleep on a pallet on the living room floor. A knock on the door and he raised up. "Yes?"

"Sheriff Baker?"

He recognized the voice of Wally Simms, a night guard from the jail. "What is it?"

"Trouble, sir."

"I'm coming," he said, shoving his feet in his pants. While she wrapped herself in a blanket and went for a lamp, he threw on his shirt and went to the door. The door cracked, he could see Simms.

"What is it?"

"I hated to bother you, but—"

"Speak up, I'm up."

"Rupart MacDavis hung himself."

Herschel considered the words—*hung himself.* He nodded. "I'll be there in five minutes. Don't touch a thing."

"We already cut him down and sent for Doc."

"I'm coming." He rested his head against the door facing. He didn't want it this way.

Sheriff Herschel Baker stood at the back of the funeral crowd, mouthing the words to the same hymn. He could see all the expensive hats on the well-dressed men and women in the front rows. No tears, only stern, hard faces. Floury fresh snow dusted the dirt excavated for the grave, and the expensive coffin shone in the light dulled by the thick clouds overhead.

"Let us lay, Rupart Cyrus MacDavis to rest—amen," the preacher said, and they began to lower his body.

Someone was shaking Herschel by the arm. "Let's go to my new house for supper," Marsha said.

"Yes, I'd loved to," he said. Maybe Jack Diehl could look down and see this. He sure hoped he could. Then he glanced over at her on his arm. He'd have to play that mouth harp for the girls; they all could stand some cheering up. And the badge under his coat meant another new serious obligation in his life.

He shook several hands of well-wishers and then helped her upon the buckboard. "Let's go home, Mrs. Baker." And they did.

EPILOGUE

Billings Herald editorial, April 15: The recent legal execution by hanging of the cold-blooded murderer "Buck" Palmer this past Tuesday closes another chapter in territorial history. Palmer was aided in his black deeds of murder and extortion by Undersheriff Copelan, who is now incarcerated at the Deer Lodge Territorial Penitentiary for ten years at hard labor, which means to all the God-fearing citizens that legal justice has finally prevailed in Yellowstone County. No longer will barbaric vigilante courts be necessary.

Our appointed sheriff, Herschel Baker, continues to campaign for his own election this fall. In our opinion, when a brave private citizen like Baker steps forward and risks his life and property (they beat him up and burned his house) to uphold the law, regardless of his party affiliation he should be elected to that office. Sheriff Baker will run as an Independent.